CROSSING THE LINE

A Dirty Angels MC/Blue Avengers MC Crossover

JEANNE ST. JAMES

Copyright © 2019 by Jeanne St. James, Double-J Romance, Inc.

All rights reserved.

No part of this book may be reproduced in any form or by any electronic or mechanical means, including information storage and retrieval systems, without written permission from the author, except for the use of brief quotations in a book review.

———

Acknowledgements:

Photographer: FuriousFotog

Cover Artist: Golden Czermak at FuriousFotog

Cover Models: Austin Standage (Nash) and Zach Fox (Cross)

Editor: Proofreading by the Page

Beta readers: Whitley Cox, Andi Babcock, Sharon Abrams & Alexandra Schwab

Warning: This book contains sexually explicit scenes and adult language and may be considered offensive to some readers. This book is for sale to adults ONLY, as defined by the laws of the country in which you made your purchase. Please store your files wisely, where they cannot be accessed by under-aged readers.

Dirty Angels MC, Blue Avengers MC, and Blood Fury MC are registered trademarks owned by Jeanne St. James

---

Keep an eye on her website at http://www.jeannestjames.com/ or sign up for her newsletter to learn about her upcoming releases: http://www.jeannestjames.com/newslettersignup

Join her readers' group for all the inside scoop here: https://www.facebook.com/groups/JeannesReviewCrew/

Down & Dirty 'til Dead

A special thanks to Cathy Torrible and Pam Nelson who suggested the bar name The Cockpit.

*Also, thank you to ALL my readers who belong to my readers' group: <u>https://www.facebook.com/groups/JeannesReviewCrew/</u>
You all encourage me to keep writing!*
Love to you all!

Crossing the Line's Playlist

Songs mentioned in Crossing the Line:

Sweet Child O' Mine - Guns N' Roses
With Arms Wide Open - Creed
Holding Out for a Hero – Ella Mae Bowen version
Let me be Myself – 3 Doors Down
Secret - Heart

Chapter One

NASH JERKED his chin up at the bartender, who was finishing up serving a patron down at the other end of the noisy and crowded bar. He pointed to his empty whiskey glass and the bartender, who was wearing nothing but a black leather jock strap with matching leather wrist cuffs and collar, nodded back in acknowledgment.

The long bar wasn't the only area noisy, the whole place was. That was because a band was rocking out on stage and while half of the patrons at The Cockpit were paying attention, half were not.

Fuck no.

Half were there for the entertainment; the other half for *their* entertainment.

The Cockpit was a known pick-up joint. But that's not why Nash was there tonight.

That wasn't saying he'd say no if the right person came along, especially since he hadn't hooked up with anyone in a while. His main reason for being at this well-known meat locker on the outskirts of Pittsburgh was strictly for business.

His band, Dirty Deeds, needed a new guitarist and

singer. Normally, Nash was the front man, singing and playing guitar for the AC/DC cover band he'd started almost fifteen years ago. He could also play the drums and bass himself, but he couldn't do it all. And it was nice to have someone else in the band who could be the lead singer when Nash's voice was in the shitter.

Like after a night of heavy partying, which tended to happen after playing a few sets at one of the many Dirty Angels MC pig roasts. Which had been his band's main gig, until recently.

Problem with that main gig was it didn't pay, except in beer, booze and pussy. While Nash would partake in the first two, along with whatever fat joint was being passed around the bonfire, he rarely took part in the third.

He could fake it, but he preferred not to take it.

And while occasionally he was drunk enough to fall face first into pussy, it wasn't his preferred meal.

No, he preferred to sink his teeth into something a little different. Like the guy sitting three stools down to his left. The blond man caught his attention when Nash went to break the seal a half hour ago.

While Nash was a biker, he didn't come out to other bikers, even his own club brothers.

That would be just plain fucking stupid.

He also tended to drift toward men who were more clean-cut. Men opposite of him. Plus, he knew those types of men would never travel the same circles as any of the bikers he knew, so his secret would remain safe.

Even so, if anybody saw him here, his excuse was trying to poach the band's lead guitarist. Though, in this case, he wasn't. He'd lost interest not long after hearing him play. While the guy playing the Fender was good, he wasn't great. So, he was taking a hard pass on this one. Unfortunately, he'd have to keep searching.

He threw a crumpled ten spot on the bar when the bear

of a bartender dropped off his Jack on the rocks. Nash waved a hand, indicating the man should keep the change. Especially since the bartender couldn't afford clothes, apparently.

As he raised his glass to his lips, someone bumped his elbow and he barely recovered his drink before it splashed over the rim.

"Fuckin' watch it," he muttered. His life revolved around loud music and crowds but only when he was on stage. He didn't enjoy being bumped into, stepped on and talked over any other time.

"Problem?"

Nash set his glass down slowly on the bar and eyed the man who now perched on the stool next to him, his knee pressing into Nash's thigh.

"Yeah," Nash mumbled just loud enough to be heard over the music.

The guy leaned in to ask, "What?"

Nash gave him the side-eye. "You."

"Didn't mean to bump into you, man. Got shoved from behind."

"Whatever," he grumbled.

"Is broody asshole still a thing?"

Was the guy trying to be funny? Nash ignored him and knocked back half of his whiskey before slamming the glass back on the bar. "Don't know, is it?"

"Haven't been out looking, so I'm not sure what's hot right now."

"Wouldn't know, either."

The guy settled more solidly on the stool, but left his knee touching Nash. And as he leaned forward to grab the bartender's attention, his chest brushed against Nash's arm. Once he placed his order of a draft beer, he turned enough where his knee slid along Nash's thigh.

Wasn't being too fucking obvious.

Problem was, Nash was trying to ignore him but was having a hard time doing so.

The guy leaned closer to Nash again to make sure he was heard over the din of the bar. "Name's Cross."

Cross. How fucking gay was that?

"Yours?" The question was yelled in his ear.

Nash dropped his chin and eyed the fingers this *Cross* wrapped around his bicep. The grip was firm, his fingers long and, for a split moment, Nash wondered how they'd feel wrapped around his dick.

Again, he reminded himself that wasn't what he was there for and, in truth, he was too close to home to hook up. It was risky. Even if it would be a random, anonymous fuck.

But since the guy introduced himself—assuming that was his real name—the anonymous part was no longer true.

"Got a name?" the guy asked again, his dark brows dropping low over his light blue eyes.

"Everybody's got a fuckin' name," Nash answered and turned back to the bar, picking up his glass and downing the remainder.

He put the empty glass back on the bar and slid it down past several other patrons toward the bartender and gave him a nod.

"You driving?"

What the fuck. What a nosy fucker.

"Nope." Nash was riding, not driving. His sled was tucked out front between a light blue Mini Cooper and a pink Mazda Miata.

"Do you come here often?"

Jesus fuck. Nash slammed his palm on the bar top. "Can't a man just grab a fuckin' drink and enjoy a band?"

Cross dropped his hand from Nash's arm and even though he pulled back, Nash could still hear clearly, "In a gay bar?"

"Is that what this is?" From the corner of his eye, Nash could see the guy studying his profile, an amused half-smile on his face.

Cross snorted next to him. "You want to play dumb?" He shrugged. "Then play dumb, but you don't look stupid. If you haven't noticed, the name of the bar is The Cockpit. Pretty fucking obvious. Plus, our bartender is a big, burly bear wearing leather gear and letting his hairy ass hang out. That's not a normal sight you see at a typical neighborhood bar."

"You might not be hangin' out at the right bars."

"This is the right bar," Cross said softly, but Nash still caught it since the band wrapped up their first set and walked off stage to a smattering of applause. A DJ started up almost immediately but was nowhere near as loud as the band.

That was his sign it was time to go, especially since the DJ was playing techno dance music. Not his scene.

He dug out another wrinkled ten from his front pocket and threw it on the bar just as the bartender snagged it and slid another glass in front of him before dropping off a fresh beer for Nash's nosy neighbor.

Nash didn't notice Cross requesting it. Maybe the bartender knew him, and he was a regular.

"Must be here often," Nash muttered.

"Haven't been here in a long time."

"Why not?" Now he was being the fucking nosy one.

"Was tied up for a while with someone. Problem was, he was out and proud, and didn't like I wasn't. Not that I'm ashamed, but I can't go publicly blasting that I like cock."

Nash turned his head toward him. Besides the light blue eyes, the man had a full head of short dark brown hair. Cut neat. A beard, trimmed way cleaner than Nash's own, which tended to stay on the scruffy side. He'd cut it back recently because it was becoming annoying as fuck, especially when he ate, but he still didn't keep up after it on a daily basis. And he certainly didn't remember the last time he cut his hair. Most of the time he put it up in a ponytail or a man-bun which some women liked, some didn't.

Not that Nash gave a fuck what they thought.

He was a rocker and a fucking biker, and his hair was for himself, not them.

If a woman wanted to drop to her knees and suck his cock, he was fine with it, but the second they started giving him suggestions on his look or whatever, he couldn't get shot of them fast enough.

And it wasn't like he would keep a woman long-term anyway, because what he preferred was sitting next to him being a pain in his ass.

Now, if that one was on his knees gagging on Nash's dick, he might listen to a suggestion about trimming up his facial hair. Not that he would do it, but he'd listen.

"You're not out?"

Cross shook his head.

"Why?"

"My job."

"Which is?"

"Not very tolerant."

Nash understood that completely. A couple of his bandmates knew how he leaned, but that was it. And they didn't talk, not if they wanted to remain a part of Dirty Deeds. Right now, with a new manager, their band was starting to book all over the east coast. And the money was finally starting to roll in. Most of them, except for their guitarist, wanted to benefit from that.

However, his lead guitarist had a ball and chain around his ankle, consisting of a wife and three kids. He couldn't just up and go do multi-state tours for weeks at a time.

Nash had a lot of freedom when it came to that. The

only ball and chain he had was his MC and even that was a light one.

"So, you're into women and you're sitting in a gay bar, not just any gay bar, but one known for random pick-ups. Why?"

"Why the fuck not? There's a band playin' and I'm a musician."

Cross's eyebrows rose. "What do you play?"

"Guitar, drums, bass. Sing, too."

"You good?"

Nash lifted a shoulder. "So I'm told."

"Ever play here before?"

"Fuck no."

"Why? Because it's a gay bar?"

No, because it wasn't a biker bar, which was most of the gigs they'd had recently. While they wanted to expand, gay bars were not on their radar. One of his band members was a homophobe and would flip the fuck out if he or their manager suggested it.

Another reason Nash kept the fact that he was bi on the DL.

Plus, it wasn't anyone's business but his and whoever was on the receiving end of his dick.

Even so, Lenny was a great drummer and Nash didn't want to risk losing another band member, homophobe or not.

"Yeah, since I'm not gay."

Cross jerked his head toward the now empty stage. "Think any of them are gay? As long as they're getting paid, bet they don't care whose pocket that money came from."

While Nash agreed, he wasn't going to say that out loud. "Time for me to go." He shifted to get to his feet, but long fingers snagged his bicep again, this time giving it a squeeze first.

"Hold up, you didn't give me your name yet."

Nash's heart began to thump like a bass drum. He should've left the moment the guy began to chatter, but something had kept him in his seat.

The guy was good looking and Nash's type, but something bothered him. Something Nash couldn't put his finger on.

Then it hit him. Something he should've caught from the get-go. Maybe the beard had thrown him off.

Cross's eyelids got heavy and his blue eyes heated as Nash leaned in close, inhaling deeply as he slid his nose along Cross's jaw, not touching, but close all the same. His cock twitched when the subtle cologne the man wore filled his nostrils, but he could still smell that identifiable stink beneath it.

Cross's fingers tightened painfully around Nash's arm when he got even closer, putting his mouth to the man's ear, murmuring, "You smell like a pig."

Cross froze but didn't let go of Nash. Instead, he glanced down at himself. "Did I spill something on myself? I swear I showered. Do I stink?"

"Yeah, you stink," Nash growled in his ear. "Got that distinctive odor that comes with badges and jail cells."

"You forgot about the handcuffs."

"Never forget about the handcuffs," Nash murmured, then sat back, studying the man once more. From what he could see, the maroon button-down long-sleeved dress shirt the man wore pulled at his shoulders, which meant there were muscles under there. His gut was trim and his thighs pretty damn thick in his jeans. His face, though handsome, was a bit baby-faced for Nash. He wasn't super young, but he wasn't old enough, either.

Nash didn't like to mess with anyone who needed direction. He didn't have the time to waste on lessons. He wanted a man, or woman, who knew what the fuck they were doing.

This way they could do their thing and Nash could bounce shortly afterward.

So, no. Nash didn't need a headache like this one. Even if it was for one night.

Pigs and bikers didn't mix, anyway.

"Gotta go."

Chapter Two

THE MAN with the long dirty-blond hair, whose name he still did not know, jerked away from him and moved from the bar and through the crowd. Cross saw a few sets of interested eyes following him as he went. He understood that interest because he was feeling it himself.

The man they were watching had long, lean legs which could eat up real estate fast. His hair was a bit shaggy for Cross's taste and his beard a bit haphazard, but his hazel eyes held a story Cross wanted to hear.

He doubted he'd ever get the chance, but he still wanted a shot at it.

How the man knew he was a cop, Cross didn't know. He didn't have a severe haircut like most, nor did he carry an arrogant air. When it came to his job, he tried to be fair. He treated others as he'd want to be treated if he was in their shoes when dealing with an officer of the law.

But the nameless man whose back he watched as he shifted through the crowd, didn't seem to want to give Cross a chance.

Ignoring his beer, he quickly got to his feet and decided

to follow. The more the man refused to give him his name, the more Cross was determined to learn it.

He wasn't one to give up so easily.

He also wasn't the one who gave up on his last relationship, his former boyfriend did. Being a cop, he didn't want the hassle of coming out. Other cops usually didn't like it when "one of their own" wasn't quite "one of their own."

And luckily, his department was one which pretty much stuck to "don't ask, don't tell," so Cross kept that shit to himself.

But Jeff didn't want to keep their relationship a secret. He didn't want to go back in the closet. He wanted to go to Cross's station functions, like the annual Christmas party, as a couple. Or attend their own parties and fundraisers.

He also wanted to ride on the back of Cross's Harley when the Blue Avengers, the law enforcement MC Cross belonged to, did their monthly runs.

That was never going to happen because things with him and his career would never be the same again. He wanted to make corporal by the end of the year, and he figured if he was outed that might not come to fruition. Excuses could be made why Cross wouldn't get that fucking promotion, even though he was qualified and had time enough on the job, but Cross would know the truth of why he kept getting passed up.

If Cross had to decide between getting dick and his career, he was choosing the one that would most likely last the longest. All he needed was another fifteen years on the job and he could retire with a nice pension and full bennies.

So why the fuck he was tracking the man who refused to give him his name and who had something against cops, Cross didn't fucking know.

And even though he knew it wasn't smart, his feet wouldn't change direction.

No, instead he pushed out the front door of The

Cockpit and into the late fall night. The paved lot was well lit, so he spotted his target immediately moving between two rows of cars.

Cross began to jog. He needed to stop him before he left. It would bug the shit out of him if the guy left before Cross ever got to know his name.

Cross was a detail type of guy. Being a cop, that was important. While he could easily see what vehicle the man got into and run his plate, that would be an abuse of power and if he got caught doing that shit, he could kiss his promotion goodbye.

He caught up with him a few vehicles down from the entrance.

"Wait. Hold up." Cross reached out to grab his arm and stop him. But the man spun on him, taking a defensive position by planting his feet wide.

Cross stepped back giving them space in case the guy tried to take a swing at him.

"What the fuck do you want?"

This was a bad idea. A really bad fucking idea. Cross should go inside and find someone a lot more willing. But for some reason, he couldn't let this go. He hadn't had this strong of a reaction to anyone in a long time, even to Jeff. Which probably was why when Jeff broke it off, Cross didn't give a shit. Yes, he'd miss the sex, but that was it.

The only time Jeff didn't bore him was when they were in bed, which was another major problem between the two, as well. Cross should've known they were doomed from the start.

Not that Cross was looking for any kind of meaningful relationship with this guy. The one who clearly had a thing against cops, which was a big part of who Cross was. But they didn't have to discuss their career choices or anything much personal at all.

He simply wanted a name.

Fuck, maybe he wanted more than a name. But a name would be a start.

"Hey, I just want to apologize. I didn't mean to run you out of there."

"Was done anyway. The guitarist didn't pan out."

Cross looked back toward the entrance of the bar. "The guitarist? Were you interested in him?"

"Yeah."

"I don't think he's gay."

"Was interested in him for my fuckin' band, not to fuck him. Told you I'm not gay."

"Where are you playing next? Maybe I'll come listen."

Fuck, that was lame. Since when had he become a desperate fool?

"Tryin' too hard," the guy muttered, shaking his head and turning away.

Cross grabbed his arm again, swinging him around and said, "Maybe not trying hard enough." He pushed the guy against the SUV they were standing next to and took his mouth.

Maybe he was wrong, the guy really wasn't gay, and he was only scouting out another musician for his band. Because the guy stiffened and began to push on Cross's chest. His lips remained tightly sealed no matter what Cross did to try to open them.

Was he molesting a stranger in the fucking parking lot?

He gathered his common sense and stopped kissing him.

But the guy hadn't hit him, hadn't complained, hadn't done anything to stop him. He just didn't take part. In fact, his hands were fisted in Cross's shirt, tight enough that Cross couldn't step back.

They stared at each other, Cross trying to gather his thoughts, along with his breath.

While the light wasn't enough in the parking lot for Cross to see the color of the guy's eyes, it was enough that he could see a spark in them, as well as catch the slight flare of his nostrils.

The guy wasn't turned off.

Not at fucking all.

Which meant he was either lying when he said he wasn't gay, or he just wasn't admitting to it. Either to himself or others.

"I'm—" Before Cross could apologize, the man had his hand gripping Cross's throat, spinning them both around and with a grunt, shoved Cross into the side of the SUV. He lost all his breath and as he opened his mouth to suck air, the man had his mouth on his and was shoving his tongue inside.

Cross drew oxygen through his nose as the guy stole the air from his lungs. The stranger tried to dominate the kiss, take control, still holding Cross by his throat, using his hips to pin Cross to the vehicle.

Cross didn't fight him. He let it happen. Because for insisting he wasn't gay, the man's erection was hard to miss since it was jammed against Cross's own.

Cross also didn't fight the groan rising from his throat as the man's fingers flexed against his neck. Cross didn't worry about being strangled, he could break free easily, if he needed to.

But he didn't want to.

The man tasted good. Like whiskey and a touch of smoke. Maybe even a touch of bud.

No surprise he didn't like cops if he was a regular pot smoker. It wasn't a deal breaker for Cross, since legalization was on the horizon.

The hard shit? No. A little grass got a pass.

But the only hard stuff Cross was paying attention to was what was straining against the guy's zipper. His fingers itched to touch him, but he wasn't stupid enough to push it.

He was currently going to walk away from this without a black eye and would like it to remain that way.

Their tongues clashed and twisted, and their kiss got even more intense. Cross was having a hard time finding his breath, especially since this guy could *kiss*. No doubt remained this guy had kissed men before. He wasn't tentative at all, instead he was going full bore.

And Cross was all for it.

He raised his hand and brushed his fingers along the wiry hairs covering the guy's jaw, then slid his fingers into the man's hair. He normally wasn't into long hair on men, but it fit this guy. The scruff, the shaggy locks, with him being a rocker it made sense.

Suddenly the kiss ended, the guy pulling away only enough so they could both catch their breath. Though, they were both struggling with it. The thumb of the guy's hand that gripped his throat took a few passes over Cross's pounding pulse.

"That what you were lookin' for?" The man's voice was gruff, raw and sent more blood rushing to Cross's cock.

Admittedly, it was a start.

Still not able to control his breath or his racing heartbeat, Cross whispered, "Not gay, huh?"

The man didn't avoid his gaze when he answered, "Nope."

Cross couldn't resist anymore and swept his hand over the bulge in the man's jeans. "Could've fooled me."

The guy jerked one shoulder up but didn't pull away from Cross's touch. In fact, he pressed into it.

Not gay, his ass.

Cross tried again. "What's your name?"

"It matter?"

"Since I got you hard, then yes, it fucking matters."

The guy's eyes landed on Cross's lips, then slid down his

chest to his waist and where they were pressed together. "Nash," he finally said.

Nash. First name? Last name? Stage name? Fake name? Cross decided not to push it. He got something out of him. For now.

"Yours?"

Cross arched a brow at him. "Told you what it was."

Nash shook his head. "No one names their kid Cross."

"It's Aiden Cross."

His lips twitched. "Least you didn't say Christopher."

"I would've run away from home if they named me that. At least your parents didn't name you Graham Nash, which would be ironic since you're a musician." He'd hoped that tease would give him the rest of Nash's name. It didn't, instead Nash jerked against him, then pulled away abruptly.

He had shut down.

Fuck.

The joke was meant to open him up, not close him down.

He pushed on. "Would like to see you play one night. On stage... or otherwise." Why was he working so hard to get this guy's dick? He never had to work this hard.

While he sometimes liked a challenge, there were too many other easy hook-ups back inside The Cockpit.

A drink. A smile. Exchange of names, real or not, and then someone was coming down the other's throat. Even if it was only in the parking lot.

It was that easy. This Nash was not being easy.

Cross needed to just walk away.

But he could leave a breadcrumb.

Releasing Nash's evidence of his lie about not liking men, he pulled out his wallet, and from that, a business card. He tucked it into the man's front pocket, making sure his fingers brushed against Nash's erection once more.

"If you decide you are gay, give me a call. If you want to meet on neutral ground, I'm willing. In fact, I'd prefer it."

"'Cause of that job of yours."

Cross dipped his head. "That's one reason."

"Don't do pigs."

"You also indicated you didn't do men. And anyway, I never said I was a cop."

"Never said you weren't."

Cross tilted his head and studied the man who still had him pinned against the SUV with his hips. They were almost the same height, so they were eye to eye, dick to dick.

Cross wanted to kiss him again, but he knew that might not fly, so instead, he brushed his thumb over Nash's bottom lip.

"One admission for another," Cross suggested softly.

Nash jerked his head away and Cross's hand dropped to his side.

"I'm good. Gotta go."

Suddenly, Cross was no longer pinned to the vehicle, and Nash's long legs were taking him quickly away from him.

Cross moved out from between the two vehicles where they'd been kissing and watched Nash approach a bike.

He should go inside and just forget this whole thing happened.

Or maybe just go the fuck home and call it a night. He had a bottle of lube and an experienced fist, as well as a good imagination, so he could use his memory of Nash to get him off, if needed.

Unfortunately, he lost interest in finding someone else in the bar. His interest was still on the man digging into one of his saddlebags. He pulled what looked like a leather vest from it, then shrugged it on.

Cross's heart started to pound in his ears.

From where he stood, he couldn't read it, but it was an

MC cut like Cross wore being a member of the Blue Avengers MC. Only Cross knew Nash wasn't a part of any law enforcement-based MC.

He didn't like "pigs," so he definitely wasn't one.

The roar of the straight pipes, which were illegal in the Commonwealth of Pennsylvania, filled the night air.

Holy shit.

Cross tracked him as Nash rode past him on his Harley, his eyes glued to the rockers on the back of that vest.

He just made out with a fucking biker. Not just any biker but a member of an MC.

Not just any MC but the Dirty Angels MC.

He knew of them, only too well.

Some members of the BAMC had connections with the DAMC.

So, messing with Nash wouldn't be random, it would be stupid.

Shit could easily get out.

Any kind of interest in Nash would be a big mistake, he could not only lose his chance at a promotion, but possibly lose his job. Outlaw club or not, Nash was part of an MC which his superiors wouldn't take too kindly to Cross having any kind of connection to.

Not only being gay but hooking up with a biker like Nash could fuck him up one side and down the other.

He reminded himself one more time the choice between dick and his career should be an easy one.

Now he just needed to convince his brain and his own dick of that.

Chapter Three

NASH LEANED back against the counter of his fully furnished kitchen in his fully furnished house.

A kitchen he never cooked or even ate a fucking meal in. A house he never slept in. Not once.

The only reason it was fully furnished was Mercy and his woman, Rissa, had holed up there all those months ago when her life had been threatened.

Nash had done a walk-through of the house in the DAMC compound once the construction was complete. He'd done a walk-through again once Mercy and Rissa had moved out.

And both times right after those walk-throughs he'd walked right the fuck back out, got on his sled and headed back to church, which felt more like home than this house did.

He was alone, why did he need such a big fucking house? Especially since he'd been on the road more often, too. He liked rolling loose and easy. When he was home in Shadow Valley, he had a free room above church where he stayed. A commercial kitchen downstairs, which was a part of The Iron Horse Roadhouse, where he could have one of the cooks or Mama Bear make him grub.

Living in his own house would not only be too quiet, but he'd have to make his own shit, for the most part. He could get a house mouse, but he didn't need some young female living with him and in his business. Fuck that.

Anyway, he wasn't ready for domestic bliss for him and his fist, since he didn't have anyone else to share it with. Probably never would.

All his brothers, who had an ol' lady or a family, now lived behind the gate and concrete walls of this neighborhood. Zak, the DAMC president, wanted everyone, especially the ol' ladies and the kids, in one spot for good reason. He wanted everyone safe after dealing with the Shadow Warriors being a threat and wreaking havoc for decades.

Now that rival MC was extinct, it was still smart to keep the families in one location. Everyone looked out for everyone else.

Safety in numbers.

It also didn't hurt that a couple of Diesel's Shadows lived in the compound, too.

Even so, Nash didn't belong here. He ought to just pass the house on to one of his brothers. But anyone not living here was single yet. Moose, Coop, Crash, Rig, Rooster and Jester. None of them wanted the burden of owning a house like this. They were happy to live above church, too.

He reached into the back pocket of his jeans and slid out his wallet, finding what he was looking for. What his mind kept going back to.

It wasn't fucking smart.

In fact, it could be a disaster.

He flipped the card over and over within his fingers, then flicked it onto the counter. He should burn it.

Then burn the memory of that kiss out of his head.

The card had landed face up on the counter and the name on it stared him right in the fucking face.

Officer Aiden Cross
Southern Allegheny Regional Police Department

Aiden Cross.

Officer Aiden Cross.

Nash usually picked men not running in the same circles. Officer Cross certainly didn't run with the same crowd, so there was no threat of that.

But still, there was a threat. Of a different kind.

He could see it now. Getting caught with not only another man, but a pig to boot.

Fuck. Might as well filet the club colors off his back himself now.

Diesel still took issue with Bella being with Axel. He tolerated the cop because the man had DAMC blood running thick through his veins, was married to D's cousin, was Zak's brother, and Linc's brother-in-law. Not to mention, founding member Bear's grandson.

So, at best, Diesel tolerated Axel. For Bella's sake.

Aiden Cross had nothing but pig's blood running through his veins.

There'd be no tolerating of shit.

Especially when Diesel's business consisted of a crew of special forces veterans who did some questionable things.

A fuckload of questionable things.

Things which needed to be done and in which D wanted to keep the club's hands clean of. But he still was not only their boss, but the club's Sergeant at Arms, so there was a tie there.

So while D took exception to Axel being close, he wouldn't give that same allowance to anyone else who wore a badge.

The club was Nash's family. If it wasn't for the club, he wouldn't be able to concentrate on music. He would be like every other fucking schlub working a nine-to-five.

His soul would whither up and die if he had to do that.

He loved his freedom. He loved his music. He loved his life.

He loved his brotherhood.

But he was tired of being fucking alone, even when surrounded by his brothers, his bandmates and even crowds of people at his gigs.

He watched almost every one of his brothers find an ol' lady who fit them perfectly. A woman who didn't put the hammer down and force them to change.

They also fit right into the club life. Either because they were also born into it or were adopted into it by way of their ol' man.

True love. True loyalty. They all had that.

And still, Nash stood in his quiet kitchen alone.

The DAMC family had expanded over the past few years. Exploded, more like it. More than doubled in size with new members, prospects, their women and, now, a whole new generation of DAMC blood.

Not that Nash would contribute to the fourth generation. Hell, he wasn't even born into the club, had no DAMC blood running through him when he became a prospect all those years ago.

He'd been approached at a biker bar out near Greensburg when he was twenty by a young biker named Jag Jamison. The only thing Nash had to his name at the time was a beat-up guitar, an even more beat up sled and about five bucks in the pocket of his ratty jeans.

Jag slid onto the stool next to him, bought him a beer, started up conversation and then offered to fix up his Harley for him since he was learning to work with metal and paint.

The man was teaching himself to design custom bikes and cars. And he needed guinea pigs who wouldn't give a shit if he fucked something up.

Nash's bike couldn't get any more fucked up than it had been. In truth, fucked up would have been an improvement.

At first, Nash thought Jag was trying to pick him up. Turned out he wasn't. His story held true. But that didn't mean Nash didn't have a hard-on over Jag for a couple of years. Until he kept watching Jag chase Ivy like a dog chasing a tennis ball.

Even though Ivy didn't want shit to do with Jag, the man never gave up.

Eventually, Nash had no choice but to give up. Even so, he was still grateful to Jag for bringing him back to Shadow Valley like a stray puppy. Tossing him a prospect cut, giving him a free place to stay, free food, free booze, and then giving him one badass bike in the end.

He owed Jag a lot.

He owed the DAMC a lot.

And the last thing he needed to do was kick them all in the nuts by not only coming out as bi, but also bringing home a cop he wanted to fuck.

He picked the card up off the counter, crumpled it in his fist and searched for the trash can. If Rissa and Mercy had one, it was gone.

He'd burn it outside instead.

He unlocked the back sliders and stepped out onto the deck, letting his gaze roam over the trees behind "his" house that had turned colors and were getting ready to drop their rustling leaves.

Could be a song in there somewhere.

He heard the faint strains of an acoustic guitar and looked to his right, past the empty lot to the next house over. Jazz and Crow's.

Jazz was outside doing what she loved. The same that Nash loved.

Playing music.

Music soothed Jazz's healing soul.

Music *was* Nash's soul.

Without it, he'd be nothing.

With a curse, he shoved the balled-up card into his front pocket and headed down the deck steps and over to Crow's place.

The closer he got, he still couldn't recognize what she was playing and softly singing. He hoped it was something she wrote.

She had a lot of talent, she only needed a lot more confidence in it.

Some people were born to make music. She was one of them.

Her eyes were on him as he approached but she didn't stop playing. Her fingers still picked at the strings, but her words trailed off as she gave him a genuine smile that filled his chest.

"Hey, babe."

"Hey," she greeted back.

"Your stuff?"

She nodded, making her blonde ponytail bob, and stopped strumming.

"Sounds good." He wanted to hear more.

She lifted one shoulder and dropped it.

"How's the kid?"

Her smile widened, her face lighting up. "Good."

He couldn't see her belly because the guitar covered it and he was sure it wasn't big yet. Good things took time.

Jazz having Crow's kid was a good thing. For her and her ol' man.

"I need to get serious about writin' shit, too. Next tour our manager wants all originals. Even though we'll probably be playin' at shit holes, he wants to test out the material. Will take anything you want to share, babe."

Her face closed up again. "I'm not good at writing my own songs."

"He wants us to stop doin' so many covers."

She twisted her head to look at him. "You're called Dirty Deeds for a reason."

"No shit." While they started out being an AC/DC cover band, through the years they expanded to different genres, but stuck with rock and heavy metal for the most part.

"The only reason to do originals is to get picked up by a label. Is that what you're looking to do?"

Nash settled his bones on the lounge chair next to her. "Dunno. Haven't thought that far ahead. Just wanna make more scratch. I'm thirty-six now and don't have a fuckin' pot to piss in."

With a furrowed brow, Jazz's green eyes landed on his house. "You have a house."

"Not sure I want it."

"You have a sled that's the shit," she reminded him.

"Yeah." True. Thanks to Jag and his skills.

"You have some awesome Gibson Les Pauls."

"Yeah." That he did. One was worth some major scratch.

"And you have us."

And that right there was fucking priceless.

"Can't afford that house without more dough, Jazz. Electric, water, sewage, all that shit costs money. Still owe the club for the lot and the construction, too. That's a big motherfuckin' IOU hangin' over my head."

"The club's in no rush to recoup that. You know that," she said softly.

"Shouldn'ta given the go-ahead."

"You must've had a reason."

He glanced over his shoulder at a house that would fit in any typical middle-class neighborhood. That was not him. Not even close.

What the fuck had he been thinking?

"Yeah, babe, musta fell off the stage while shit-faced and cracked my skull."

Jazz laughed. "I must have missed that."

"It was more like a rash decision after a night of listenin' to Rooster cock-a-doodle-fuckin-dooin' as he's stickin' it to one of the sweet butts. Fuckin' asshole makes a helluva racket when he's dippin' his dick in snatch."

Jazz dropped her head and shook it, but her shoulders shook, too.

He grinned. "Baby's not gonna hear any of what I just said and remember it, right?"

She lifted her head, eyes sparkling. "I hope not. Because if this baby is hearing things, he's going to come out already corrupted with what Crow and I..." Color tinged her cheeks. "Though, I do sing to him every day."

"Fuck, I want to sing to him, too."

Jazz glanced over her shoulder toward the house.

Nash looked in that direction, too. "He here?"

She shook her head. "At the shop. But if any of his appointments bail he sometimes comes home early."

"Think he'd mind?"

Jazz chewed on her bottom lip. "Not sure."

"We're singin', not fuckin'."

"Yeah," she said on a breath.

Nash tamped down the disappointment which was rising from his gut. "Forget it, if you're worried about it."

"No, I want to." She pulled the guitar over her head and offered it to him. "You play and choose a song. I'll follow your lead."

She placed a hand over her belly, which was a noticeable bump, and sat back in the chair, waiting.

He dropped the strap over his head and tapped his hand on the body of the guitar, getting a beat started.

He closed his eyes, let his fingers find each note and chord, then let the words of *Sweet Child O' Mine* by Guns N' Roses flow from his lips. He kept it slow and easy and Jazz joined in, her sultry voice blending perfectly with his.

She kept a hand to her belly, her chin tipped down, a small smile on her lips as she sang to her growing child.

Watching that, seeing everything beautiful that had come to Jazz after everything so ugly, he was happy for her, but something else pulled at him.

Something he himself was missing.

When they were done, she lifted her head, met his eyes and gave him a bright smile. He returned it but his wasn't as bright.

And, fuck him, she caught it.

He braced because he could see her gearing up. He wasn't wrong.

And it extinguished that bright smile of hers. "You need this in your life, too, Nash. I see it sometimes. You look lost. Lonely. I see it because I lived it."

"Yeah."

"The only time it goes away is when you're up there on that stage. I know that's your true love, but you need more than that. We all do."

"Jazz—"

She kept going. "You have a house waiting. You just need to fill it."

If he moved in, the only thing that would fill it was music. That was his one true steady. He could live without the rest.

But, for fuck's sake, he needed to change the subject. "Gonna ask you again to think about writin' for us. Know Crow won't let you join us on tour, even for a few stops, and I get why. Plus, now with the baby..."

"I don't write rock."

"Just gotta write the lyrics, I'll write the music to go along with it. I'll make it rock."

"I don't know..."

"If you're like me, you got a notebook full of scribbled words. Some of those words might be shit, the others might be gold. Think about it."

Nash didn't miss her glancing back at the house again. She loved her ol' man, she loved their life, she didn't want anything creating waves on the calm sea she worked so hard to find.

"When you sang that version of *Holding Out for a Hero* to Crow that night, you took us all to our knees, babe. Fuckin' every last one of us. You got skills. He saw it. He's an artist, too. He'll understand."

When she didn't say anything and sat only staring towards the woods behind the house, he wanted to kick himself for pushing her.

"One more before I go, Jazz. One for you and the little one. *With Arms Wide Open* by Creed. Yeah?"

She nodded. "Okay."

He played the music and let her start with the lyrics and after a few bars, he joined in.

When she played and sang, the happiness she found beamed from her. It touched everyone around her. He wanted to reach out and grab it, but he knew if he did, it would slip right through his fingers.

It wasn't meant to be.

After the last note was played, the last lyric sung, he stood, leaned over, pressed his lips to her forehead and handed her back her guitar.

Before he could pull away, her hand touched his and lingered.

With a squeeze to his fingers, she whispered, "I found my happy, Nash."

"Yeah, babe."

"You need to find yours, too."

Nash sucked a sharp breath through his nose, turned and, instead of heading back to his big empty house, he strode directly back to his sled, hopped on and rode away.

Chapter Four

CROSS CHECKED his cell phone for the hundredth time in what seemed like just as many days.

It hadn't been that long, but it sure as hell felt like it.

He was obsessing over a man he couldn't—*shouldn't*—have. And also a man who didn't want him.

He had given Nash his card. If the man didn't want to make use of it, there was nothing Cross could do. He didn't have the guy's number or even his full name. He wasn't even sure if Nash was only the biker's road name. He had nothing.

In truth, he needed to move on.

Especially when he, stupid shit that he was, had been pulling over every bike for even the most minor of infractions just in case one of them would be Nash.

He'd also gone back to The Cockpit a couple times, as well as every other gay bar he could find in the Pittsburgh area and near Shadow Valley.

Even went as far as stepping foot into a couple underground clubs.

While he found a lot of men in those establishments, not

one of them was Nash. Which meant Cross had gone back to his townhouse every one of those nights alone.

Today, he'd been assigned a patrol zone at the southernmost part of his PD's jurisdiction. Actually, he'd switched with another officer who wanted to work Cross's assigned zone since it was near his home and he could stop there for lunch. That was good news for Cross because the southern zone bordered Shadow Valley PD's coverage. So all day, Cross had been sitting on the township line watching vehicles fly by, spot his cruiser parked behind a roadside sign and then slam on their brakes.

If he'd been timing them, their reaction would've been too late. But he wasn't necessarily looking for speeders. He was once again searching for bikes. Not just any bikes, one with straight pipes and a well-known brand name on the gas tank.

Because, again, he was a stupid shit. He sighed.

His radio chirped and he listened with half an ear to a call someone else got in another zone. Dogs barking. Cross was thankful that nuisance call wasn't his.

If his cruiser didn't have GPS, letting his dispatchers know his twenty, he'd risk swinging through town to ask around about Nash. He was sure someone would be able to point him to the Dirty Angels MC clubhouse.

Maybe he'd do that on his next day off.

Jesus.

He needed to get over this guy. It was one fucking kiss.

Okay, two, technically.

But every night when he closed his eyes, he pictured releasing Nash's long hair from its ponytail, and wrapping it around his fist while Nash was on his knees sucking his cock.

Last night his imagination had gone even further, which spurred him into watching porn on his tablet to relieve some of that pent-up need.

Even now his cock was chubbing up at the memory.

He needed to get his mind off an unavailable biker who could even possibly be a felon. Cross had no idea if the man had a sheet on him. And if he did, how long it was.

Gay. Biker. Possible felon.

The perfect trifecta to fuck up Cross's career.

A racket caught his attention and an old, beat up red and white Ford pickup with a missing license plate, a dragging exhaust pipe and a cracked windshield approached him. The driver eyeballed him as Cross did the same as the truck rattled its way passed.

Another law-abiding citizen. Probably didn't have a dime's worth of insurance, a valid registration or a fucking driver's license.

He sighed again, put the cruiser in drive and flipped on his party lights.

As the truck slowed, but didn't stop, Cross called in the vehicle description and advised dispatch he'd be making a traffic stop. He also noted the back window had an NRA, "Don't Tread on Me," "My Ford is Protected by Smith & Wesson," and "These Colors Don't Run" stickers.

Great.

Cross was pretty sure the driver was one of those who declared being gay was a mental illness, too.

Oh, and a choice Cross willingly made.

If it was a choice, it wasn't one Cross would've picked. No one voluntarily wanted to live a life full of discrimination, plus the fear of being outed on this job.

Despite what some people believed, being gay didn't stop him from being a good cop, friend, neighbor and son.

And, maybe one day, a good father.

Even husband.

But none of that was going to happen any time soon.

"Fuck," Cross muttered as he pulled up behind the truck which finally pulled off onto the shoulder a half mile after he'd flipped on his overhead lights.

Right now, he had to have a serious discussion with the operator of the vehicle he pulled over.

He sat in his cruiser a couple minutes more just to make sure the driver didn't decide to flee. When he didn't, Cross unfolded from the car, using the door as cover.

He considered yelling orders to the driver instead of approaching. But so far, the man had cooperated and besides having a run-down truck, the driver hadn't done anything that warranted a felony stop.

But that didn't mean Cross wouldn't be overly cautious in his approach.

He shut the door, hiked up his duty belt and gave an update to his dispatcher into his shoulder mic. Then as he stepped up to the rear of the truck, pressed his thumb to the tailgate so if anything went down, law enforcement could prove this was the truck and guy who did something to injure or kill him.

But hopefully nothing happened, because that would suck.

He kept his body close to the side of the pickup and stepped up to the window that hadn't been rolled down yet.

Cross shook his head and said, "Roll down your window."

His gaze swept the interior of the cab as much as it could for weapons or any illegal substances, but it was so full of trash, the man could be hiding anything in there.

"Roll down your window," he repeated louder and a bit more firmly.

Cross tensed as the man complied, then leaned out of the window and spat tobacco juice on his boot.

This would be a hell of a fun stop.

"Need your license, registration and insurance, sir."

No answer.

Fuck me.

"Do you speak English, or do you need an interpreter?"

The man, probably in his fifties, sporting a long salt and pepper beard, heavy on the salt, whose face showed he hadn't lived an easy life, turned his head and said, "I speak American."

Alrighty.

"Okay then, let me repeat my request in *American*. Need your license, registration and insurance, *sir*."

"Don't got none of that. As a resident of this great nation, the United States of America, home of the free, land of the brave, I'm at liberty to do whatever I goddamn please."

Cross sucked in a breath. This was getting more fun by the second. "It doesn't quite work that way. There are laws—"

"Fuck your laws."

Cross pursed his lips and studied the man. He needed a plan. A good one. The man might be a bit older than Cross, but from what he could tell, the guy looked pretty fucking big. And solid. Like a damn lumberjack.

The type of man who could down a beer in one gulp and then crush the can on his forehead.

"You want to tell me your name and social?" he asked, even though he already knew the answer.

Another wad of tobacco juice splattered on his other boot. "Nope."

"All right, then. Sir, how about you step out of your vehicle and come sit in the back of mine while we figure this all out." He didn't make it a question, because it wasn't.

Cross stepped back from the driver's door and planted his spit-stained boots wide enough for balance, kept his knees unlocked, one hand on his taser, the other on the butt of his Glock, which was angled away from the driver.

"Step out of the vehicle and—"

The door pushed open slowly and the man unfolded

out. Cross was right. The fucking man stood a few inches taller than him and was heavier, too.

While Cross was good at holding his own when it came to taking down people, he also knew his limitations.

This would be a fight.

This man did not give a shit about the law, which meant he didn't give a shit that Cross was a police officer. He lived in his own world, by his own rules and fuck everyone else.

Cross pressed the button on his shoulder mic. "Dispatch, subject out of the vehicle, taking him back to mine for questioning."

"Dispatch copies."

Cross pressed the button again, adding, "Send another unit."

Before he got an answer from dispatch, he heard, "Why you need another unit? You're steppin' on my freedoms by detainin' me."

"Sir," Cross started, trying to keep his tone level and calming. "I have every right to stop you for traffic violations and detain you because you're not carrying identification."

"Bullshit."

"I have to make sure you don't have any warrants. And if you don't have current insurance and registration, I'll have to get this vehicle towed." He should call for a tow truck and get them rolling. He wasn't going to let this pickup back on the road in the condition it was in, no matter what.

"You ain't takin' my truck. I paid for that fuckin' truck. It's mine."

"You'll get it back once—"

"I paid for that fuckin' truck," the man repeated louder, his face turning red. "You ain't takin' it!"

"Just until—"

Cross saw it coming, braced for it, but what struck him wasn't a fist, it was like a sledgehammer. Even though he got an arm up for a partial block, it still caught part of his face and whipped his head back.

Cross swore he heard every bone in his neck crack from whiplash.

He brought up another arm just in time to block another direct blow to the face. He dropped one hand to his taser again, but before he could unholster it, he found his legs swept out from underneath him and fell backward onto the pavement hard.

He dug deep, referred back to his training, trying to keep his cool and think clearly. He didn't want to use deadly force but would if necessary. He had every right to escalate to that level, but he grabbed his taser instead and pointed it at the man standing over him. He didn't hesitate to pull the trigger and watched the barbs sink into the guy's chest and deliver a shock.

Unfortunately for Cross, the guy didn't even react. Probably because the man who reminded him of a lumberjack was wearing a thick flannel shirt, one that looked lined. The barbs hadn't gotten a good hold. The voltage was probably only an annoying tickle to him.

Fuck.

He released the spent cartridge and before he could do anything else, a big boot made contact with his head.

The impact made him struggle to fill his lungs and to keep the darkness at bay.

His only thought was, he didn't want to die on the side of a fucking road.

Fighting his narrowing tunnel of vision, he felt for the mic that had been knocked off his shoulder. As soon as his fingers made contact with it, he pushed the emergency button and then tried to concentrate on what the man was about to do next.

Which was reach for Cross's gun.

Cross dug deep again, drew his knee back and nailed the

guy directly in the chest with his boot.

Besides a loud grunt and a half-step back, it hardly fazed him.

Jesus.

The man grabbed Cross by his uniform shirt and began lifting him. Then suddenly Cross dropped to the pavement like a sandbag as the man stumbled back.

Cross had no idea what the fuck was happening, he just knew he was free. He scrambled to his feet, catching his breath and fighting the dizziness, only to see another man squaring off with the lumberjack. He couldn't see who it was, though. The guy was just that big.

He looked around and saw no other cruisers but his.

What the fuck was going on?

Whoever was in a struggle with the big dude didn't have the upper hand but Cross could still see the lumberjack taking blows. He was also delivering them.

Then suddenly the big man dropped to his knees, crumpled to the ground, and landed face first onto the pavement like a felled tree.

Cross watched it all happen as if in slow motion, made sure the fucker wasn't getting back up, then lifted his gaze to the man who was bent over, seemingly out of breath, long dark blond hair falling around his face, and wearing a black leather vest.

That man also had a black leather object in his hand.

Cross had never used one, never even seen one in real life, but he knew what Nash held.

A blackjack.

Completely illegal. Something cops carried back in the day and it could do some real damage. Which was evident by the big man knocked out on the berm of the roadway.

Nash lifted his eyes and theirs locked.

"Get rid of that," was all Cross could think to say.

Nash looked down at his hand and the bloody weapon,

then turned and whipped it far out into the field next to the road.

Once it landed out in long weeds, his eyes went back to Nash, whose chest was heaving and his eyes, looking a bit wild, were on Cross.

Wiping at his mouth, Cross realized it was bleeding. "Fuck," he muttered, moving over to the downed man and grabbing his cuffs. He went to his knees and restrained the unconscious man. He really needed two sets but only had one, so fuck the guy if they were too tight.

Once the lumberjack was cuffed and Cross made sure he was still breathing, he pushed to his feet and turned to find Nash.

He tried to shake the dizziness from his brain, but it lingered. Even so, he moved quickly toward Nash, who stood there watching him approach.

Now Nash's hazel eyes were glued to his lips, which Cross was sure were bleeding and he could feel them starting to swell.

He stepped toe to toe with Nash, let his gaze rake down his body, making sure the man didn't need medical.

He didn't. Besides a small cut on his cheekbone that was already beginning to bruise and a fat lip that would match Cross's, he looked okay.

Thank fuck.

"Jesus, you saved my life," Cross whispered.

Nash just stared at him but said nothing. The hair on the back of Cross's neck rose at the look in Nash's eyes. It was almost feral.

Cross reached out and, using his thumb, wiped a spot of blood off Nash's bottom lip. "Hey—"

Without warning, he was down on the ground again, the breath knocked out of him, all of Nash's weight crushing him, as their mouths melded, their tongues touching and tasting.

Metallic but sweet. Both of them were bleeding, both of their lips were split but they ignored the pain, the blood and deepened the kiss.

This was crazy. A knocked-out guy, who almost killed him, laid only feet away from him while he and Nash made out in the weeds by the side of the fucking road.

But Cross couldn't pull himself free. Even if Nash didn't have him pinned down, he wouldn't want to break the kiss he'd been dreaming about for the last two weeks.

It was just as good, if not better than that night in the parking lot of The Cockpit. Even though it was on the painful side.

Cross's fingers twisted in Nash's shirt, holding him close, encouraging the man to kiss him harder.

Cross tilted his hips and ground his cock into Nash's. Even with the cumbersome duty belt, Cross groaned at the contact.

He was struggling to think straight, to remember where they were, who they were and, *hell*, more importantly, that they were out where anyone could see them.

But no matter how many times he told himself they needed to stop, that he needed to break away, he didn't.

He didn't want it to end.

Well, he did, but if it ended the way he wanted, they could both be arrested for indecent exposure.

And the first time he fucked Nash, he didn't want it on the side of the road in the dirt.

Finally, Nash lifted his head enough to break their kiss. He stared down into Cross's eyes, his hair falling around them like a curtain, his breath ragged. Cross still kept his hands fisted on Nash's cut because he knew if he let go, he might never see him again.

As he opened his mouth to tell Nash he needed to leave before his backup came, he heard thundering footsteps and shouts.

Fuck.

They were too late.

Nash's cut was ripped from his grip when hands hauled the man off him. Before he could yell at them to stop, he saw his fellow officers, one with a hand yanking Nash off his feet by his hair, another had a grip on the collar of his cut. Then he was shoved to his knees and tased.

Cross opened his mouth to scream "No!" but nothing came out.

Absolutely fucking nothing as he stared up into the concerned eyes of his sergeant. Then he was surrounded by his fellow officers and had no idea what happened to the biker who had pulled over to save his fucking life.

EVERY MUSCLE SEIZED and cramped as the taser was pressed point blank to his chest. Nash tried to catch his breath, but he was frozen and there wasn't shit he could do about it.

He had to ride those fifty thousand volts for five whole fucking seconds and before he could recover, ride it once more.

This would teach him for saving a pig's life.

He should have just kept motoring and ignored the scuffle on the side of the road. But, fuck him, as soon as he saw who was getting his ass kicked, he had jerked his sled to the berm.

He'd seen nothing but fury as he'd pulled the blackjack out of his saddlebag and rushed to help Cross. Then he took action.

It took longer than it should have to take down the big man, but he did it. And once down, Cross quickly had the guy cuffed.

But now, it was him being hauled to his feet, cuffed and shoved into the back of a cruiser.

Him, the good fucking Samaritan. The stupid fuck who

helped out one of their brothers in blue.

He hated pigs. He hated them even more now.

A blow to the side of the head had him seeing double as he was hauled from his knees and dragged across the pavement, thrown into the back of a cruiser onto his stomach and the door slammed shut, barely missing his feet.

Fuck those motherfucking assholes.

His chest heaved. He could feel the tightness in his jaw as it swelled, his nose and mouth were leaking blood at a fast rate. His left ear rang from being cuffed upside the head.

Lying on the back seat, he couldn't see the driver's door open and slam shut, but he could hear it.

With a groan, Nash planted his boot on the floorboard and pushed himself up to a seated position, tossing his loose hair out of his face. As the cruiser pulled away, he glanced out the back window, but he couldn't see Cross since he was surrounded by more cops.

Almost like a fucking army of them.

A blue army.

"Didn't do shit," Nash grumbled, jerked on the cuffs pinching his wrists, then spit a mouthful of blood onto the floor.

"I'll use your fucking hair to mop that shit up, you filthy fucker."

Nash met the pig's narrowed eyes in the rearview mirror. "Didn't do shit," he mumbled again.

"Agg assault, asshole, attacking a cop."

They thought he'd been attacking Cross.

He was. But not in the way they were thinking.

He had lost his head when he saw Cross getting his ass beat. He had lost his head again when he saw Cross was okay.

But the cop's fellow officers delivered an important reminder he wouldn't soon forget and Nash wouldn't lose his head again.

Chapter Five

CROSS TOOK LONG STRIDES down the empty corridor, an ice pack pressed to his right eye. He had just returned to station from the ER, where his sergeant had insisted he get looked at.

His nose had been bloodied but not broken. He had a bruise and swelling at his temple and he sported a black eye.

Truthfully, he'd been lucky. He was still upright and breathing.

And whatever the other officers witnessed between him and Nash, it wasn't what they thought.

Unfortunately, he was about to land in his sergeant's office to explain everything that went down so they knew what charges to file against the asshole lumberjack.

And also against Nash.

They caught most of it on his MVR, which began recording as soon as he'd flipped on his lights, but luckily once Nash got on scene, everything with him from the blackjack to the kiss happened off camera. *Thank fuck.*

Even so, Cross needed to come up with some excuse as to why Nash was on top of him.

Kissing and grinding their cocks together because they

had both lost their heads in a moment full of adrenaline wasn't going to cut it.

But when the rest of the officers rolled up on scene, the driver had already been subdued, was no longer a threat and the only action they witnessed was between him and Nash.

He had no fucking clue what to tell his sergeant and the other officers, but he needed to come up with something and fast. He had run several scenarios through his spinning mind while at the ER, but they all seemed lame and not plausible.

As he stepped into the sergeant's office, he took a breath to bolster himself and closed the door behind him.

Game time.

A HALF HOUR later his long strides were taking him in the opposite direction from where his sergeant ordered him to go.

"Go home, rest, take a couple days. We'll get someone else to question that biker, get a witness statement from him and then, as long as he cooperates, we'll let him go."

Right.

Cross needed to make sure Nash cooperated. The sooner he did, the sooner he'd be free.

He also needed to make sure their stories were straight.

Last thing he needed Nash to say, even in jest, was that they'd been making out in the middle of a bad situation. While they had been, it wasn't smart on Nash's part to admit it.

Even if he was pissed off.

Which Cross was sure Nash was.

The man had been detained for hours and hadn't even

had anyone look at his injuries, which, hopefully, were minor.

Besides getting their stories in line, Cross needed to see Nash with his own two eyes to make sure the man was okay.

He also needed to thank him. As well as apologize for the way he was treated.

And then ask him if they could see each other again. Hopefully, in much better circumstances.

He had a feeling Nash wasn't going to give a shit about any of that. But at minimum, Cross could advise the guy what to do to be released as soon as possible. And, with any luck, a lot less fuss than what happened back at the scene of the traffic stop.

Fuck.

He combed his fingers through his hair as he relived Nash getting tased twice while Cross did nothing to stop it. His step stuttered as it replayed in his head once more. He slammed his back into the hallway wall and dropped his head.

Fuck.

He should've stopped it.

He wasn't expecting the officer who tased Nash to do just that and before Cross could react, force the words past his lips, it was over, and Nash was being dragged to one of the cruisers.

When Cross went to rush in that direction, he'd been detained by his sergeant and circled by fellow officers, concerned with his welfare. Then he was shuffled against his will into the back of another cruiser and hauled off to the nearest hospital.

He was a goddamn fucking coward.

He should have screamed at them, made them listen as he told them the truth and insisted they release Nash.

Now, he could only hope what he told his sergeant

would be good enough, so they didn't harass Nash anymore before letting him go.

The biker didn't deserve the shit pie he'd been served.

It was Cross's responsibility to wipe up the mess. Not to mention, hope Nash forgave him for being that goddamn fucking coward.

He squeezed his eyes shut, then smacked his head back against the wall once, twice, then pushed away and went to find where Nash was being held.

He walked into the holding room, relieved to find Nash alone there. He had no idea if the lumberjack-sized asshole had ended up in the hospital or had already been processed and sent to county.

He didn't ask and he didn't care about the driver.

He only cared about the man sitting in the narrow room, his back to the wall and his hands still cuffed and secured to the metal bench. Nash's head was leaned back against the wall, his hair falling away from his face, so Cross could see his eyes were closed, one due to being swollen shut like Cross's.

The man's beard also did nothing to hide the purple, swollen bruise that ran along his jaw.

Dried blood clung to his wiry beard, his long hair, stained his ripped Sturgis long-sleeved tee and speckled his DAMC cut.

His long legs weren't restrained so he had them extended out and spread, the edges of his boot heels planted on the concrete floor. Blood splattered his scuffed and worn biker boots, too.

His dirty, worn jeans had grass stains on the knees and Cross could only guess those stains weren't there before the two of them had rolled around in the weeds before the rest of the officers arrived on scene.

"Fuck," Cross muttered under his breath.

But it was loud enough for Nash's eye to open and for him to roll his head against the wall to look at him.

Or at least look at him with his one unaffected eye.

"They're going to release you. I gave my accounting of what happened to my sergeant. They now know you helped and didn't hinder. You were aiding me and not that crazy fucknut."

Nash turned his head back and stared across the room, ignoring Cross.

He pinned his lips together and moved deeper into the narrow area to stand between Nash's boots.

"Could do damage with you standin' there."

Yes, he could. "You won't."

"You don't know that." Nash's voice was rusty as if it had been strained from yelling.

"I know that."

"Awful fuckin' trusting with a prisoner."

"Yes. But you won't be in custody for long."

"Been here long enough."

"Sorry about that. They forced me to the ER and this was the first chance I could get back here to clear your name."

Nash huffed and raised his gaze to meet Cross's. "Clear my fuckin' name." He shook his head, his long hair, now dirty and stiff, brushing over his shoulders. "Clear my fuckin' name."

Cross grimaced. "One of the other officers will come get you, move you into an examination room and get your accounting of what happened. You need to cooperate. As soon as you do, they'll release you."

A muscle ticked in Nash's cheek as his one good eye narrowed on Cross. "*I* need to fuckin' cooperate?"

Nash was getting loud and angry, so Cross quickly glanced at the open doorway to make sure no one was overhearing him. "Nash, man, you need to just keep your cool, answer their questions and they'll let you walk."

"Got no fuckin' reason to have me detained. None what-so-fuckin'-ever."

"I know."

"You tell 'em what they saw was you grindin' your dick into mine?"

Again, Cross's eyes slid to the doorway of the holding area. "No."

"You tell 'em if we hadn't been on the side of that fuckin' road, you woulda been bendin' over and takin' my dick up your ass?"

Cross coughed and sucked in a breath at the same time. "No."

"What d'you tell 'em?"

"I told him you were assisting me by being a good Samaritan. I had blacked out after the struggle with the driver, so you cuffed the prisoner and then came to check on me. I had just come to when they arrived."

"Fuckin' liar."

Air rushed from him. "Yes. I lied."

"But you didn't do shit to stop what they did to me."

"I had no control over—"

"Bull-fuckin'-shit."

A pain shot through Cross's chest at the emotion behind Nash's curse. He was trying to hide it but it was there. The air was thick with it, not only could Cross taste it, it was making it hard for him to breathe. "You need to stick to that story."

"They don't know their boy is gay."

His heart skipped a beat and began to pound. "No."

"They don't know you woulda begged for my dick up your ass."

"Nash..."

"Why? 'Cause you're afraid they'd treat you like they treated me? Like a piece of fuckin' trash?"

"I—"

"Stepped in to help and this is the fuckin' thanks I got. Exactly why I hate pigs. Thank fuck your fellow pen mates reminded me." Nash tilted his head and stared up at Cross. "Fuckin' was tased—twice, for fuck's sake—beat upside the head while my hands were cuffed, thrown onto the backseat face first, *accidentally* kicked and punched when I was pulled from the car, then dragged through the parking lot into your pigpen. Can't forget searched, fingerprinted and then had my record run like a fuckin' criminal. Only thing missin' was a cavity search. But maybe they were leavin' that up to you since you probably enjoy shovin' your fingers up a man's ass." He huffed and shook his head. "Bet that motherfuckin' asshole who took you down was treated better than I was."

Cross wanted to fucking puke. A simple sorry wasn't going to cut it.

As it shouldn't.

He needed to show Nash how much he appreciated him stopping and helping even though it was dangerous for him to do so. Not only dealing with the driver, but with the very people who were sworn to uphold the law. His brothers had failed.

They judged Nash by how he looked, by who he was, without even knowing why he was there.

Cross was ashamed for them.

And he was ashamed at himself for not stopping them.

He needed to do better. They all did.

But this was not the place to continue this conversation. He said his piece, which he hoped Nash would repeat to whoever questioned him, and, now, he needed to go before he got caught with Nash when he had been officially sent home by a superior. "You still have my card?"

The crack of Nash's cuffs against the metal bench when he jerked them filled the small room. "Fuck no."

Cross took a step forward until he stood between Nash's extended legs, his uniform pants brushing against the man's jeans. Not quite touching but a connection all the same. "Want to thank you for saving my ass and also apologize for how you were treated. There's no excuse for it."

Nash didn't answer right away. Instead he drew his legs up and widened his bent knees, so their legs didn't touch, his one-eyed gaze searing Cross. "Don't want nothin' from you or your *brothers* 'cept my freedom. Can you get the fuck outta here now?"

"I want to make it up to you."

"Just need you to leave me the fuck alone."

"I *need* to make it up to you."

"You hard-headed motherfucker, you don't fuckin' listen."

"I know what I felt in that parking lot outside The Cockpit. I know what I felt on the side of that road. You do, too."

"Didn't feel shit."

"Deny it all you want. But I know. You know. I get you're pissed right now, I would be, too. But when you've had time to think—"

Faint voices coming down the corridor had Cross leaning closer and whispering, "Just think."

Then he stepped away and headed out of the room. He heard, "Nothin' to think about," as he moved down the hall away from the voices and out the back door to the parking lot.

Nash was stubborn.

But then, so the fuck was he.

―――――

CROSS BLINKED HIS EYES OPEN, and they landed on the alarm clock next to the bed. 11:45.

He heard the ring again as his phone lit up his nightstand.

With a groan, he reached for his cell. Even though the traffic stop had been two days ago, he still hurt like hell. Hot showers and aspirin only helped so much.

He snagged his phone and looked at the screen. It was a number with a local area code, but one he didn't recognize. Normally, he wouldn't answer an unknown number and would let it go to voicemail. But being this late, it could be an emergency.

Right.

His pulse picked up speed as he slid his finger across the screen and stuck it to his ear. "Hello?"

When he cleared the sleep from his throat, he almost missed the deep, but rough, answering, "Hey."

Holy shit.

Someone hadn't gotten rid of his card. Even if he hadn't before the incident a couple of days ago, he expected Nash to rip it to pieces and set it on fire after.

He settled his head back on the pillow and burrowed deeper under the covers, his trembling hand sliding up his bare chest and over his jaw. "Hey," he whispered back.

Then nothing.

Silence.

Complete utter silence. His gut churned and he pressed his palm to it, doing his best to wait Nash out, but having a hard time doing so.

Nash's voice finally came through the speaker a bit hesitant, "Just checkin' to see if you're okay."

He had to be dreaming. He was still asleep, wasn't he? There was no way Nash was calling to check up on him.

No fucking way.

But in case he was, in case this wasn't a dream, Cross answered, "Yes. You?"

Again, another excruciating long hesitation, which made Cross want to reach through the phone and shake the words out of Nash.

"That guy kicked your ass."

Great. Maybe not those words.

"My brothers kicked yours." One corner of Cross mouth tipped up. The anger from that day was now gone, and he guessed they were to the stage of joking about it, even though none of it had been funny.

Not in the least.

"Unfair advantage."

Cross's lips flattened out at Nash's bitter tone, because that part wasn't a joke. "I was at one, too. You saw how big that fucker was."

"Yeah, he didn't give a fuck you wore a badge. Shoulda shot his ass."

Cross grimaced, rolled his head back until he stared up at the ceiling through the dark, his thumb sliding back and forth over the phone's protective case, wishing it was Nash's skin instead. "Not a good way to get my promotion."

"Not gonna get a promotion if you ain't breathin'."

"True. But I am, thanks to you."

"No thanks to your pig buddies."

Cross's fingers stopped sliding and instead tightened on the phone. "Again, sorry about that."

"Probably best they thought I was attackin' you rather than dry humpin' you on the side of the fuckin' road."

"Yeah," Cross agreed, then pinned his lips together. He didn't know if he should laugh over that or regret they were interrupted. But it was best his fellow officers didn't see it for what it really was. "I explained to them it was a misunderstanding, that you really were helping me out. Hopefully that's what you told them, too."

"Yeah, heard your instructions when I was chained to the bench like a fuckin' dog."

Cross closed his eyes and that moment replayed in his head. "They dropped the charges."

"Yeah, I know, Cross. I was fuckin' there. Told 'em what you wanted me to tell 'em."

Right.

Cross pulled a breath through his nose. At almost midnight, while lying naked in bed, with the deep, smooth voice of the man he wanted to fuck in his ear, was not a time to replay the clusterfuck that happened that day.

His palm brushed over his pebbled nipples and down his abdomen to the trimmed nest of hair at the base of his cock.

While he was soft because of the current topic of conversation, it wouldn't take much to change that.

Nash called for a reason and it wasn't because the man was concerned with Cross's injuries. Especially since his had been worse.

"Nash?"

"Yeah?" The question was just as quiet as Cross's.

"Where are you?" His cock twitched within his fingers and he circled it, beginning to stroke the life into it.

"In bed."

Cross pictured the man naked, reclined in wrinkled white sheets, one arm tucked behind his head, the other reaching down and stroking his own cock.

Damn. Now he was hard as a rock and his balls were pulling tight as he remembered how good it felt to grind against him that day, even with all the turmoil surrounding them.

He wished it was Nash's mouth, fist or ass surrounding his cock right now, not his own fingers.

"Where?" His voice was thick, rough, with the possibility of getting that.

"Somewhere you can't be," came the just as thick answer.

"I'm in bed, too... Somewhere you *can* be." Cross's heart began to thump more heavily in his chest and his breathing turned shallow at the thought of Nash showing up at his door.

Of walking through that door.

Of joining Cross in his bed.

He got nothing for the longest time. Only quiet breathing on the other end of the phone. Then it sped up and there was a hitch to it.

Was Nash touching himself, too?

"Nash," Cross groaned softly. "Got your number now. I'll text you the address."

The breathing stilled.

Did he hang up?

He pulled the phone away from his ear. No, he was still there.

"Don't bother."

Cross wasn't giving up so easily. "You show up, no colors. Got a townhouse in a complex with a lot of nosy neighbors. They see you representing something other than what I represent, it might become an issue."

Still no answer.

Cross's thumb slid over the crown of his cock and his hips twitched as he swept away the bead of precum that had accumulated.

He was willing to take a risk to get what he wanted, but he needed to keep that risk limited. "No colors, Nash. Just you."

Cross was about to scream in frustration from not getting a response, when Nash's tight voice hit his ear. "You were right. My ass was already kicked once, don't need it kicked again, this time by my own fuckin' brothers."

Both Cross's hand and heart froze. He struggled with

one breath. Then a second. Finally, "I'll text you my address."

It needed to be repeated. Because he wasn't going to give up so easily.

Because he was a stupid fuck who wanted a man he should forget.

"Waste of your time."

Cross pulled his phone away again and saw it had gone dark.

It lit up once more as he pulled up the last received call, saved it into his contacts and texted his address.

Then he waited.

Chapter Six

CROSS SHOT straight up in bed, his heart racing, his hand automatically reaching for the .38 he kept in his nightstand drawer. The digital clock read 2:45.

Two fucking forty-five and someone was laying on the doorbell.

He was going to kill whoever the fuck it was.

It had been a week since he'd texted Nash his address, so it most likely wasn't him. It was probably some drunk asshole who was standing in front of the wrong townhouse, since they all looked alike, wondering why his key wasn't working.

He shoved the covers off and rolled out of bed, tagging the grey cut-off sweatpants-turned-shorts he kept nearby since he slept naked.

Yanking them on, he twisted his head toward his bedroom door when the ringing stopped.

Thank fuck.

Then it started again without a break.

Normal people rang once and waited. Gave it a reasonable amount of time, then rang again, just in case the occupant of the residence had missed it the first time.

Normal people. Not drunk assholes.

He left his gun concealed in the drawer and stomped to the front door of his second-floor townhouse and leaned in, putting his right eye to the peephole.

Then he closed his eyes and straightened. "Fuck."

The ringing stopped.

Cross waited.

The ringing started again.

He twisted the double deadbolts and yanked the door open. "What the fuck?"

"What the fuck!" was the answer he got back. "Been waiting out here for-fuckin'-ever."

"Like two fucking minutes."

"Two minutes too fuckin' many."

"What the fuck are you doing here?"

"You fuckin' invited me."

"A fucking week ago!"

"Didn't know there was an expiration on the fuckin' invitation."

Cross closed his eyes again, sucked in a slow breath and shook his head, trying to tamp down his irritation.

That was until two palms slammed him in the chest, making him lose the air he just sucked in, and he stumbled back a few steps, trying to catch his balance.

Before he could recover and block Nash from entering, the man stepped inside, slammed the door shut and twisted the two deadbolts.

"I have neighbors."

"And? I didn't wear my colors like you said."

"I'm talking about the noise."

Nash shrugged. "Move somewhere you don't have neighbors."

Cross raised his brows. "Just like that."

"Yeah. You pack your shit and go."

"Just like that," Cross repeated.

"That asshole give you brain damage or somethin' when he kicked your ass?"

Cross stared at the man who he had hoped would show, but didn't, and right now he was wishing never did.

Why the fuck was he here? Now? At this time of the night, being a dick? "You drunk?"

"It look like I'm drunk?" Nash took a step toward him and kept stepping until they were toe to toe. Then he brushed his beard along Cross's, making his heart do a flip. "Smell like I'm drunk?"

Cross's nostrils flared. He smelled like a man he wanted to fuck and... "You smell like weed."

Nash went nose to nose with him, their gazes locked. "Do I taste drunk?" He took Cross's mouth, shoved his tongue inside, swept through Cross's mouth once, then stepped back, leaving him wanting more.

No, Cross only detected a faint taste of beer. Not strong. But the weed was slightly stronger.

"So, you're stoned instead." It wasn't a question because Cross had no doubt he was. Or had been.

"I like to partake in a bit of the natural stuff for a gig."

"Before, during or after?"

"Yeah."

Cross rolled his eyes. "How fucking stoned are you?"

"Not really. Just a bit mellow. That's it."

"Didn't sound mellow when you forced your way into my place."

"I was gettin' impatient."

"Karma's a bitch."

Nash jerked his head. "What'dya mean?"

"I mean, I texted you a week ago. I expected you to show up that night."

"Again, didn't know there was a time limit."

"Usually invitations aren't good for infinity unless it clearly states it in the fine print."

Nash's lips twitched. "Then I'll go."

When he stepped back, Cross's hand snaked out and grabbed his wrist, keeping him in place. "You're already here, I'm already awake, you might as well stay. Plus, you shouldn't be driving under the influence."

"I'm ridin', not drivin' and pot just takes the edge off."

"The edge of what?"

Nash ignored that question, his eyes dropping to where Cross still held his wrist. "Holdin' on pretty tight there, Cross."

Because I don't want you to leave.

Nash grinned as if he'd read Cross's mind. "All you gotta do is ask me to stay."

"Stay."

The grin flattened. "Didn't sound like a question. Sounded like a demand."

"Consider it a strongly worded request."

"Pigs tend to be bossy."

"You can stop calling me a pig at any time. This isn't *Deliverance* and I'm not going to squeal like one when we fuck."

"Aren't you?" Nash asked with a cocked eyebrow.

Cross's mouth parted and he slowly released his breath.

Nash lifted his free hand, swept his thumb over Cross's bottom lip and whispered, "Got a purty mouth there, piggy."

What. The. Fuck.

This had to be some bizarre dream he was having. Because this conversation could not be really happening.

Cross grabbed Nash's other wrist, so now he had a tight grip on both. "So, what are you doing here?"

"Just told you I was invited."

"I didn't think you were going to come."

One side of Nash's lips curled up at the accidental

double-entendre. "That's why I did." His gaze dropped to Cross's sweat-shorts. "Looks like you're glad about it, too."

Cross didn't have to look to know his grey terry cloth shorts didn't hide the evidence of his reaction of not only holding Nash's wrists, but with what was about to happen. "I'm not your first, right?"

"First what?"

Cross ignored that. "You're not here to experiment? You've done this before? This isn't just something on your bucket list? Something you're only here to check off that list?"

"That'd be an interesting bucket list."

Cross smirked. "Yes, it would. I just want you to be aware of what you're getting into."

Nash's eyes got serious. "Know what I'm gettin' into. That's why I'm here. Hopin' it's the same for you."

"Only ever been with men," Cross admitted. He loosened his hold on Nash's wrists and immediately Nash broke free. "I've never been with a woman. Never wanted to be."

"Well, I'm definitely not a fuckin' woman."

Cross let his gaze roll down Nash. From the messy man-bun with some of his dark blond hair escaping it, to his hazel eyes, his scruffy beard and lower. He was wearing a long-sleeved thermal that promoted the band Rush, but it was worn, like he'd had it for a long time and loved wearing it.

One side of the thermal was tucked in at his hip, the other side loose, his jeans were also worn to the point they had a tear at his left knee. He had a black leather belt cinching his lean waist above his narrow hips. The brass buckle was large and clunky and was made up of the letters DAMC. So, even though he wasn't wearing his cut, he was still representing his brotherhood. A chain was hooked to one belt loop and disappeared behind him. Cross could only imagine he had one of those large leather wallets tucked into his back pocket.

Lastly, his legs were long and ended at heavy black biker boots.

Cross normally didn't go for this type. But when he'd seen him at The Cockpit something had drawn him. It was like the man didn't have a fucking care in the world. That he just lived his life, not giving a shit.

Live free, ride free. Cross could see Nash living by that motto.

And that drew him.

Cross didn't live free, he lived in a fucking cage that he couldn't break out of.

He had picked a career that stifled who he was. He lived a life in hiding, always worried he'd be outed.

And it wasn't just his sexual preference that had turned the lock on that cage. Being a cop, you lived by certain rules. You were expected to live and act a certain way. Not all cops did, but Cross loved his job. He'd wanted to be a cop ever since he could remember. From a very young age, he remembered his father coming home in uniform, tired, but even so, he'd still take the time to tell Cross about his day. And Cross ate that shit up. The job sounded exciting even on the days it wasn't. Cross didn't want anything more than to grow up to be just like his dad.

He also wanted his dad to be proud of him. He thought that would happen when he went to follow in his footsteps by attending the police academy.

At first, his dad *was* proud of his son.

Until he no longer was. Which was the day his father found out the truth about that son. A truth his father couldn't accept.

"Hey," Nash murmured. "Where'd you go?"

Cross shook himself mentally. "Nowhere."

"Good. Didn't come here for conversation. Prefer to use

my mouth for somethin' other than talkin' or singin'. Already did enough of that tonight."

Cross pushed away the last of his memories. "I've got some suggestions."

"Any of those suggestions have to do with campin'? 'Cause you're pitchin' a fuckin' tent."

Cross stepped back and pushed his shorts over his hips until they fell around his ankles. "Let's go camping."

"Always wanted to be a Boy Scout."

"Doubt that."

"Yeah, they probably don't have one of those badges for suckin' cock."

"Tried to earn one of those my last year as an Eagle Scout," Cross admitted.

"Why are we still talkin'?"

"Good qu—" Cross was knocked off his feet and he lost his breath as Nash's weight landed on him, pinning him to the floor.

Jesus. This man did not know how to take it slow.

He groaned as Nash captured his mouth and began to slide his jean-clad erection against Cross's bare one.

That wasn't going to work for very long. If he got brush burn on his cock from the denim, that might put a damper on things.

But after a few seconds of their tongues tangling, Nash was moving down Cross's body, licking a path from the hollow of his neck, around each beaded nipple, down his sternum, around his navel, until he reached the dark line of hair that led to Cross's cock.

He held his breath, hoping Nash would keep going. Hoping the man wouldn't bail. He wanted nothing more than to have Nash's mouth on him.

Not just there. Everywhere.

But he'd be happy if Nash did start there.

Very happy.

Nash's mouth hovered over that trail of hair. Not touching, not licking. His warm breath tickled the dark, short hairs, which made Cross's cock flex and his balls tighten.

He swallowed down the words that threatened to explode from him. He wanted to beg and plead for Nash to keep going.

Cross needed this.

He needed Nash.

And he hoped to fuck this wasn't some cruel trick the biker was playing on him.

Because if it was, it was a dangerous game.

It didn't seem to be a game when Nash shifted down even more, his tongue tracing that dark path, skimming the tip of his tongue across the crown of his cock, down the length, taking Cross's balls into his mouth and sucking.

Cross just about jumped out of his skin as Nash's warm, wet tongue swirled around his delicate sac.

"Fuck," he groaned. Cross got no response except for two fingers squeezing the root of his erection so tightly it cut off the blood flow. Cross tipped his head down until he could see his cock turning purple and Nash's head between his thighs, though his hair was now partially loose and covering the man's face.

Then he could no longer see his cock when Nash lifted his head and took him into his mouth.

Cross planted his feet on the floor, sucked in his gut, and drove his hips up as the wet heat and suction made him lose his mind.

Nash moved with him so his throat wouldn't be impaled. When Cross dropped his hips back to the floor, Nash kept only the head in his mouth and his tongue swirled over the tip.

Cross's lips parted as he struggled to breathe from not only watching Nash doing what he was doing but feeling it all the way to the tips of his toes.

There was no doubt Nash had done this before. He was comfortable with it, and, *holy fucking hell*, knew what he was doing.

Like *really* knew.

Fingers curled around his balls, gently tugging and squeezing, as Nash slowly worked his way back down Cross' hard length, then sucked the skin at the base where his sac met the root.

Cross's hips twitched in response, he buried his fingers in Nash's hair and pulled, his voice cracking when he demanded, "Suck me."

Nash lifted his head, their eyes locking. "That a strongly worded request?"

Before Cross could answer, Nash took him completely into his mouth. His lips almost reaching his body.

Yes, that fucking deep.

It wasn't like Cross had a monster cock, but what he did have he was proud of since it was a touch above average. And no one—at least, not one other man he'd been with—had taken him that deeply without a struggle.

Cross had a second of being conflicted about that. He was impressed with Nash's enthusiasm and skills but that also meant...

Nash was older than him. Of course, he'd had more men, right?

For fuck's sake, he needed to concentrate on what the man was currently doing, not what he'd done in the past.

Everyone had a past.

Even Cross.

Now was not the time to worry about how many notches either of them had on their belts. Or bed posts.

Hell no, because now Nash was working his cock like a starving man who'd just been handed a corndog at the State Fair. He was swallowing it whole.

A guttural sound bubbled up Cross's throat and escaped before he could stop it.

That encouraged Nash to work even harder at making Cross fight the tightness in his balls and the familiar pressure which meant he was about to lose it deep within Nash's mouth.

He tried to form a courtesy warning in his mushy brain, his fingers flexing and unflexing deep within Nash's long, now totally loose hair.

Hair which was like silk brushing against Cross's heated skin.

The warning only turned out to sound like, "*Ah, fuuuuck*," mixed with a long groan as his hips surged up and Nash's mouth came down.

But just as Cross felt his cock pulsing, his cum rising, ready to shoot down Nash's throat, the man pulled free, wrapped his long fingers around Cross's wet cock and pumped the load all over Cross's stomach.

Streams of hot cum streaked his skin as he threw his head back and tried to not only catch his breath but gather his sanity.

His stomach rose and fell with each breath he pulled deep, but he froze when that fucking skilled tongue touched his skin again.

Nash was tracing it through the mess Cross made. How fucking hot was that!

Cross tipped his chin to his neck again just to watch.

Nash's eyes were glued to his as he held his hair back with one hand and licked up every last drop of cum Cross had released.

Why Nash didn't just swallow in the first place, Cross didn't know. Or care.

Spit. Swallow. Jerk it onto his stomach. He was fine with any and all of it.

What he wasn't fine with was, he wouldn't be able to fuck Nash as soon as he'd hoped.

However, he could find plenty of things to occupy their time while he recovered. And coming now meant when he got to fuck Nash later he'd last a little longer, now that he took the edge off. Kind of like Nash's pot.

He grinned up at the ceiling at that thought until Nash started crawling up his body, his square heavy-duty belt buckle scraping along his skin.

But before he could tell Nash he needed to get rid of his clothes, the other man had his hands planted on the floor on either side of Cross's head and dropped his mouth to Cross's.

The salty tang of his own cum on Nash's lips and tongue assaulted his senses. It wasn't like he hadn't tasted himself before. And he wasn't going to start thinking about all the times he had and why, but he didn't mind sharing that taste with Nash.

In fact, it was hot as fuck.

Apparently, Nash thought so, too, because he was straddling one of Cross's thighs and grinding against his hip.

This needed to stop.

Not because Cross didn't want to fuck Nash, because, hell yes, he did. But because, not only were they on the floor in the shadowed entryway of his townhouse and Nash was still dressed, that oversized belt buckle of his was going to maim him.

He twisted his head to the side, breaking the kiss. "Nash, want you naked and in my bed."

Nash stared down at him. "Don't know how to ask for shit, do you? This a regular thing for you? Bein' a pig and all?"

"Comes with the territory," he admitted.

"Not sure I like it."

"You'll get used to it."

"Not sure I'm stayin' that long for that to happen."

"You're staying long enough for us to finish what we started," Cross told him.

"There you go again."

"Can you get off me, please, so we can go into my bedroom and fuck?"

"The please was a nice touch, but unnecessary."

It was Cross's turn to shove Nash in the chest with his palms, knocking him not only off balance but off him completely. Cross rolled up, snagged his shorts and got to his feet at the same time Nash was getting to his.

"You can either follow me or you can split. The door's right there. Don't give a shit what you do." Cross turned on his heels and headed through his dark townhouse past the open kitchen and living room, past the spare bedroom and guest bathroom, toward his master bedroom in the back.

"Think you do," he heard behind him.

Right, he did. But, fuck him, he wasn't going to admit it.

He heard heavy boots quickly following him, then a hand on his shoulder. He was spun around and pushed against the wall just next to his bedroom door. Nash pinned him in place with his body. "You got yours," he growled, "now I get mine."

"Are you asking or demanding?" Cross whispered because their faces were so close their noses were almost touching.

"Takin' what's mine."

Well, that comment actually gave his cock a little spark of life, but not enough to do what Cross was dying to do. But again, they could come up with plenty of things to do before then.

"You're dressed. I'm not. And my bedroom is right there. Can we finish this conversation with both of us naked?"

Nash stared at him for a couple of beats, then backed

off. Cross continued into his bedroom, his heart thumping as he stared at his bed and heard Nash following.

He hadn't turned on any lights when he went to answer the door and wondered if he should now.

Yes, fuck it, he needed to see all of Nash. He kept the overhead light in the ceiling fan off but switched on a small lamp on the nightstand. It gave just enough light to give the room an ambient glow.

Not that this needed to be a romantic atmosphere. This was going to be anything but romantic.

Interesting? Yes.

Exciting? Yes.

Satisfying? So far, for him, yes.

But even remotely romantic? Cross turned to look at the man who now stood in the middle of his bedroom, glancing around. No.

And to suggest that this was the beginning of anything other than what it was, wasn't even realistic or romantic.

It was a sexual attraction between the two of them. At least, it was on his part, and he couldn't imagine why Nash would show up in the middle of the night if it wasn't true on his.

"Well?" Cross asked.

Nash lifted a brow.

"You're *still* dressed."

The corners of Nash's lips quirked, and the creases around his eyes deepened as he shook his head and moved over to Cross's dresser. Then he slowly and methodically began to pull off each of the many rings he had circling his long fingers and placing them in a pile on top of the dresser.

"You take your rings off when you fuck?"

Nash hesitated and glanced over his shoulder. "Yeah, they're bulky, they can leave bruises."

Cross's gaze slid to the side as he pondered that, then let it slide back to Nash, who continued to divest himself of the wide black leather cuffs he had around each wrist. While one part of him wanted to ask a follow-up question about the rings, the other part of him didn't want to know.

Either way, the thought of Nash doing something to him that had the potential to leave bruises both excited him and worried him at the same time.

He might be stepping into uncharted territory with this man.

He had been worried Nash was the one to be inexperienced being with other men. Maybe, just maybe, Cross was the one who needed to expand his horizons.

He thought he'd pretty much tried it all, but maybe he was wrong.

He'd began experimenting with sex with other boys when he was in his teens and realized males were his preference. He didn't even try to date or kiss any females. That thought had left him cold.

But through the years, he'd sought out various sexual experiences and figured out what he liked and didn't like, what was acceptable to him and what wasn't.

What made him lose his mind and what turned him off.

However, his attraction to and interest in Nash caught him off guard. He had seen him across The Cockpit and watched him for probably a half hour before even approaching.

It wasn't that he had to gather the courage to approach, but he wasn't sure he trusted what both his brain and body were trying to tell him. That the long-haired, tattooed man sitting at the bar, not actively seeking sexual companionship for the night—which was the reason most of the other men were there for—was for him.

He liked the fact Nash had been sitting alone and relaxed at the bar, enjoying his beer and the band, and not acting desperate to find his latest hookup.

Now that same man was pulling his Rush long-sleeved

thermal over his head, exposing not only lean muscle, but an enormous tattoo on his back.

In fact, Cross blinked at how much real estate that tattoo took up. Even in the low light of the bedroom, Cross had no problem reading the rockers and knowing what all that ink stood for.

Which was like a glass of cold water splashed in Cross's face, because it was a reminder this probably wasn't a good idea.

But, again, this could be a thing without being a *thing*. And Nash was already unbuckling that heavy belt buckle and unfastening his worn Levi's.

If Cross was having any second thoughts, he needed to voice them now. However, what an asshole he would be by letting Nash suck him off and then he, at least, not return the favor.

Nash's loose jeans had fallen a little lower around his hips as he bent over, unlacing his boots, again with excruciating slowness, almost as if he was purposely trying to torture Cross. Eventually he toed them off, yanked off his threadbare socks and then turned to face Cross, still wearing his jeans.

However, now his jeans gaped open and Cross could see how lean Nash really was. Amongst more tattoos, a long necklace made of black leather or cord had some kind of metal pendant hanging from it between his pecs.

He was not bulky at all, which Cross had figured, and it didn't look like he worked out or, if he did, it was minimal. He appeared naturally lean. Like he was the type of guy who could eat huge plates of food and not gain an ounce.

Unlike Cross, who worked out hard a few times a week to stay in shape, not only for his job but for attracting other men.

Nash had half sleeves covering both arms, and a large tattoo across his chest saying "Live and Learn" in script.

And if Cross could read them right, "Brothers" on his ribs, as well as the words "Never Quit." He wondered what all of those meant to Nash. "Brothers" he could understand because as a part of the Dirty Angels MC, which meant he was part of a brotherhood. The rest, though...

Live and learn.

That could mean anything.

But now was not the time to ask for that explanation, even if Nash would give it to him. Now was the time to appreciate the "V" of muscle that disappeared into his gaping jeans and the dark hair peeking between the open zipper.

That was the only hair Nash had on his torso. Other than that, his skin was smooth.

And Cross couldn't wait to touch it. So, he didn't. He moved over to where Nash stood in front of the dresser, his eyes tracking him as he approached, his hands gripping the waistband of his open jeans, seemingly ready to shuck them.

When Cross was there, he lifted the pendant that hung against Nash's sternum. It was a guitar pick made of what looked like copper that had "Where words fail music speaks" engraved on it.

Cross was beginning to wonder if Nash was more complex and had many more layers than he originally thought. Maybe the man wasn't living free and easy, maybe he wore chains, too.

He was sure being gay wasn't easy because of the brotherhood he belonged to. He couldn't imagine a typical MC accepting Nash's sexual orientation, even if he was bisexual and openly swung both ways.

Cross returned the pendant to its spot, the back of his fingers pressing against warm skin. Smooth, just like it looked.

Cross raised his gaze and met Nash's. "Drop them."

Without hesitation, Nash dropped his jeans and Cross realized he'd been going commando under them.

Keeping his gaze locked to Nash's, Cross dropped his hand from the pendant, slid his fingers slowly from Nash's balls up his length, discovered a bead of precum at the tip with this thumb, collected it and raised it to his own lips.

Still not breaking eye contact, Cross slowly licked it off the pad of his thumb. Before he could drop his hand again, Nash crushed his mouth to his and licked Cross's tongue. Then he deepened the kiss, bumping Cross backward step by step until the back of his legs hit the edge of the mattress. One more hard bump and Cross was falling back onto the bed, Nash quickly following.

Cross grunted as Nash's weight hit his chest, his fingers gripped Cross's short hair, and he took his mouth roughly again.

Twisting his neck, Cross broke himself free from Nash's plundering tongue and tried to catch his breath. He was now semi-hard, but still not ready to proceed with what he had planned. With what he hoped Nash had planned.

Instead, he grabbed Nash's right arm, tugging his weight off him and then scrambled out from being pinned to the bed.

"Hey—"

"No," was all Cross said, pulling Nash's arm hard and yanking him into the center of the bed. Even though Nash didn't fight it, Cross could see he was thinking about it.

Before Nash could think too hard, Cross had him flipped onto his belly and he straddled Nash's thighs.

Fuck, his ass was perfect. Lean, but muscular like the rest of him. It reminded Cross of a perfect peach. And he *loved* peaches. In both cobblers and on a man. And the fact he had two dimples right above that peach made it even hotter.

He squeezed both cheeks, then leaned over to lick up the line of Nash's spine, from the top of his crease all the way to the back of his neck. He fisted a handful of his loose, messy hair and moved it to the side so he could suck at the skin where Nash's neck met his spine. Every muscle in Nash's back rippled when he did. He sucked again, this time harder and got the same reaction along with Nash's hips grinding into the mattress.

He did it once more, not only sucking, but sinking his teeth gently into the damp skin.

"Fuck," Nash groaned.

Cross smiled against Nash's neck, then released him. It wasn't a hard bite, but enough to leave a red mark. Seeing it made Cross's cock take on a little more life.

Soon. He'd be ready soon.

Good things shouldn't be rushed and since he didn't work until second shift that day, he had plenty of time to spend on Nash. He also assumed Nash had nowhere to be in the morning, otherwise he wouldn't have showed up at that ungodly hour.

Using the fingertips of both hands, he traced the man's ink that defined who he was. At least, for the most part. Maybe more like who he belonged with.

Unfortunately, that was not in bed with a cop. Cross knew that much.

His fingertips followed the lines of the top rocker which read "DIRTY ANGELS," the large center insignia which represented the club, then the bottom rocker which read "PENNSYLVANIA."

Cross had something similar inked into his skin and was surprised Nash hadn't mentioned it.

He understood brotherhood and loyalty all too well. Having Nash in his bed defied his, being in Cross's bed defied Nash's.

But no one had to know but the two of them.

He wasn't worried about Nash outing him because he,

himself, probably wouldn't want to be outed. So, they were safe if they were careful.

Even if they only had tonight.

He pressed his lips to one dimple, then the other, before moving down to sink his teeth into one half of that peach. Nash's muscles twitched as he bit down even harder.

Then using his thumbs, he split that peach in two and drew his tongue from the top of the crease down.

A sound came deep from Nash's throat as Cross's tongue circled, flicked and teased, dipping occasionally just slightly in the center.

Nash's hips surged up, Cross's only indicator the man wanted more. Which he gave to him.

Without breaking contact, he moved between Nash's legs and tapped his hip. Nash rose to his knees, but kept his face hidden in the pillow.

It gave Cross much better access, not only for what he was doing, but so he could reach around and take Nash's cock in his hand.

Using a little lube would make it so much better.

He released Nash and Cross heard a rush of breath.

"Don't move," Cross ordered.

"Again, a fuckin' demand."

Yes, it was.

But the man didn't move as Cross yanked open his nightstand drawer, grabbed the bottle of lube, squirted a dab onto his palm and took the bottle with him. He left the drawer open because soon he would need what else was in there.

However, right now was all about taking care of Nash after he'd done the same for Cross.

He moved back behind Nash, reaching around him again, this time fisting the man's cock and spreading the silky gel all over it from root to tip.

Nash's hips surged forward as Cross pulled, but quickly moved back into place. And Cross knew why.

He continued to stroke Nash with a slow, lazy pace, squeezing and releasing his fingers as he did so. Then he went back to work, kissing those sexy dimples once more before using his free hand to separate Nash's cheeks again and Cross buried his face there.

Chapter Seven

Jesus fuck.
    Jesus motherfuck.
    Jesus holy motherfuck.
    Nash honestly hadn't held out any hope that Cross knew what the fuck he was doing. He couldn't stop thinking about him since The Cockpit, but after the invitation a week ago, Nash's brain was full of nothing *but* Cross.
    In fact, he hardly even remembered his gig tonight. It had been a blur and not because of pot.
    Because of Cross.
    After playing his last set at Dirty Dick's, a biker bar now run by the Dark Knights MC, he'd pulled up Cross's text—which he should've deleted—got one of his bandmates to pack up his equipment, then he hopped on his sled and came here. To the cop's townhouse.
    And now he was in the man's bed getting a rim job like never before.
    He hadn't been expecting that. In fact, the only reason for showing up at the cop's townhouse was for a quickie. Nash planned on banging one out, then splitting.

He didn't expect a bunch of foreplay. That wasn't why he was here. No, he just wanted to fuck Cross, get off, then leave.

But what Cross was doing to him made him want to stay. At least a bit longer than originally intended.

The bossiness, though. It was fucking with Nash's head. He was usually the one giving orders when it came to hookups like this.

He knew what he wanted, took it, and didn't linger. If the current hookup he was with at the time didn't like it, then fuck him, it wasn't like Nash would see the fucker again.

Wham. Bam. Thank you... Man.

Don't call me, I'll call you... never.

That was how Nash rolled when it came to fucking either sex. Men. Women. Whoever.

Though, women tended to be clingier. Another reason he preferred men. Much easier to scrape off at the end of the night.

Even some of the sweet butts—their club whores—could be hard to kick out of his bed. They usually had their claws out, trying to sink them in one of the available brothers. Which usually ended up being a big, fat fucking failure for them, since no fucking brother in their right mind would tie his dick to a woman who'd fuck anything wearing club colors.

But it wasn't a woman licking, sucking and tongue fucking his ass right now.

Fuck no, it wasn't.

It was a man who seemed to have some experience at that. It was also fucking blowing Nash's mind better than smoking a bowl of prime Blackberry Kush.

He'd never once had a woman eat his ass like that. In fact, when he'd suggest it, they'd wrinkle their fucking noses.

But, *fuck*, if Cross hadn't dived right in along with stroking Nash's dick like a gold medal hand job champion.

Only problem was, Nash was about to blow his load all over the man's sheets. When he lost that load, he'd prefer it to be when his dick was buried deep inside Cross. Which meant he needed to gather his scattered brain cells and tell him to stop.

But, fuck him, he was having a hard time forming those words.

Because, also fuck him, he wanted to come just like that. With Cross's mouth on his ass and his dick in the man's hand.

He could always go against his own rule and stay afterward this time, since he was not leaving that fucking townhouse until he got what he came for. Which was Cross's ass.

But it seemed as though he would have no choice but to linger because the cop was now doing something with his fingers against Nash's taint. And, *holy fuck*, what he was doing was stroking and pressing his prostate from the outside instead of the inside.

And...

Nash's thoughts shattered as his hips thrust forward and the build-up of pressure released everything Nash had into Cross's hand. He might have even whimpered while it happened.

Hopefully not. But he didn't give a shit if he did since that was the best fucking combination hand-job ass-eating he'd ever received.

Yep, Cross was a gold-medalist at jerking another guy off.

"Don't move," Cross ordered, his tone raspy.

There he went giving Nash orders again. Why the fuck was he even listening?

When the mattress shifted, Nash removed his face from

the pillow and watched Cross's ass as he headed to what he guessed was the master bathroom, which was confirmed when he heard a sink run.

Not thirty seconds later the man was heading back toward the bed, his cock hanging hard and heavy between his thick thighs.

Cross seemed to be ready for a second round of head, which Nash would gladly give him after that mind-blowing orgasm he just had.

As he started to drop his hips to the mattress, Cross barked out, "Don't move," again.

He'd heard that a few times from pigs before and never liked it in the past. He also wasn't so sure he liked it now. But he was curious as to what the man had planned next.

At least until the bed shifted again and Nash heard the tear of a foil wrapper.

Hold the fuck up.

"Has it been awhile? Do you need prep?" Cross asked, rolling on a wrap.

Hold the fuck up!

Nash quickly dropped to his stomach, rolled onto his back and sat up, staring at the bottle of lube in Cross's hand, his heart thumping in his chest. "You got this fuckin' wrong. I give it, I don't take it."

Cross's dark brows rose. "I was—"

"No, the fuck you're not," Nash cut him off.

"You don't—"

"Not sure where you got that fuckin' idea."

"You were taking orders."

"Yeah, because you're bossy as fuck. Doesn't mean I take it up the ass."

"Never?"

Nash shut his mouth. He had in the past, but it had been a while since the last time. Usually with the quick hookups he sought out, he was only there to get himself off. And he did that much faster by topping whoever was his volunteer.

He should've fucking known with Cross being who he was, what he was, he'd want to top.

Fuck him. He'd been fucking stupid. Panting so hard over the man who currently wore a wrap and was ready to lube up Nash's asshole, he hadn't even considered this might be a problem.

Cross's eyebrows dropped low. "You always top?"

Nash's brows got just as low. "Yeah."

"Then it seems we're at an impasse."

"That what it is? A fuckin' *impasse*? Like 'do not pass go?'"

"Well, I've bottomed before, but I haven't since..." Cross paused. "A while. It's not my preference."

"Maybe you haven't gotten it from the right man. Maybe you'd love it if you did."

Cross's lips twitched. "Are you that right man?"

"You can let me know afterward."

Cross snorted. "Or vice versa."

Nash pushed the hair out of his face and looked Cross directly in the eyes. The man didn't even blink. Yeah, they were at a fucking impasse.

"Both got off. I could go." That would be an easy solution, but one Nash wasn't really thrilled about. He had wanted more from Cross, just not what the man was willing to give him. Which was his dick up Nash's ass.

He glanced down at his own dick. He'd just shot the motherlode and it'd be a while for him to recover, especially now since he was teetering on thirty-seven. It had been a long time since he could rebound like when he was eighteen. *Hell*, no rebound was needed back then. He'd been rock hard twenty-four seven. Over men, over women. He'd even done a chick with a dick once. Okay, more than once. In his twenties, he'd stick his dick in any willing hole, be it mouth, ass, or pussy.

He was more selective now since his hormones didn't rage like they used to. *Thank fuck,* because he'd done some dumb shit he wanted to forget. And some of it had nothing to do with hormones... but that was another story.

"How about a compromise?"

Nash wasn't liking the sound of that, either. But it was a question and not a demand this time, so there was that. However, it didn't change the fact he wasn't the one going to be getting fucked.

But the look on Cross's face read that Nash was going to be the one getting fucked.

He closed his eyes and tried to remember the last time that occurred.

Too fucking long ago. And he'd only done it out of necessity, not because he wanted it.

"We can switch," Cross continued, his hand now on Nash's bare thigh, giving it a squeeze.

Nash's heart pounded even heavier in his chest. This wasn't what he came here for, otherwise, he wouldn't have come. But in no way was he ready to leave this man's bed yet. No fucking way. So to get a shot at Cross, he needed to submit first.

Was he really fucking considering it?

"Guess you'll need to be prepped," Cross said again, his voice low.

The bossy motherfucker just assumed Nash would bend the fuck over and give it up.

"Fuck me," Nash muttered.

Cross grinned and jerked his chin down, indicating his erection. "That's the plan."

"Didn't mean it like that."

"I know, but it's how I'm taking it. I'll take it slow and make it worth your while."

Sure he fucking would. "Then I'm doin' the same to you."

Cross's grin slipped. "You won't have to go as slow with me."

"Thought you only liked to top."

"Normally, yes, but I... I've switched recently with someone else."

"How recently?"

Cross's lips became a thin slash. "Get back on your knees."

Nash's eyebrows shot up his forehead. Someone was avoiding that question. *What-fucking-ever.* He didn't give a shit who Cross had been fucking or had been fucked by or even how recently.

He wasn't putting a ring on it. Unless it was a cock ring.

Grinding his teeth, he moved back to his knees, trying to keep his muscles relaxed and his mind open.

This wasn't his favorite thing to do, by no means.

He sucked in a sharp breath when cool lube hit his hole, then a finger followed it, circling and dipping just slightly.

"You're tightening up."

No shit.

He sank his teeth into his bottom lip, and shoved his face back into the pillow, covering his head with his arms.

He could do this. He could.

Then it would be his turn.

That's what he needed to focus on. How it was going to feel to sink deep into Cross's tight, muscular ass.

Behind closed eyelids, Nash's eyes rolled back when Cross worked his index finger in slowly, to the first joint, the second, then all the way in.

Nash hissed out a breath as it slid in and out of him, a generous amount of lube being distributed deeper inside.

"Prepping" him.

His breathing shallowed as Cross's heat touched the skin

of his ass and the back of his thighs. Cross held one of Nash's hips to keep him still as he kept working that finger in and out of him, occasionally pulling a groan from Nash when it would brush his prostate.

That's what he wanted more of. *That*.

He might not usually take dick back there but there had been plenty of times he'd used a prostate stimulator as he pounded one out on his own. The orgasms were long and intense, and he was always wiped afterward.

But he hadn't done it too often as he couldn't leave that toy in his room at church. Last thing he needed was one of the sweet butts or prospects finding it on the rare occasion they cleaned his room. Instead, he kept it hidden in one of his guitar cases and only got it out on the road when he stayed in a motel and he was alone.

But, *fuck*, when he did...

His thoughts were quickly brought back to the present when Cross slipped a second lubed finger past his sphincter and not only worked them back and forth, but scissored them, stretching him.

"You need to fucking relax," Cross growled, bending over Nash and nipping one of his ass cheeks.

Nash jerked from the sharp pain and after a second, concentrated on loosening that tight ring of muscle.

"That's it," Cross said softly. Curling his fingers, he teased Nash's P-spot a few more times and then he warned, "One more, then we'll try."

Cross's voice was becoming hoarse and sounding out of breath, his wrap-covered dick pressing against the back of Nash's thigh, and he could feel each pulse. The man was probably close to his limit and ready to take what he wanted.

Even so, Nash appreciated Cross taking the time to make sure he was ready. But when Cross added a third finger, Nash could feel the burn. The discomfort.

"Last time I'm saying it, you need to fucking relax, Nash. I'm bigger than this."

"For fuck's sake, you're motherfuckin' bossy as motherfuckin' fuck!" Nash screamed into the pillow, though it ended up muffled.

Then his fingers were gone.

Was he giving up? Were they done?

Before Nash could shift away, Cross's hand clamped tighter on his hip, his fingers digging in painfully, the fat head of his dick pushing in.

"Push out."

"Fuck you. Know what to fuckin' do. Fuck!" he shouted again into the pillow, clutching it so hard his hands were beginning to cramp.

Cross fell over Nash's back and growled in his ear, "If you don't want to do this, just fucking say so. But know this... You're not getting mine if I don't get yours. This is your choice. You tell me *no*. Or you tell me *go*. But choose, for shit's sake."

Nash closed his eyes and took a deep breath, feeling the pressure of Cross's head pressed against his anus. One good push, he'd be inside him.

Did he want that?

Did he want Cross that badly?

For fuck's sake... "Go."

Cross released a breath so harsh against Nash's ear that he had to have been holding it. He'd been worried Nash would say no.

Nash was a fool. He never thought he'd ever be in this position again and here he was.

All for a fucking cop.

A cop he had no business being with.

A cop who was about to...

A hiss escaped him as his breath came more quickly.

"You're still tense. Does it hurt?"

It was the slight pain, the pinch, that bothered him, that took him back...

Dad, it hurts! Stop!

My boy wants to be a fucking faggot?

Nash squeezed his eyes shut harder and struggled to suck in air.

"Nash..."

No boy of mine is going to be a faggot!

"Nash!"

"Go," he groaned, trying to push out that memory, waiting for Cross to push inside.

That's what it's going to feel like when a faggot does that to you! Does that feel good, boy? Is that what you want?

"Go." Beads of sweat popped out on Nash's forehead.

Is that what you want, boy?

Cross went. He breached the tight ring, the burn almost unbearable. The memory even worse.

"Tell me to stop if you need me to stop," came soft but strained in his ear.

What needed to stop was that memory from twenty years ago. Memories he thought had faded away.

But they hadn't. They'd been lurking right below the surface, waiting.

That was then. This is now.

That was then. This is now.

It isn't the same. It's different.

So different.

Cross wasn't moving. He was letting Nash get used to the stretch, the fullness.

"Tell me when I can move."

Nash pushed those memories out of his head and slammed the door shut behind them. Then he mentally locked that fucking door.

He needed to remain in the here and now. He needed to

concentrate on Cross. The man might be a bit bossy but so far, he seemed to be a considerate partner.

Nash nodded against the pillow. "Okay."

"Sure?"

"Yeah."

As Cross straightened, he grabbed Nash's wrists and wrenched his fists from his death grip on the pillow. Then Cross pulled both his arms around, so Nash's wrists were pinned to his back, just as if Nash was being arrested.

A very dominant move. One Nash wasn't sure he appreciated.

It pushed Nash's chest deeper into the bed, put strain on his shoulders, and kept him in place. He wouldn't be able to rise onto his hands; he wouldn't be able to move from the position. The only thing Nash could do to escape was drop his hips.

Cross continued to hold on to both wrists and began to move. It was slow. Steady. Careful. "Talk to me."

"Fuckin' ain't time for talkin'."

"Tell me what you want, what you need. It's been awhile for you..."

It certainly fucking had. But that reminder made that locked-away memory want to break free once more.

"Just shut up."

"I—"

"Just shut up and fuck me."

Cross stilled, the head of his dick barely inside him.

"Don't say another fuckin' word," Nash warned him.

Cross began to move again, this time faster but still careful, his fingers tightening on Nash's wrists.

Surprisingly, Nash began to relax. Cross was no beginner. His movements were smooth. He knew how to flex his hips, not just ram his dick in and out of Nash like a piston.

Nash never remembered it feeling this good. Not once.

It had always been awkward in the past. Uncomfortable. This was anything but.

Cross released his wrists and left one hand lightly on top of Nash's, an indication for him to remain in that position but ultimately letting Nash decide. Nash was free, he could move his arms, but he no longer wanted to.

He wanted to wait this out, see what Cross would bring him.

Which was his free hand smoothing over Nash's ass cheek as he continued to fuck him. His palm smoothed over the other cheek, over his hip and underneath him to find Nash still semi-soft. Cross gently cupped him there, giving him a slight squeeze then moved back to where he was earlier. His thumb pushed against that magic spot found in the crease between Nash's dick and anus.

Even soft, Nash's dick twitched at the pleasurable pressure.

No, being a bottom had never been this good.

Not once.

And, fuck him, it ticked him off that he found it with this fucking cop.

Cross's pace increased, and Nash's ass rippled with each thrust of the man's hips. With the pressure from Cross's thumb on the outside, and the pressure on the inside, Nash was surprised to find himself hard again, his cock swinging wildly with each pound against his ass. A long string of precum hung from the tip as Cross began to fuck him even harder, their skin slapping and Nash grunting with each thrust.

He never liked this shit before.

Never.

How could he like it now?

He wanted Cross to continue. To fuck him harder. Deeper.

"Fuck," he groaned into the pillow, tipping his hips to a

better angle, giving Cross more of his ass. Encouraging him without words.

A bead of sweat dripped on Nash's ass. Then another as Cross's breathing was loud, like a steam locomotive.

Then Cross's hand was gone from his, leaving him totally free. But only for a second, because that same hand tangled in his hair, fisted it painfully and Cross ripped his head up, forcing Nash to go along with it.

Nash rose to his knees as Cross sat back on his heels, no longer pressing on his prostate.

No, instead the man wrapped his arm around the front of Nash's chest, pinning Nash's back to Cross's front, his mouth to Nash's ear, his deep grunts filling Nash's head.

Cross's other arm wrapped around his hip, grabbing Nash's cock and pumping it furiously.

"No," he managed to get out. He was so close to coming and he wanted to fuck Cross. "No," he forced out again on a groan.

Cross released him, instead grabbing his hair again and tipping Nash's head back until it rested on his shoulder.

Cross's face was in Nash's neck, Nash's back was arched, Cross's cock planted deep as he powered up into Nash over and over again.

A thumb brushed over Nash's tight nipple, then fingers snagged it, tweaking and twisting, causing Nash to cry out with how crazy good it all felt.

Nash's cock was hard, aching, strings of precum releasing with each pump of Cross's hips.

Then Nash felt the rumble in Cross's chest before he heard it. A low, loud groan that turned into a grunt accompanied with one last hard thrust up as Cross held him tightly against him, his face buried in Nash's hair, his breathing harsh as he came deep inside Nash. The root of Cross's cock pulsated against Nash's throbbing rim.

Nash was held captive against Cross because of the

man's grip on his hair. Cross wasn't going to let him go until he was ready.

But Nash didn't fight it.

He needed to gather his thoughts, because if he fucked Cross right now, he'd come instantly. And that would fucking suck because he wanted to make the most of this short time they had together.

Because that was what it'd be. Short.

Chapter Eight

CROSS HELD THEM BOTH STILL, not saying a word. His breathing said it all. Hopefully it expressed how thankful he was for the opportunity of Nash giving himself to Cross.

He ran his tongue up the side of Nash's damp neck, tasting the salty tang of his skin, nuzzling his hair, sucking his earlobe. "Thank you," he whispered, again hoping Nash realized how much he meant that.

Nash hadn't given himself lightly.

Cross hadn't taken that gift lightly, either.

It had taken longer than Cross anticipated for Nash to relax, to give in, but when he finally did...

Fuck, Cross wasn't ready to move. He wanted to remain right where he was with Nash pressed against him, and them intimately connected.

It felt both disturbing and right at the same time. Disturbing because Nash was the wrong man, but also because Nash was the right man.

His pulse was still pounding and that thought didn't help it settle.

Cross slid his hand up from Nash's chest which was rapidly rising and falling, to his throat, his fingers curling around it lightly, his thumb finding Nash's pounding heartbeat.

His other hand smoothed over the man's stomach into the thick, springy hair, then he wrapped his fingers around Nash's erection.

"No," Nash said, his breath hitching.

"You're probably ready." He had to be on the verge of coming again.

"I'm not ready. Let me go."

Cross let him go, pulling back slightly, his hand dropping from Nash's throat as well.

"Wh—" Cross swallowed his words as Nash surged forward, breaking their connection. Nash spun him around, grabbed Cross by the throat and shoved him to the bed. All the air rushed from him as he landed, not expecting the sudden change of power.

"Hold on," Cross yelled, scrambling to remove the spent condom. But Nash had it off of him and tossed over the side of the bed before Cross could protest.

Nash planted a hand on Cross's chest, holding him down while he fisted his own cock twice.

"Hey—"

"Shut up." Nash leaned over, crushing their mouths together, smothering any of Cross's protests. The kiss was not gentle, not even close. It was the type of kiss that "claimed" the other person. Dominant. Aggressive.

And if Cross hadn't just come, he would be as hard as a fucking rock over that kiss, even though he was the one usually in charge.

Nash captured his groan and gave it back to him. And when Nash broke free, he was panting.

He wasn't the only one.

His heart had been racing when he fucked Nash. Even now, it hadn't slowed one bit, especially with the sudden switch of power.

Nash kept his hand firmly planted on Cross's chest, keeping him pinned to the bed as he leaned over and grabbed the lube and another condom, tossing them on Cross's chest.

"Get me ready 'cause I'm not waitin'."

Without a word, Cross did just that. Rolling on a condom, lubing up his cock, then with two fingers, lubing up his own hole inside and out. He trembled with anticipation and a little bit of trepidation.

Like Nash, being a bottom wasn't his preference. But they'd made a deal and now Cross had to keep his end of it.

"Knees to your chest."

Cross didn't like being controlled. He'd already had someone who tried to be bossy. It didn't work. In fact, it was a disaster. And if Nash was that way, tonight might be the only night they'd be together.

It might be better that way, anyway.

This could be a thing without being a *thing*.

Even so, Nash bossing him around the same way Cross had done to him...

Was kind of...

Hot.

Unexpectedly hot.

Why he'd want that from a man he hardly knew versus a man he had lived with and thought he was in love with was a mystery.

Though, one not to be solved tonight. So, he held his knees wide, pulled them to his chest and willed his muscles to loosen.

If he tensed, it would hurt.

If he didn't, it would...

Be worth it.

Fuck, he hoped it was.

Cross closed his eyes and blew out a breath, waiting for

the pinch, the pressure, the ever so slight discomfort of the stretch.

It had been months for him.

Since that last time.

Before that last fight, that last straw.

That moment they both realized it would never work.

Neither was willing to give in.

And here Cross was again in the same possible situation. With a man who might never give up the power.

This could be a thing without being a *thing*.

Keep things easy. Loose.

Between just the two of them.

Then Nash pulled Cross out of his thoughts when he pushed, pressed, demanded entrance.

Cross let him in. Accepting him, encouraging him with the tilt of his hips to take him completely. Nash did so, then hesitated, his palms planted in the mattress, his dark, unreadable eyes meeting Cross's.

He remained still at first, just like Cross had done with him. Letting Cross's body adjust around him, preparing for what was to come.

Then with a grimace and a growl, Nash began to fuck him. Hard. Fast. Slamming deep. Cross's body jostling with each thrust.

Cross had taken care.

Nash was not.

Each thrust was fueled with anger. Cross wasn't sure if it was directed at him or at Nash himself. Was Nash beating himself up for giving Cross the upper hand?

Nash clamped his fingers around Cross's wrists, pinning them to the bed, one on each side of his head, driving all of his weight into them to hold Cross down.

It was uncomfortable but exhilarating, too.

And now he was glad Nash took off his rings. They would have left marks, possibly even bruises, behind.

But he didn't complain, he didn't tell Nash to stop. He let the man work out whatever demons he was trying to rid himself of.

The pounding got even more intense. Nash's balls slapped loudly against Cross's ass like the beat of a drum. If Cross was going to bottom, he didn't mind it rough. But this was more than rough, it was almost emotionally detached. Mindless. Cold.

And then... it wasn't.

Nash fell over him, sucking one of Cross's nipples into his mouth, flicking the tip with his tongue.

His pace had changed to slow, lazy.

Nash's powerful hips flexed with each drive up and into Cross. Cross threw his head back, his mouth fell open, sounds escaping each time Nash bottomed out. Driving deep, grinding even deeper.

Not so desperately now.

Controlled. Deliberate.

Nash moved to the other nipple and scraped his teeth over the tip, then licked it, planting a kiss on it before his lips traveled a path to the center of Cross's chest, then up. Up his exposed throat, the underside of his jaw, to the corner of Cross's mouth.

The instant Nash captured his mouth but released his wrists, Cross tangled his fingers in his hair, holding him close, deepening the kiss. Until they inhaled each other's breath. Their breathing became one.

In. Out.

In.

Out.

Their breaths coming slightly faster than Nash's thrusts.

When they stopped kissing, their mouths remained fused. Their breaths still merged.

Cross's hand slid from Nash's hair down his back, feeling his muscles move beneath his fingertips, until he got to

Nash's ass, where he held on, feeling each pump, inside and out. Pulling him balls deep.

He defied Nash's order to keep his knees to his chest because he needed to hold on tighter, so he wrapped his legs around Nash's hips, holding him close, squeezing him tightly.

He felt the tremble begin to start, to take over Nash's body. The drive now more determined. The goal close. The peak within reach.

Nash broke his mouth free of Cross's, their beards brushed, and the wiry hairs tangled. But, *fuck*, the rough of Nash's beard felt good against his cheek, his lips, his neck.

Cross dug his fingers more firmly into the muscles of his ass, whispering, "That's it. Give me everything you've got."

Nash's breath shuddered and he shoved his face into Cross's neck, a long groan pulled from him as he curled over Cross one last time, driving his cock home as deep as he could go.

And then he stilled, pumping cum deep within Cross.

Cross imagined him bareback, raw, filling him with every last drop of his seed.

Then something happened which never happened before. He orgasmed without an erection. His climax radiated from his soft cock and through him, surprising the shit out of him.

He didn't even know that was possible.

Nash pushed up on his arms and glanced down between their bodies. "Damn," he whispered. "I felt that from inside you, too."

"Yeah," Cross breathed. Every cell in his body deeply satisfied, every bone like rubber and he was now ready for a nap.

No, not a nap, to sleep like the dead.

He had not one ounce of energy left and he knew they had to clean up yet.

As it was, he was sure Nash would be hitting the door and the road soon, anyway.

"Shower?" Cross suggested, hoping he'd stay a little longer.

Nash lifted his head and his hazel eyes met Cross's. "Yeah."

Cross whispered his next question. "Want to conserve water?"

"Fuck yeah," Nash whispered back.

Cross bit back his grin.

It was obvious, so did Nash.

———

HE SHOULD'VE LEFT but he hadn't. He'd stayed.

It was fucking stupid. Dangerous. Out of his norm.

A broken rule.

But what they did in the shower didn't leave him itching to leave.

It made him want to stay.

They had taken their time, sudsing each other up using their hands, washing each other's hair. Touching, playing, lingering here and there.

Appreciating every line and curve of each other's body. Exploring them, too, using their mouths and fingers. Until the water turned cold and they were forced to shut down the shower and dry themselves off.

It was fun and they could forget who they were for a little while.

After switching out the messy sheets, they both collapsed into Cross's bed, exhausted, content. But they kept a gap between them, both lying on their backs. Both tucking their arms under their heads, staring at the ceiling. Quiet.

Both unwilling to discuss anything that had happened that night.

In the bed. In the shower.

Inside of them.

But there was something he spotted in the shower that was fucking bugging him.

Something he'd missed earlier he shouldn't have.

Something he wished he'd seen prior to sucking Cross's cock.

And now he laid there in the dark staring at what that was since Cross was asleep on his stomach, his breathing steady, snoring softly, his face turned toward him.

His right upper arm bore a tattoo. The only one Nash found in that exploration earlier.

But it was one he wished he hadn't.

He recognized the logo. He knew the fucking meaning.

There were no six degrees of separation.

There were none. Zero.

This was too close to home.

Mitch Jamison was president of the Blue Avengers MC. Mitch Jamison was Zak's fucking father.

Axel Jamison was the VP of the Blue Avengers. Axel Jamison was Zak's fucking brother.

Zak Jamison was the president of the Dirty Angels. Z was Nash's fucking prez.

Z's father and brother were both fucking cops and wore the BAMC colors. Two men Nash knew all too well.

Cross was a cop and also wore the BAMC colors.

Cross had said *nothing* to him.

Fucking nothing.

They might not run in the same circles, but those lines were blurred, those circles now overlapped.

His original plan was to fuck Cross again later in the morning after they got a few hours of sleep. But there was no point in staying, there was no way he'd be able to sleep now.

And it was a bad idea to fuck Cross again.

He slipped out of bed, careful not to wake up Cross and, ignoring his pile of clothes, walked over to a door partially gaped open.

He opened it wider and wasn't surprised to see what he already knew... A lineup of neatly pressed uniforms on one side of the closet. But hanging at the end of those uniforms, a leather vest.

Cross's cut.

Nash grabbed it and pulled it out, staring at the back. He ran his fingers over the rockers, the center insignia, the square patch to the right of it which read "MC", the square patch to the left that read "LE."

Law enforcement.

The top rocker read "BLUE AVENGERS," the bottom, "PENNSYLVANIA."

The center patch consisting of a skull and crossbones and skeleton hands holding two guns, one saying "Loyalty," the other "Honor." It also included the "thin blue line" shield.

A rectangular patch on the front read "CROSS" and below that another one read "W. REGIONAL."

Hell, their club was large enough they had to split the state. He knew it was because their MC was full of law enforcement from all areas, not just local.

Cross was a weekend warrior, belonging to a club of fucking pigs who were wannabe badass bikers.

But no matter what they thought, they weren't. Never would be. Although they rode Harleys and stole the customs of true bikers, they were still pussy-assed pigs down to their core.

They had no love for real bikers.

And Nash and the rest of his brothers had no love for cops.

Nash put the cut back where he found it, then turned to stare at the sleeping man.

He shouldn't be here.

He didn't belong here.

He needed to get the fuck out of there.

He forced his feet to move, to gather his shit, get on his sled and get gone.

Chapter Nine

CROSS CRAB-WALKED his Harley back into a line of other bikes. There were a lot of them. But that was to be expected since The Iron Horse Roadhouse was a biker bar.

A *real* biker bar. One where MC colors were worn proudly. As long as they didn't belong to a rival club.

Most bikers knew the deal. They didn't drink in enemy territory.

As a cop, The Iron Horse was one hundred percent enemy territory.

But he was also a stupid fuck who had a hard-on for someone he shouldn't.

Someone who could have a beer in a bar like this and fit right in. Truthfully, Nash fit in here better than at The Cockpit.

At least to the outside world.

Cross's balls should be shriveled at the thought of doing what he was about to do, but he was fucking doing it.

When he woke up alone two weeks ago, he'd looked for a note left behind.

There'd been none.

When he'd sent a text later that morning, he got no

response. When he'd tried to call, it went to voicemail. He tried it a few more times in the last couple weeks. His texts and calls went ignored.

So here he was, being fucking stupid. What he was about to do could be dangerous.

He dismounted from his bike and turned to study the building. He filled his lungs, held it for a few seconds before blowing it back out. He ran a hand over his hair, and down his beard. Took one more inhale, dropped his head and shook it while staring at his boots.

Then he hoped like hell he walked out of that roadhouse the same way he walked in.

All in one piece.

If he'd been wearing his duty belt, he would've hitched it up at this point to bolster himself, but he wasn't. Instead he was wearing the oldest Levi's he owned, a Harley Henley he'd had for years he found at the back of his drawer and a heavy black, well broken-in leather jacket he wore when riding in cooler weather.

He stepped inside the door, let his gaze slice through the room to do a quick assessment, along with checking for any possible and immediate threats, then went directly to the bar and nabbed an empty stool.

The place was packed for a Sunday night, probably because it sounded like a live band was playing even though he had no idea where.

If it was a recording, it sounded damn good.

Each pool table was full, each table was occupied. And Cross had taken the last empty spot at the bar.

He glanced over his shoulder and took it all in once more.

No drugs. No underage drinking. No prostitution. No fighting.

Nothing.

Just a bar full of bikers, their women, and a group of

what appeared to be some military in a back corner. When he turned back to face the bar, Cross figured out why. There was a sign above the cash register stating that military, active or retired, drank for half price.

Cross had gone from high school directly into the Navy, did a two-year stint of active service before entering the police academy. During training and his time as a rookie, he remained in the Reserves until he finished serving his obligated time with the government.

Now he served his community.

A young biker wearing DAMC colors stopped in front of him on the backside of the bar, interrupting his thoughts. "Beer?"

"What do you have on draft?"

The twenty-something, still wet-behind-the-ears biker answered, "Beer."

Cross blinked to avoid rolling his eyes. "I'll take that."

The man whose patch said his name was Jester gave him a nod and moved down the bar.

Cross only hoped whatever beer was on tap wasn't Iron City. Even though it was a local beer, Cross preferred something more full-bodied.

He threw a five down on the bar seconds before Jester was back, slamming the pint glass in front of Cross so the head of the beer spilled over the rim. Cross grimaced at the color of the beer, knowing full well whatever he'd been served was not full-bodied, but more like swill. Jester snagged his five and disappeared again.

Cross took a sip. Yep. Monkey piss. He should have just ordered a bottle of ale. Too late.

He took another sip then sucked the foam out of his mustache before spinning around to survey the room again.

The only people in the place wearing DAMC cuts were the two bikers working behind the bar. Everyone else was wearing various colors or none at all.

But they all seemed to be enjoying the music. Either by singing along, dancing, moving to the beat and the like.

"Is the music live?" he asked his neighbor, who was scarfing down a plate of wings so hot they even singed Cross's nose hairs from where he sat.

The older, heavyset gentleman with a spider-web tattoo taking up the whole side of his neck, released a loud, toxic belch, then said, "Yeah."

Great. "Where's it coming from?"

"The courtyard," he said before shoving a whole chicken wing into his yapper.

"Is that part of the bar? Like an outside deck area?"

His neighbor didn't answer him since he was too busy sucking the fried and sauced chicken skin and flesh off the bones.

Instead, he heard Jester's voice behind him. "The courtyard's only for DAMC members an' their invited guests."

He turned his head and met Jester's eyes. The young guy's heavily tattooed arms were crossed over his chest. Cross ignored the body language and asked, "How do you get back there?" anyway.

Jester's eyes narrowed on him. "You don't. Got me?"

Cross nodded and turned back to the room, muttering, "Got it."

"Good."

Out of the corner of Cross's eye, he saw Jester move down the bar again.

He eyed his stool-mate and the mountain of bare bones on the plate. It looked like a massacre. "The wings any good?"

"Fuckin' best."

"You come here often?"

The man's jowls shook, and he dropped a half-gnawed wing on the plate. "You tryin' to pick me up?"

What? Cross quickly raised his palms. "No! Fuck no. I didn't mean it like that."

"Better not have."

"I was just curious how often the band played and figured if you were a regular, you'd know."

"I know."

He waited. The guy went back to inhaling his wings and Cross sighed.

"Hey, watch my beer, will ya?" Cross finally said, climbed off the stool and headed toward the exit, not waiting for the answering grunt.

He hit the parking lot, walked past his bike and around the side of the building.

Damn. From the front, the building was deceiving. As he moved down the side, he realized it was a lot longer than it looked. He got to a fence that was made of solid metal panels. Even though the gate was closed, the padlock on the chain hung open.

However, the sign on the front of that gate was not at all welcoming. Cross ignored that, just like he'd ignored Jester, his chicken-eating stool-mate and his own common sense for showing up at the bar in the first place.

After opening the gate just enough for him to slip through, he kept moving, staying close to the building in the shadows.

Another parking lot sat at the back of the building, actually larger than the one in the front, if that was possible. It was also packed with bikes, trucks, and SUVS.

He squinted at something at the far end of the parking lot.

Yep, just what he thought. Some woman had her skirt pushed up to her waist as she was bent over a bike, her palms planted on the seat. The guy fucking her had his jeans dropped to his knees and was drilling her like he was searching for oil. Of course, right out in the open where anyone could watch.

So, Cross watched for a few seconds and realized that shit didn't do anything for him. Now, if he had Nash bent over his Harley...

Cross adjusted himself and kept moving. He stayed between vehicles and kept away from the back door where anyone could step out at any moment.

He followed a line of tall half-dead bushes that seemed to be a natural "fence" of some sort and above it Cross could see the roofline of what appeared to be a pavilion. He wondered if that was where the band played. The closer he got, the louder the music became, so he knew he was on the right path.

At a gap in the bushes, he squeezed through and found himself at the back corner of the pavilion. His attention was first grabbed by a guy sitting on one of the picnic tables, his thighs spread, his boots planted on the seat and a woman's head buried in his crotch.

None of these guys apparently had any shame in their game. They got it where ever they could get it.

Staying in the dark corner by the bushes, he assessed the area. While the parking lot was full, the courtyard wasn't. A few people hung out under the large pavilion; a bunch of chairs, filled with more people, sat around the bonfire which burned in the center of that courtyard.

A few kegs lined the front fence separating the courtyard from the front public parking lot. A meat smoker, which sat near the beer, was open with a half-picked apart pig still spinning.

However, he wasn't there for a beer or a pulled pork sandwich. His gaze landed on the stage which sat on the other side of the roaring bonfire at the side of the courtyard farthest from the building. An actual stage with lighting, a professional sound system and everything.

On that impressive stage, Nash was the front man, singing into a mic clipped into a stand while he played an electric guitar.

And, *holy fuck*, he sounded really fucking good. He looked even better.

His long dark blond hair with sun streaks was flying free, except for some sweaty tendrils plastered around the edges of his face. He was putting everything he had into the song he and his band were playing, which was *Let Me be Myself* by 3 Doors Down.

How fucking fitting was that? He wondered if Nash's "brothers" or his bandmates recognized the irony of Nash singing that song in their midst.

Probably not.

Most likely no one but Cross understood those lyrics most likely held more meaning to Nash than anyone would know. Or cared.

Cross shifted forward, dying to move closer to experience the energy Nash was exuding up there on stage.

And, *damn it*, he wanted to lick the sweat off Nash's brow.

That would not be a good idea.

He'd been worried about leaving The Iron Horse in one piece and now he was even deeper in enemy territory. Licking a biker in front of a whole bunch of other bikers would be stupid.

When a hand clamped on his shoulder, he just about shit himself.

He spun around, his heart beating faster than the drums on stage, to face none other than Axel Jamison, the VP of the Blue Avengers MC and corporal at Shadow Valley PD, whose jurisdiction he was currently standing in.

Thank fuck it was him and not one of Nash's club brothers.

"What the hell are you doing here, Cross? Are you doing a stakeout or something?"

Ah, shit. He should've come up with a cover story. Now he had to wing it. "Heard there was some illegal activity going on here. Is that why you're here, too?" *Fuck*, he hated to lie. Especially to a friend.

Even in the dark, Cross could see Jamison's eyebrows drop low as he studied him. "Are you working undercover?"

"I recently got assigned to a special task force." *Fuck.* Another lie!

"What task force? I haven't heard of any task forces involving MC's."

"It's a new gang task force. A county thing." He bit back a groan. More fucking lies!

"Most MC's aren't even gangs, they're clubs. Brotherhoods like ours. You could call some outlaw MC's gangs but even that's stretching it. If you're going to go that route, they should be considered organized crime, not gangs."

Why was Jamison schooling him? Why the fuck did Axel care if an MC was called a gang? But Cross wasn't going to question him on that since he needed to pick his battles. And Jamison wasn't done yet.

"Even so, this is SVPD's jurisdiction. And if there was a new county task force, I'd know about it. More importantly, my brother is president of this MC. My sister's husband is a member. The club's clean."

Cross shot him a dubious look, trying to play the part as a member of a made-up task force. "No drug use? Nothing?" Because he knew for a fact Nash had come over to his townhouse smelling—and tasting—like weed. But he wasn't going to share that with Axel, either.

Plus, looking around the courtyard he could see plenty of people smoking. What they were smoking, he wasn't sure because it was too dark to see, but he could guarantee it wasn't only tobacco.

It didn't matter anyway, pot wasn't on his radar, the man still singing on stage was.

"Look, it's as clean as it's going to get. Took me a while to get my head on straight about it. I might be a cop, but this club's in my blood. It's also my wife's family. Both my granddad and hers were the founders of this MC. In fact, mine died for it. So when I say the club's clean, just accept that. You start digging, we're going to have a problem."

Cross had no idea that Axel or his father, Mitch, had ties running that deeply to the Dirty Angels. That meant both of them knew Nash well, which now made the whole situation between them even stickier.

The whole situation.

Like there was a situation between the two of them.

The only true situation was Cross being a dumb fuck, standing on DAMC ground wanting something he shouldn't want from a man who probably didn't want the same from him.

Because if he had, Nash wouldn't have just disappeared the other morning or would have responded to all the texts or messages Cross sent him like a desperate asshole. This was all proof a little bit of good dick could make a gay man lose his fucking marbles.

He certainly had to be losing his marbles when he imagined some monster lumbering in their direction.

Holy shit.

He might as well kiss his ass goodbye. Forget not leaving this place in one piece, he might not be leaving it at all.

"Fuck," Jamison muttered under his breath next to him, which wasn't reassuring.

Cross realized he could hear that mutter because the music had stopped. His eyes flicked to the stage. Empty.

His eyes flicked back to The Incredible Bulk, which was fitting for the man who now stepped toe to toe with a smaller Axel Jamison, who, in reality, wasn't really small.

However, those beastly eyes were glued to Cross and even in the dark, he could see those eyes were not happy to see him.

"Smellin' some fuckin' bacon, Axhole. Love fuckin' bacon but not the kind with two legs. Had this discussion with you before. Thought you got it. Maybe you didn't. Maybe you need a bit of a fuckin' reminder."

"How do you figure he's a cop?"

Cross was impressed Axel was bold enough to play dumb with this guy.

The big man sniffed the air loudly. "'Cause all you fuckers stink." He leaned closer to Cross and sniffed again. "He stinks like a pig. Plus, he's talkin' to you."

Jamison shot Cross a quick look and said, "We're on a task force together. He needed to pass off some important information to me in person that couldn't wait. He did it, now he's leaving."

"Don't give a shit 'bout your pig business. This is DAMC property an' not a livestock pen. Don't need your kind hangin' out here, Axhole. Bad enough you live in our compound." Diesel leaned in. "If it wasn't for Bella..."

Cross didn't miss Jamison puff out his chest and lean in, too. *Brave fucker.* "You're fucking right, D. Doesn't matter about Jayde and Z being my siblings, right? You only tolerate me because of Bella."

"You *think* I tolerate you," Diesel growled. "Woulda squeezed the life outta you a long time ago if it wasn't for her. The day Z got out—"

Jamison cut him off. "We're going to hash that shit out again?"

D's head snapped up. "No. Fuck no. You ain't worth it." He swung his gaze to Cross, then back to Axel. "Get 'im the fuck outta here. He don't belong here. Neither do you. Don't make me fuckin' regret the freedoms I give you." Then his head swung around as he surveyed the courtyard. "Woman!" he bellowed, then lumbered off.

Crossing the Line

"What the fuck?" Cross mumbled. "After that, I'm not sure I'll be able to unpucker my asshole any time soon."

Jamison watched the big man get farther away. "Yeah, don't get on his bad side."

"Are you on his bad side?"

"Does it look like I'm on his good side?"

"No." Cross swiped a hand over his brow. He needed to check his balls to make sure they dropped back to where they belonged. "Fuck."

"Unfortunately, I have to deal with his grumpy ass. His ol' lady's my cousin. My wife's his cousin. His president is my brother." Axel blew out a breath. "Fucking family tree is so fucking twisted I can't even break it all down. Knows he can't kill me, that's why he gets so frustrated. He also knows I watch out for Bella so he doesn't have to anymore."

"Bella? I met her on some of our runs, right?" Cross remembered the beautiful dark-haired woman who rode on the back of Jamison's bike during some of their club runs. But she wore a "Property of Axel" cut. That wasn't something the women, wife or girlfriends, normally wore. While all the law enforcement members wore the club colors during runs, the women just wore whatever they wanted.

"Yeah."

"Had no idea she had ties to this club."

"Mitch knows, of course. Now you. That's it. Appreciate it if you keep that to yourself."

So Cross wasn't the only one with a secret to keep. Jamison not only had blood ties but ties through his wife. "Not a problem."

"Now, you want to explain to me why you're really here? The task force excuse is total bullshit. So, who are you trying to bust?"

More like bust a nut. "Nobody."

"You didn't just wander back here out of curiosity. Any

of the women here are either an ol' lady, a sweet butt or a stripper from the club's strip joint."

The MC owned a strip club? And what the fuck was a sweet butt?

"So, if you're panting after one of them, I'd say you might want to look elsewhere."

"Thanks for the tip." Cross inhaled a deep breath, then stated, "I like sweet butt but I'm not sure your meaning is the same as mine." He hesitated, then let it go. "I'm gay."

Jamison's mouth dropped open before snapping shut. "Oh. I... didn't know that."

"No one does. At least no one at my PD or our MC."

Jamison's eyebrows pinned together. "What does that have to do with this club?"

Fuck, he was stepping in it, but Axel Jamison could be a possible ally. "I came to see the band."

Jamison shook his head. "Okay? You're seeing someone in the band?" Jamison turned to scan the now empty stage. "It's someone in Dirty Deeds? All those guys are married or have girlfriends... except for..." He turned back to Cross, his eyes so wide Cross could see the whites of them even in the dark. "Holy fuck." Jamison pursed his lips. "Does he know?"

"Does he know he's gay?" Cross's question came out a little higher pitched than he liked.

"I meant about you being interested in him. I'm not sure... I don't think..." Jamison twisted away from him, his head rotating as he surveyed the whole courtyard before it snapped back to Cross. "I don't think Nash is gay." He lifted his chin toward the fence in the corner between the kegs of beer and the building.

Cross looked in that direction and his head jerked back. Was that... Could that be...

Of course it fucking was.

Nash was standing with his back to the solid metal fence, his head dropped forward so his face was covered by his hair, but still recognizable. He had two hands on a woman's head, who was on her knees, and he was...

He was...

Fucking her face.

Maybe he was wrong.

Fuck no, he wasn't wrong.

Nash's head jerked up and tipped backwards, his hair no longer hiding anything. And, yep, there was no doubt whoever was on her knees in front of him was taking it like a champ. Nash's hips were pumping at a pretty fast clip.

Then he did one last thrust and stilled.

"Yeah, I don't think he's gay," Jamison murmured next to him.

"My mistake," Cross muttered back.

Jamison turned and blocked Cross's view of Nash. "Where'd you meet?"

Cross tried to rein in his spinning thoughts and ignore his churning gut. "Uh, a bar."

"Where his band was playing?"

"Yes. We... had a conversation. I just must've misunderstood."

"I'd say. Good thing you found out the truth before you embarrassed yourself."

Of course. Because sneaking into a MC's club and getting caught wasn't embarrassing at all. Especially when he just confessed he was gay and the man he was interested in just got a blowjob by a fucking woman! "Yeah," Cross breathed, a burn filling his lungs.

"I've only ever seen him with women. Let me tell you, he's not shy about it, either. He pretty much hits whatever isn't nailed down."

Cross lifted his eyes to Jamison's, his temples now throbbing and his fingers itching to rub them. "That right?"

Jamison slapped Cross on the shoulder. "Well, glad I

could help you keep from stepping in shit. I'll keep your secret. You keep mine. Deal?"

"Deal."

"Now, you need to get the hell out of here. If Diesel comes back and finds you still here, I'm not taking a punch for you. His fucking fist is like a sledgehammer. Trust me."

Cross was sure The Incredible Bulk, whose name was apparently *Diesel*—not surprising—could put a hurting on another man easily. Cross preferred that it wasn't him.

However, there was no way he was leaving.

No fucking way.

He'd just have to take that risk.

And anyway, remaining all in one piece was overrated.

Chapter Ten

NOT ONLY WERE his marbles lost, they were never going to be found again. Keeping out of sight from all the bikers, along with the other partiers, had been a challenge. He certainly didn't want to be caught "lurking" like some stalker. Or have The Incredible Bulk find him.

But he found a spot where he had a pretty good view of most of the courtyard and had watched Nash zip up his jeans and simply walk away from the woman who rose to her feet and tried to hang all over him.

If Nash said a word to her, Cross couldn't tell from where he stood. Even so, he couldn't miss the woman yelling something at Nash after he peeled her off and pushed her away. Exactly what, Cross didn't know. But whatever she said, it probably wasn't pleasant since a lot of heads turned toward her as she had done it with her arms flailing.

Nash ignored the dramatic outburst, grabbed a beer, a plate of food, then ambled over to an empty lawn chair that sat near the bonfire, and grabbed another empty chair, pulling it toward him to use as a table. As soon as he sat his beer and plate down on the spare chair, he leaned back, drew his hair back into a ponytail and pulled what looked like a hand-rolled cigarette out of his wallet.

Cross guessed it wasn't a "cigarette." Especially when someone else stopped in front of him, took a toke off it after it was lit, then wandered away again.

Nash sat there for a whole fucking hour, chatting with anyone who'd stop by, occasionally picking at his food and nursing his one beer.

Then he simply stared at the bonfire for another half hour.

By that time, Cross was ready to scream. So, what did his foolish stalker ass do? Sent the man another text.

Cross held his breath as Nash pulled his phone from his back pocket, glanced at it, then shoved it back where he found it.

Dropping his head, Cross scrubbed his palms over his face. Then he took a breath and told himself he should leave. Give up this fool's errand and get his head back on straight.

Was that what he did? Fuck no.

Luckily, a few minutes later Nash was on the move, which was toward the side door of the building. Cross slipped back through the bushes.

The private parking lot was almost empty now. Just a few bikes and vehicles remained. They probably belonged to the people who lived at the clubhouse or were too drunk or stoned to drive.

He made sure the coast was clear before heading toward the back door he avoided earlier. Above that gray steel door was a sign that read *Dirty Angels MC* and in smaller letters below that, *Down & Dirty 'til Dead.*

Great. That was promising.

He opened the door slowly, snuck inside and hoped like hell he didn't get down and dirty until he was dead by going face to face with The Incredible Bulk.

Crossing the Line

NASH WAS BEAT. His band sounded on point tonight. They were soon ready to hit the road on their east coast tour. They just needed a few more original songs.

Unfortunately, the words had escaped him lately.

That was because his mind had been on something else.

Or someone else.

He thought about the last text he received from Cross earlier, which he ignored, as well as the five hundred and eleven the man had sent before that. Every time he received one, he was tempted to respond. But he didn't.

It would be fucking stupid.

Plenty of available pussy hung around church, so it wasn't like he needed to even go out and search for it. It was always right there. Unzip your fly and some snatch, be it a sweet butt or one of Moose's strippers from Heaven's Angels Gentlemen's Club, would be there to take care of you.

Did they want more?

Fuck yes.

Were they getting more from him?

Fuck no.

Just like he could always find available strange when he played gigs. Some woman was always willing to put out. At worst, they wanted a drink or two in exchange.

He sighed as he hoofed it up the dark, narrow steps off the clubhouse's common area.

But none of it was what he was looking for. Yeah, those women took the edge off, but none of it was deeply satisfying.

Not like it had been with Cross.

It would be best to block the pig's number. Then he wouldn't be so tempted to call or text him back.

But he couldn't do that, either.

And that right there pissed him the fuck off.

He dragged his ring of keys from his pocket, found his room key, slid it into the lock and as he pushed the door open, he was hit hard from behind.

The impact made him stumble farther into his dark room. Before he could spin around, his door was slammed shut, and the room went completely black, except for a thin strip of light coming from under the door.

"What the fuck!"

Was it the sweet butt who was pissed he wouldn't take her upstairs? He shoved whoever it was against the door and before his eyes could adjust to the zero-light situation, every nerve ending in his body crackled and popped. It wasn't Mini, the club's head-loving whore.

Hell no, it wasn't.

But Nash's head exploded with the fear of Cross being caught in his room. Not only because he was a gay man, but because he was a cop. He wasn't sure which one would be worse in his brothers' eyes. "What the fuck are you doin' here? Are you fuckin' crazy?"

Nash released the grip at the base of Cross's neck and slid his hand down to the man's chest which was rising and falling as quickly as Nash's. Cross's heart thumped heavily beneath his palm.

"No one knows who I am... except Axel."

"Axel," Nash repeated, his own pulse trying to escape his throat. "Axel knows you're fuckin' here?"

"He won't say shit."

Cross's warm breath crossed Nash's parted lips. He licked them, hoping for a little taste of the man. Because that's all he'd allow himself. Nothing more. "How do you know?"

Cross didn't answer.

Nash tipped his head back and let out a searing, "Fuck." This was stupid and dangerous on Cross's part. He had to have a screw loose to take the kind of risk he had by following Nash upstairs. Anybody could've spotted him.

With one hand still on Cross to keep him pressed to the door, Nash flipped on the light switch to the left of it. Then he reached into Cross's back pocket, pulled out his wallet, opened it to where his shiny badge was kept and shoved it into Cross's face. "This might give it away, too."

Cross's mouth remained shut.

Nash released another, "Fuck," flipped the wallet closed and pushed it into Cross's chest, who pried it from Nash's grip and tucked it into his pocket. Nash stepped back and turned away to stare at the wall over his bed, trying to get his shit together.

His pulse, his breathing, his spinning thoughts. All of that. He needed to lock that shit down tight.

He wasn't expecting to see Cross tonight... Hell, he wasn't expecting to see Cross ever again and, fuck him, if the man wasn't in his room above church, of all fucking places.

Nash spun as he felt Cross approach. He was about to tell Cross to get the fuck out when the man's next words made his mouth snap shut.

"Saw you at the fence."

Nash quickly hid his wince with a frown. "What?"

"Saw you at the fence." Cross's cheeks were flushed, and Nash guessed it wasn't from embarrassment.

Nash had heard him the first time. He just didn't want to believe it. That meant Cross had been in the club's courtyard, too. "Not what you think." Did he even care what the cop thought?

He shouldn't.

What he had done with the sweet butt was his own fucking business, not the cop's. Cross had no right to even remark about it.

"Know what I saw."

Nash tilted his head and narrowed his eyes. "What'd you see?"

"Do I have to give you the literal *blow-by-blow*?"

Nash dropped his head to avoid something in Cross's eyes he didn't want to see. But it was more than anger. "It wasn't what you think."

"Could've fooled me."

No, not just anger. Hurt stained his words. Disappointment. Which Cross had no right to be.

They fucked once. Once. That was it. It was just a hookup. Nothing more. And even that had been a mistake.

Even so, why did he feel the need to explain himself?

I wasn't fuckin' her face, I was fuckin' yours. Nash lifted his head. "It's a game I gotta play, Cross. An image I gotta uphold. No one... No one in this fuckin' club turns down free head unless they have an ol' lady. Sometimes not even then."

"Convenient."

Nash stepped forward and bumped Cross in the chest with his own, making the man take a step back. Then he went toe to toe with him. "When the fuck did I start answerin' to you? Don't owe you shit. Especially loyalty. We fucked once. That's it. Don't act like it meant somethin' more to you than that. Don't get confused about what we did."

Cross's lips flattened out and his jaw got tight. "You're right. It was just a thing."

A thing. Yep, that was what it was. Just a thing. "Now get the fuck outta my room before someone sees you." He stepped back and pointed toward the door.

However, Cross didn't head in that direction. "How often do you fuck women, Nash?"

Why was this *any* of his fucking business? Nash blew out a breath and dropped his arm. "A lot."

"So you power through it to save face?"

"No, Cross. That's where you're wrong. I like pussy."

Cross's head tilted. "You're not gay."

"Never said I was. Didn't know I needed to hand you my résumé before stickin' my dick up your ass. Why you still standin' here in my room? What part of *you need to get gone* didn't you fuckin' understand?"

"You don't want me to leave."

"Pretty fuckin' sure I'm speakin' English."

"Your words aren't matching your body language."

"What're you? A shrink now?"

"You don't think I can't see how fucking hard you are right now? Why is that? Because you're reminiscing about the head you got downstairs? Or is it because I'm in your room and we're inches from your bed?" Cross stepped forward and put his hand on Nash's chest.

"Can't get dick elsewhere?"

"Don't want it elsewhere," Cross whispered. "Neither do you."

Nash went to remove his hand and deny that claim. But instead he held Cross's hand right where it was. He stared at the man before him. The dark trimmed beard, his blue eyes, his fucking lips. Nash closed his eyes and pictured Cross naked as he walked across the bedroom a couple of weeks ago.

Fuck, that vision was burned into his brain. And Cross's ass. His fucking ass. He wanted to take it again, but what he *wanted* to do and what he *should* do were two different things.

Cross's hand slipped from beneath Nash's and slid down his belly, over his belt buckle until he found his target.

Nash bit back a groan as Cross cupped his hard-on, giving it a light squeeze. "Proof you want me as much as I want you."

"I just want your ass."

"I'm attached to that ass."

Nash huffed out a breath. "That's the problem."

"Can we just forget who we are for tonight? Like the other night?"

"Problem was, I got a reminder when I saw your fuckin' tattoo."

Cross got quiet, letting his hand drop away. Nash felt that loss but also thought it was for the best.

"Then I saw your fuckin' uniforms all lined up in your closet like good little soldiers and behind them your cut."

"Okay? I belong to an MC just like you. How is that a problem?"

"MC? You mean MC light. Embarrassin' to call them a fuckin' MC. You're all wannabes."

"We wear colors, got a brotherhood just like yours."

"Weekend warriors. Don't live the life."

"So fucking what? That's like me calling you a wannabe rocker. You don't live the life. If you did, you'd have a recording deal, right? You'd be on the radio. Your shit would be streaming on music apps. You wouldn't be living here in Shadow Valley but in LA."

Nash's jaw worked and his fingers curled into fists. "Between your *MC* and mine, there's too many fuckin' connections. Don't need to be outed to my brothers."

"I don't need to be outed at my job or my MC, either. So here we are at an impasse again."

"Must like that word."

"And you keep making me use it. Look, I'm already in your room. I wasn't caught. I'm going to ask again, why can't we simply forget who we are tonight?"

"Ain't that simple."

Cross licked his lips and Nash's eyes followed, his pulse kicking up a beat. "Stop making it hard," Cross whispered.

"It's just a thing."

"It's just a thing," Cross repeated.

"Nothing more."

Nash expected Cross to echo those words, too, but he

didn't. Instead he said, "This *thing* will be give and take, though, Nash. No other way. You're not getting the upper hand, and neither am I. I'm willing to do that for you. Are you willing to do the same?"

Was he? They switched last time and he'd made it through. It turned out it wasn't as bad as he thought, as long as he kept his memories locked down.

Apparently, Cross wasn't willing to give himself unless Nash was willing to do the same.

"Thinking since you were getting head down there, you fuck them up here. Means you must have condoms."

Thinking since you were getting head down there, you fuck them up here. Not if he could help it. "Got wraps." Why was he even considering this? He needed to kick this cop out of his goddamn room.

"Wraps?"

"Yeah, the shit you wrap your dick in."

"Wraps. Okay then... Are you going to deny what you want?"

Nash huffed out a breath. "Been doin' that for a very long time."

"If anyone understands that, it's me," Cross said softly.

"Don't need you to understand. Need you naked."

A rush of air escaped Cross. "Need you naked, too. But have to say..."

Nash cocked a brow.

"I'll have a hard time concentrating if I see lipstick on your cock."

With a nod, Nash pushed past Cross to head into the tiny bathroom off his room, throwing over his shoulder, "Better be on my bed naked, ass in the air, your fuckin' hole lubed when I come back out. Because this time I'm goin' first."

FIRE BURNED through Nash's veins as he watched the head of his dick breach Cross's tight ring.

When he came out of the bathroom after washing off Mini's spit and red lipstick, Cross had done exactly as Nash demanded.

He was ass up, head down, naked.

In Nash's bed.

Just that sight alone blew away any desire to have any of the women who hung around the club give him head ever again. Yeah, having them do it got him off and that was the only purpose. Nothing more.

But when he'd walked around his bed to see how slick Cross's asshole was, he just about went to his knees. And his dick got even harder.

Cross had found Nash's stash in his drawer next to the bed, had applied lube generously and a wrap had been placed by his leg, so it was easily accessible.

Nash wanted to touch the man all over, kiss him, lick him, explore every inch of him. But he didn't.

Instead, he picked up the wrap, tore it open, rolled it on.

This was just a thing.

Doing anything other than getting off would make it more than a thing.

Once he settled between Cross's legs, he only pushed his hips forward to give him the tip, then he pulled back and broke their connection.

Then he did it again.

And again.

Denying himself what he really wanted, which was to take Cross completely.

In actuality, he withheld what they both wanted.

A punishment for both of them for being weak. For giving into temptation when they knew better.

Punishment for not recognizing this *thing* could only ever end up being a fucking disaster.

Nash grimaced with the struggle to hold back. Cross was struggling, too, evident by the way the sheets were fisted in his hands as he smothered words into the pillow.

He was begging.

There was no doubt that he wanted Nash badly. As badly as Nash wanted him. But, apparently, not enough to let Nash hear him beg.

So, Nash denied himself. He denied Cross.

Because Nash wanted to hear Cross beg.

Cross surged back, trying to impale himself on Nash's dick, but he'd been ready for it. He slipped out of Cross completely, his fingers digging into the man's hips, pushing him away. "You'll get what I fuckin' give you."

"Then give me more than what you're fucking giving me," Cross growled.

"What the fuck do you want?"

"More."

That answer wasn't good enough. "Fuckin' tell me. More of what?" For fuck's sake, while he wanted to hear Cross beg, Nash wasn't exactly sure for what.

What did he want from Cross?

Maybe the danger of them being together wouldn't come from the outside but from right there, from the inside. Between the two of them.

Maybe that was the most dangerous of all.

"I want you."

"Where?"

"Inside me."

The blood rushed through him. What Cross was asking for wasn't just about sex. Unless he was misunderstanding the meaning behind those words.

As a musician he was good at reading between the lines. Good at interpreting the heart and soul behind each syllable of spilled words, of sung songs, of written lyrics.

What was on the surface wasn't always the truth. Sometimes the truth was deeper within those words, you just had to find them.

He pressed the head of his cock to Cross's tight hole once more.

He shouldn't do this. He should end this right here.

But he did it anyway against his better judgement. Against his instinct to survive in a world where men who liked other men weren't accepted and men who were cops weren't, either.

Why can't we simply forget who we are tonight?

Could either of them ever forget?

Fuck no, they couldn't.

Nash dropped his head, closed his eyes and simply breathed.

He started when a hand wrapped around the back of his head and pulled him into a kiss.

He grabbed Cross's face and kissed him back, their tongues tangling and tasting, their groans mingling. Their beards scratching each other's skin.

He couldn't get enough of kissing him. Of touching him.

This was wrong. All wrong.

But then it became right. When Cross pushed him backward, not only breaking their kiss but sending Nash onto his back. And before Nash could stop him, Cross was straddling his hips and sinking down onto Nash's cock.

Planting his palms on Nash's chest, Cross caught his eyes and held them as he began to ride him.

At first it was slow, Cross would rise to the very tip, then slide back down, doing a grind at the end. Then he'd do it all over again.

Each time was a little faster. Each grind a little longer. Until Nash couldn't take any more.

Digging his feet into the mattress, he flipped them over, taking control. With one hand planted in the bed, the other rolling and tugging Cross's nipples, he began to power deep. Driving hard, relentless. As if trying to rid himself of those demons that haunted him. If he fucked hard and came even harder, he might break free.

Be at peace.

But that was only a fantasy.

Not the true reality of who they both were.

Maybe not to each other.

But to everyone else.

Chapter Eleven

CROSS'S BODY rocked with each pound. His ears rang with each slap of skin against skin.

If Nash kept that up, Cross was going to come before him and then he wouldn't be able to fuck Nash.

And he wanted to fuck Nash.

He needed to be inside him. To feel that connection, that closeness they would probably only find in moments like these. Where they had shut out the rest of the world and it was just the two of them.

Nash dropped forward, shoving an arm under Cross's hips, lifting them to a better angle. Thrusting forcefully. Pounding deep. Driving hard. Cross wrapped his legs around Nash's waist, grabbed his ponytail and pulled him into another kiss.

But he gave a warning against Nash's lips first, "You need to come before I do."

Nash pulled his mouth away just a fraction. "You close?"

"Too fucking close." That was too true.

Nash took his mouth, curled his body over Cross's and with a loud groan, surged forward one last time.

Thank fuck.

Cross gritted his teeth, fighting the strong urge to come, trying to think of anything but the man who just busted deep inside him, whose weight was now pressing him into the mattress. He didn't want to rush him, he normally enjoyed the whole "afterglow" thing, but right now he was ready to blow like a geyser and it would totally fucking suck if that happened.

"Remember what I said about give and take? I need to start giving soon."

Nash turned his head from where it was next to Cross's, saying low into his ear, "Or what?"

"Or I'll make you suck me afterward until I'm hard again. Your lips are pretty skilled when it comes to singing. Think they can take an hour of sucking, too?"

Nash's body shook. Was he laughing?

Cross wasn't joking, he was dead fucking serious!

With a groan Nash slid out of him, but before he could remove the spent condom, Cross stopped him and removed it instead, holding it between two fingers.

Nash shot him a suspicious look.

"Wrap me up," Cross demanded, hoping Nash doing so didn't send him shooting into orbit.

Nash kept one eye on the full condom within Cross's fingers and the other on what he was doing, which was rolling a fresh condom onto Cross's cock.

"What're you gonna do with that?" Nash asked, reaching for the lube.

"You don't need that," Cross told him.

Nash's brows dropped low. "The fuck I don't."

"On your belly."

Nash gave him one more wary look before rolling onto his belly and facing the headboard.

Cross emptied Nash's condom into his palm then threw the empty "wrap" onto the floor like Nash had done at his place.

He took the handful of cum and said, "Watch me."

Nash twisted his head enough to watch Cross take that cum and spread it all over his latex-covered cock. Then he moved onto his knees until he was between Nash's parted thighs.

"Spread your knees farther. Tip your ass up just slightly. That's it." His commands were starting to sound breathless instead of firm, but Nash complied. His eyes appeared darker than normal as he watched Cross take the remainder of the cum in his hand and use it to lube Nash's own hole.

Nash made a strange noise, then shoved his face into his pillow.

A burn started in Cross's stomach and moved outward, up into his chest and all the way down to his toes at the thought of fucking Nash using the man's own cum as lube.

Instead of wiping the remainder off, he took his slick fingers and ran them up Nash's spine, following with his tongue. Nash's back arched in response and a deep groan came from the pillow.

But Cross hesitated. He knew he wouldn't last if he entered Nash now. He was struggling with control. He wanted and needed this to last as long as it could.

He wasn't sure how many opportunities like this he'd have with Nash. If any more at all. So, he needed to gather his wits, slow his breathing, slow his racing heart, slow everything down.

However, seeing Nash's ass tipped up, slick with his own cum, just about undid him.

Cross closed his eyes, concentrating on his breathing for a moment, until he heard Nash groan, "Fuck, Cross. Don't leave me fuckin' hangin'."

Which to Cross's ears meant Nash wanted this as much as he did. For some reason, both of them, neither who liked to bottom, didn't mind it with each other.

That was saying something, wasn't it?

For shit's sake, why was he analyzing that now?

Oh, right. Because otherwise, as soon as he touched Nash, he'd blow his load.

"Thought you didn't like the bottom?" he managed to ask. Though, words that made sense were currently a struggle.

"I don't."

Cross opened his eyes, saw Nash watching him, and gave him a smile. "Tell me that again afterward."

"Won't be an afterward if you don't hurry the fuck up."

Nash being impatient helped Cross rein in his control, even though his cock was throbbing like crazy. "Are you in a rush?"

Nash rolled his eyes and tucked his face back into the pillow. Cross swore he heard, "What-the-fuck-ever," coming from it.

He shifted forward and pressed the crown to Nash's anus, sliding the tip back and forth, gathering and spreading around the drops of cum that had escaped.

"Keep low on the bed but your ass just like that."

A noise came from the pillow which may have been a curse.

Cross smacked Nash's ass hard, making his head shoot up. "What the fuck?"

"Head back down, body low, ass up."

"Fuckin' bossy motherfucker."

Cross smacked his ass again, making both Nash's head and hips jerk this time. Nash's ass cheek became flush. Cross leaned over and kissed where his hand left a mark.

"Fuckin' pushin' it, dude."

Dude.

Nash was not restrained in any manner. He could move, he could turn over, he didn't have to stay where he was. He could bitch all he wanted, but it was easy to see Nash liked what Cross was doing.

Cross smacked him one more time in the same spot as the other two, making sure that spot would sting.

"Fuck!"

And with that, Cross lined up his cock quickly and pushed inside of Nash, feeling the tight heat, the stretch of Nash's muscles as he accommodated Cross's length and width, the tight squeeze that was a thousand times better than any fist. Especially his own.

Every muscle in Nash's body had locked, so Cross hesitated, waiting for him to relax. When he did, Cross fell over him, pinning him to the mattress with his weight, pressing his chest into Nash's back. Sliding his arms over Nash's, finding his hands under the pillow and intertwining their fingers.

Nash didn't fight it. In fact, he squeezed Cross's fingers in response.

Cross saw that as a good sign. A sign of connection. Of acceptance. Of more than a *thing*.

He quickly tossed that out of his mind. He couldn't hold out hope, because he didn't want to be disappointed. It wasn't realistic to believe anything more could ever come of this. But for a split moment he wanted to believe things were different and they could.

"Let me know if my weight gets to be too much," he breathed into Nash's ear.

"I'm not a pussy," came the low rumble.

"If this is what pussy feels like, then I may have to try it."

Another growl rose from the pillow.

"You don't want to watch me get head by some woman and come down her throat?"

"Fuck you."

"Would that bother you?"

"No."

Cross pumped his hips once, twice, then stilled. "Sure?"

"No."

He pumped his hips again. Two times, then stopped. "Picture me standing by a fence, a woman on her knees at my feet, her lips wrapped around my cock."

Nash's fingers twitched in his. "Wouldn't care."

He ground against Nash's ass. "I think you're lying."

"Think whatever the fuck you want."

"How about if it was another man?"

Nash's body tensed beneath his. "Fuck you, Cross."

"No, I'm fucking you this time."

"Just pissin' me off."

"Why?"

"Wasn't her suckin' me off. It was you."

Cross stilled, his heart beating furiously at Nash's admission.

"Picturin' you doin' it was the only way I could come."

Cross wasn't sure what to say to that. He'd been hurt, even jealous seeing it. Things he shouldn't be. And even though he fought it, those feelings had won.

Even so, he understood the need for Nash to be what people expected him to be. To be accepted.

Cross had to play that same game. He'd never taken it as far as getting head from a woman, especially in public, but there had been times where he'd taken a woman as a "date" to functions. He felt bad pretending, using them only for that purpose and never calling them back afterward.

But he'd done what he needed to do to survive.

Nash might be bisexual instead of gay, but in most people's eyes, there was no difference. To them, being attracted to and having sex with other men made Nash gay.

Like Cross, Nash did what he needed to do to blend in and survive. Why he chose the life he did, when his sexual preferences ran as they did, baffled Cross. Though it shouldn't.

Cross knew he was gay for as long as he could remember

and was old enough to know what being attracted to other boys meant. But he willingly went into a career where he knew his sexual orientation might not be accepted. He made that choice and took that risk.

Maybe it was the same for Nash. Though, being a biker wasn't a career. Maybe he had no family other than his club brothers.

There were so many things he wanted to know about Nash, and they hadn't even scratched the surface.

Nash confessed he'd been thinking of him while getting head. Should that make Cross feel better about it?

He had no right to forgive the man, because Nash had been right. They owed each other nothing. They had fucked once and now again tonight.

And here he was, ruining his time with Nash by overthinking what happened earlier out in that courtyard. He was not here to judge Nash's choices.

It was true Nash didn't owe Cross shit, but the man gave him an explanation anyway. He didn't have to, but he did.

And that meant everything to Cross.

Everything.

"Cross."

"Yeah?" he breathed, coming back to the present.

"You ain't movin'."

No, he wasn't. He was laying on top of Nash, both of them connected from feet to fingertips. His nose behind Nash's ear. And he was simply breathing.

"Don't got all fuckin' night."

Cross smiled into Nash's hair. That complaint was soft, the tone not holding the same weight as the words.

Why did this man fascinate him? Why did he want to peel away his layers? Nash was a biker to his brothers, a musician to his fans. But he could be so much more to Cross.

If things were different...

But if they were, Cross might never have spotted him across the bar that night.

"Cross."

"Yeah?" he breathed again.

"You forget your dick's in my ass?"

Again, Cross smiled. "Hard to forget that."

"Ain't that the fuckin' truth." Nash jerked his hips beneath him.

Cross took his time, brushing his lips along Nash's bearded jaw, then followed his hairline to the back of his neck, tasting the salt on his skin there. He nipped Nash and swirled his tongue over the bite before moving to the top of the man's spine and doing the same. Then he sank his teeth in that vulnerable spot where Nash's neck met his shoulder.

Cross didn't have to move because Nash began to rock his hips as if he was fucking someone beneath him. Cross wondered for a moment if Nash was hard again and trying to get himself off.

But he didn't care, he let Nash set the pace to an extent because Cross's weight still pinned Nash to the bed, so he had the ultimate control.

"Is it too much?"

"Not enough," Nash groaned, rocking his hips even faster.

Cross had meant his weight, but apparently Nash didn't mind it. "Are you hard again?"

"Check."

"No," Cross whispered, unwilling to unclasp their hands to find out. Instead, he gave Nash's fingers a squeeze. "Just tell me."

"Not yet. Want you to get me there."

"What do you need for me to do to get you there?"

"Fuck me."

Yes, neither men liked to bottom. Until now. Funny how that was. How that changed.

Cross began to move with purpose since he was given a challenge. To get Nash hard and maybe even get him to come a second time before Cross did.

They started slow until slow wasn't enough for either of them.

After a while, the pounding of blood in Cross's ears matched the pounding of his hips. And Nash surrendered to him. Gave his all to Cross. A strangled moan. A soft curse. The tip of his hips. Cross accepted everything Nash gave him.

He pulled his chest up and pushed their clasped hands deeper into the bed, holding Nash there. He didn't stop or slow down, even when his control began to splinter. He drove deeper, harder, finding an angle that had Nash writhing beneath him. The man, both pleading with him to stop on one breath and begging him not to on the next.

Their heated skin was so slick with sweat they struggled to maintain clasped hands. But they did. They both held on. Neither wanting to let go.

Their breathing became harsh, loud, the sounds Nash made filling Cross's head as he echoed them back mindlessly.

In a haze, Cross demanded, "Tell me when you're going to come." He got no answer except a sharper tilt of Nash's hips.

Their damp skin made the slapping of his hips against Nash's ass sound deafening. But he couldn't slow down, he needed to get Nash there, so he could quickly follow behind.

Nash didn't need to say he was coming. His clenching muscles, the arch of his back told Cross he was there. Then Nash forced their joined hands beneath his body and, with a long grunt, spilled into their cupped palms.

Cross's rhythm faltered, and he buried himself deep one last time, a low groan coming deep from his center to be released into the world, as he lost another piece of himself to the man beneath him.

THE DOOR to Nash's tiny bathroom opened and Cross exited after disposing of the wrap and cleaning up. Nash was already out of bed and heading in there next because if anyone was messy, it was him. Especially since Cross used Nash's own cum as lube.

He'd never thought of doing that before and it not only worked well but was hot as fuck. He'd have to remember that trick in the future.

Cross said in passing, "I'm both surprised and appalled you have your own bathroom, because maybe you shouldn't. It's pretty fucking gross."

Nash snorted. "Think that's bad? Hoof it down the hall to the common one. That'll make you puke." Then he closed the door behind him.

A few minutes later he came out to find Cross back in his bed, acting like he belonged there, not dressed and ready to head out, like Nash had hoped. Or at least, that's what he told himself he wanted. "What are you doin'?"

"What's it look like?"

Nash should tell him to go. Cross got what he came for, there was no other reason for him to stay.

Like it or not, Nash had to admit the man looked good in his bed. And, fuck him, he wasn't ready for him to go. Cross just needed to leave before the dead started to rise in the morning and wander like zombies through the upstairs quarters and the downstairs common area, looking for their brains, grub and coffee.

Cross's lips twitched as Nash studied him in his bed. Then he shook his head, sighed and climbed in. His bed was only a queen, so it was small for two grown men. That meant, unlike in Cross's bed a couple weeks ago, they couldn't lay in it together without touching.

When the back of Cross's hand brushed against the back of his, Nash didn't pull it away the first time. Nor the second.

Without a word, they turned their hands palm to palm and their fingers interlaced again like they had when they were fucking.

Nash didn't want to think about what that meant. But, again, he didn't fight it because it settled something deep within his center. This connection with a man he never would've sought out if he was in his right mind.

But maybe he wasn't.

Maybe his mind was broken.

Maybe Cross was what he needed to make it whole again.

But that couldn't be right.

Chapter Twelve

"My boy wants to be a faggot?"
"Dad!" Panic. Sweat. Tears.
"My boy wants to be a fucking faggot?"
"Dad, no!" Lots and lots of tears. Endless. Hot, wet streaks.
"No boy of mine is going to be a faggot!"
His father had him pinned to the dirty floor with a knee on his back, holding him down with his bulky weight.
"Dad!" Helpless. Terrified. Shaking.
Warm blood. Searing pain. Sharp cramps. Hot daggers.
"That's what it's going to feel like when a faggot does that to you! Does that feel good, boy? Is that what you want?"
Screaming. Begging. Pleading. Wishing for it to end.
Not soon enough. Not soon enough. Not soon enough.
From a distance, his mother shrieked, "John! What are you doing!"
"Teaching your son not to be a fag."
Not soon enough. She was too late.

Nash struggled for air as his eyes flew open and a bead of sweat ran across his forehead, down his temple and disappeared into his damp hair.

He released a shuddered breath. *Fuck.* He hadn't had that nightmare in a long time.

It might have been twenty years ago, but that nightmare could bring it back like it was yesterday.

He'd been a month away from seventeen when he got caught in his father's tool shed with a neighbor boy who'd been just as curious as him.

Only that boy hadn't been punished for kissing another boy. That boy hadn't been taken to task for touching another boy.

Only that boy's father hadn't shoved a wooden broom handle up his ass to teach his son a lesson.

Only that boy hadn't passed out during that never-to-be-forgotten lesson.

Afterward, Nash had woken up alone in his room on his belly with his jeans still caught around his ankles. He'd fought the severe cramps and nausea that almost crippled him to clean up the blood that had dried on his skin. And also in an area too painful to touch.

He'd gingerly pulled his clothes back into place, then stuffed his school gym bag full of his most important belongings and carefully but painfully walked out the door. He didn't know where his parents had disappeared to and he didn't care. His only thoughts had been to escape undetected and to get far, far away as fast as he could.

He almost blacked out and had to wait until the spots disappeared from his vision when he mounted his motorcycle. The one he'd bought for only $950 with the money he earned mowing lawns in the summer, raking leaves in the fall and shoveling snow in the winter. Jobs that had landed him a look of pride from his father and a pat on the shoulder from his mother.

But that day everything changed and that moment in the tool shed changed everything.

He left with only thirty dollars to his name shoved deep into his pocket and his second-hand, beat-up guitar.

Ignoring his pain, he rode as far as the gas in his tank

allowed and an extra five dollars on top of that took him a little farther.

Then he did what he had to do to survive alone at sixteen, on the cusp of seventeen. Still a teen but forced to be a man.

He sang and played his guitar on the streets for money.

He gave blowjobs and hand jobs in exchange for weed and food. Sometimes he gave up pieces of his soul for a roof over his head and a warm bed to sleep in.

But he kept moving. Until one day he landed in Greensburg, Pennsylvania, at a bikers' hangout named The Handle Bar, hoping the manager would let him play for an hour on stage so he could earn tips. And it was there he met a man not much older than him named Jag.

That day everything changed and that moment in the bar changed everything.

He stopped moving. He stopped hustling.

Even so, his father had taught him an important lesson twenty years ago.

One he never forgot. And never would.

Cross curled into him, his eyes opening, his hand sweeping over Nash's chest tattoo that read "Live and Learn."

Live and learn.

He saw it in the mirror every day.

Sometimes life lessons were hard ones.

Ones hard to swallow. Ones which could strangle you.

And right now, he was choking with what all this meant. What Cross being in his bed, being in his room at church, meant for the two of them.

What it might mean to the people who surrounded them. What would happen if they discovered the truth.

For a couple of hours it had been possible to forget who they were. Now lying in his bed, it was slapping him in the face once more. While his tattoo was a good reminder, his memory served as an even better one.

"You okay?" Cross asked, his voice scratchy from lack of sleep. The man's hand slid from Nash's chest to his sternum, where his fingertips pressed into his skin.

Nash was tempted to hold his hand again, to feel Cross's fingers slide between his and hold on.

But he resisted. Instead, he closed his eyes and said, "I'm done with you."

Cross's head lifted from Nash's shoulder as he asked, "What?"

Nash couldn't open his eyes; he couldn't look Cross in the face because that might make him change his mind. "What we did was a mistake. We fucked up."

Those fingers on Nash's sternum fisted. Cross no longer was curled against his side. Instead, he'd become wooden. Hard. Lifeless. "We fucked up?"

Cross's voice had caught but Nash ignored that, too. "Never shoulda showed up at your place. You never shoulda showed up at mine. So, yeah, we fucked up."

Cross moved from Nash's side and he felt the bed shift. When he finally opened his eyes, the man was sitting up, his head in his hands. Then he dropped his hands and twisted his neck to stare at Nash, his light blue eyes searching.

Maybe they were searching for his soul.

Nash tightened his jaw, determined not to give in. Determined not to ask Cross to stay. Because that would be an even bigger mistake than what they'd already done.

This needed to end.

Nash wasn't going to pay the price for getting caught with another male again.

He had too much to lose.

And, in truth, so did Cross.

This *thing* wasn't worth what it could cost them both.

He had a good life, an easy life. His freedom to do what he loved. A loyal brotherhood.

He wasn't going to let sex ruin that.

Cross had a good life, a good career, a possible upcoming promotion. A loyal brotherhood.

Nash wasn't going to let sex ruin that.

So again, he said, "I'm done with you."

"Just like that."

Nash nodded, avoiding direct eye contact. "Just like that." His eyes slid to his ancient digital clock. "You gotta go before my brothers get up."

Cross looked at the time, too, then his gaze landed back on Nash. "I have to go before your brothers get up." His words were robotic and empty.

But still, Nash resisted.

Cross slipped from the bed and tugged on his clothes, keeping his back to the bed. Then, as he reached for the knob, he said softly, "I'll call you."

Nash dug deep to say, "Don't. Lose my number."

Still facing the door, Cross nodded and murmured, "You got it."

The soft click of the closing door might as well had been a knife stabbing Nash right in the heart.

———

EVERY STEP DOWN those narrow stairs into the common area was agony. Nash wasn't sure if even an IV of coffee would help, but it would be better than nothing. He'd had zero sleep since Cross left and even if he tried again, he doubted it would come.

His plan after grabbing food and caffeine was to grab his notebook, head out to the pavilion and maybe let the fresh air try to spur some new words.

The deadline was looming. He needed to concentrate on

his music and not the man he'd kicked out of his room because shit was getting real.

He hit the bottom of the steps and let his gaze slide through the large room until it caught on a new prospect mopping the floor. He didn't know the prospect's name and didn't pause to find out. He honestly didn't give a fuck who the young guy was. If he ran the gauntlet, made it to the end and was patched in, then Nash might care. Until then, fuck no.

He ignored the newbie and focused on his destination, which was the commercial coffeemaker at the corner of the club's private bar. And, of course, though the area was, for the most part, empty and quiet, Grizz, the oldest member of the MC, was already glued to his seat. That was good news for Nash. It meant his ol' lady, Momma Bear, was already in the kitchen, hopefully cooking.

Which also meant he'd get a good fucking breakfast this morning. He could use a large plate of eggs, bacon and toast to give him back some energy from his lack of sleep and the sex he and Cross had.

But as he passed the nameless wannabe, he heard something muttered under the prospect's breath.

Nash swore it was "faggot." That couldn't be right.

"My boy wants to be a faggot?"

Nash stopped his forward motion and twisted his head to eyeball the young asshole. "What the fuck did you say?"

The prospect lifted his eyes and leaned on the mop. "Nothin'."

"The fuck you didn't. Repeat the shit you just said."

The prospect shrugged, then went back to mopping, his gaze back on the floor.

Nash heard it much more clearly this time, even though it was once again muttered. "Cocksuckin' faggot."

Nash set his jaw and turned, pulling his chin down to his

neck and staring at the prospect, who soon might not be one. "Gonna look me in the fuckin' eye and say that?"

The prospect kept mopping, giving Nash his back.

Nope, that wasn't going to fucking fly with him. In a few steps, he had his hand on the young prospect's shoulder, spinning him around. He ripped the mop from the guy's grip and tossed it to the floor.

"Look me in the fuckin' eye and say that one... more... time."

The prospect took a deep breath, lifted his chin, looked Nash right in the eye and said, "Heard what you were fuckin' doin'. Saw who walked outta your room. No pussy was in there with the two of you."

Nash's nostrils flared and ice slithered down his spine. "What the fuck were you doin' upstairs?" Prospects weren't assigned rooms at church. They had to live elsewhere until they were patched in.

Even though the kid's dark eyes had narrowed, Nash couldn't miss the loathing in them. "Was drunk an' crashed there. Got up to take a piss an' saw it with my own two eyes. Saw what you were fuckin'," he leaned closer, sneering, "and it wasn't pussy."

"Musta been so drunk you were fuckin' seein' things."

"Yeah, and saw a fuckin' dude with a dick come out of your room which makes you a cocksuckin' fa—"

Nash interrupted those words with his fist to the mouth they were spewing from. The prospect's head snapped back. And when it came forward again, Nash nailed him center face.

Blood splattered from the prospect's nose, but he didn't go down. Fuck no, he took a defensive stance, ignoring the stream of blood rushing down his chin and dripping onto his cut, his shirt and the newly mopped floor.

Nash shook the blood off his own knuckles and planted his feet just in time. The prospect launched himself at Nash, knocking him backward. Before Nash could recover, his hair was being used to take him to the ground.

Nash twisted before his back hit the concrete floor and he struck the prospect's arm in the funny bone.

Then he was free. Nash rolled away, got to his knees, but was tackled before he could rise.

"All faggots need their asses kicked. Need to be taught a fuckin' lesson."

"John! What are you doing!"

"Teaching your son not to be a fag."

Nash lost his breath when he took a right hook to his cheek and his neck twisted painfully from the blow. He quickly gathered his wits and swept his leg out, kicking the prospect's legs from under him. He crumpled to the floor and it was Nash's turn to launch himself.

He got in one good punch before someone was grabbing him under the arms, pulling him off and dragging him away.

He glanced over his shoulder to see that someone was Linc.

Hawk, whose face was red, unlikely from exertion, yelled, "What the fuck's goin' on?"

Nash wiped the back of his hand across his mouth and checked to see how badly he was bleeding. It was nothing compared to what the pigs had done to him the day he saved Cross's ass.

"Asked a motherfuckin' question!" Hawk bellowed.

As the prospect went to stand, Hawk used his boot against the guy's chest to push him back down. "Ain't gettin' up 'til you answer."

"Can I let you go, brother?" Linc said quietly.

Nash nodded, still trying to catch his breath.

Linc released him and stepped next to Hawk so the two of them were between Nash and the prospect. A wall neither the prospect or Nash would ever be able to breach.

Hawk was huge in every way possible, and, though not quite as tall, Linc was now a solid wall of muscle.

"Don't fuckin' hear shit yet. Gonna make your VP wait?" Hawk yelled some more. He scowled at the prospect. "Think that's fuckin' smart?"

Nash didn't want to answer, either, so he didn't. And the heat was on the turd on the floor and not him, anyway.

But Grizz decided to be more than helpful when he yelled from his stool, "Asshole there called Nash a cock-suckin' faggot. Even heard it with my old fuckin' ears all the way over here."

Hawk leaned over the prospect, whose eyes widened. "You call 'im that?"

The prospect's mouth opened and closed a few times before it spat out, "Fucker was up there suckin' dick an' takin' it up the ass."

Hawk's spine snapped straight, and his dark, unreadable gaze landed on Nash for a *very* long, *very* uncomfortable moment before swinging back to the prospect.

The growl that came out of the man was enough to make anyone's balls shrivel. Including Nash's. "Think you forgot who you are. Forgot where you are. That bottom rocker says prospect. You haven't earned your fuckin' colors here. Now you never fuckin' will. Never fuckin' disrespect a member, you piece of shit. Never."

With that, Hawk reached down, gathered the prospect's cut in his fist, hauled him to his knees and landed a punch so hard the guy's head flopped back and stayed there. The former prospect crumpled to the ground when Hawk released him to rip off his cut, then he threw it on the closest pool table.

Nash stood frozen on the spot as Hawk whipped out his dick and pissed on the passed-out guy. He shook it off, tucked it back in, then jabbed a thick finger at Linc.

"Get another one of those pussy-ass bitches to clean up

this mess an' finish moppin' the floor. Then grab Coop so you an' him can drag this piece of shit out back. Don't stop there. Drag his ass through the parkin' lot, out the gate, all the way out front, an' leave him at the fuckin' curb like the trash he is. You need to take a piss, he's a good target."

Linc grinned. "Drank a bunch of coffee already. Just might have to break the seal." He turned to Grizz and yelled, "Grizz, you see any more of these 'pussy-ass bitches' around?"

Grizz jerked a thumb toward the kitchen. "Momma's got one scrubbin' the kitchen down an' another prospect's moppin' The Iron Horse."

Linc gave him a nod and headed in that direction. After Linc disappeared, Nash turned his attention back to Hawk, who was staring at him, his face not showing any kind of happy. "Gonna have a fuckin' shiner."

"Yeah." Nash did his best to keep his expression neutral as Hawk pursed his lips and continued to stare at him.

"We need to have a fuckin' discussion?"

"Nope."

Hawk nodded. "Gotta do inventory." He continued through the common area and pushed through the double doors that led to the commercial kitchen between church and The Iron Horse.

Nash blew out a breath, moved behind the bar, grabbed a few napkins and ran them under the sink before starting to clean up his face and his split knuckles.

"Woman!" Grizz bellowed, making him jump.

After a couple moments, Momma Bear's grey head popped through the double doors where Hawk had disappeared. "You yellin' for me, ol' man?"

"You're the only woman here right now, ain't ya?"

Momma rolled her eyes. Then her gaze landed on Nash's eye and her lips flattened and she got a hard look in her eyes.

"Get 'im a bag of ice an' breakfast," Grizz ordered.

"Don't need your cranky ol' ass givin' me orders. I know how to take care of my boys," she huffed, nodded to Nash and disappeared.

Nash threw out the bloodied napkins, moved over to the coffeemaker and saw it was empty. "Fuck," he muttered.

"Nobody made coffee like Crow," Grizz grumbled.

"Yeah, well, fuck me." He grabbed the shit to brew a pot and when he was done, he leaned back against the counter to wait, looking over at Grizz. "Want some?"

"Does it fuckin' look like I need coffee?"

No. Grizz already had a pint glass of beer in front of him.

"It's morning," Nash started.

"It's eleven, boy." The old man laughed as he pulled at his long salt and pepper beard. "Musta had a rough night." His faded blue eyes stared at him just as intently as Hawk's had. "Had a man up there?"

Nash returned the stare, wondering where this line of questioning was going to go. And whether he was willing to take it there.

"You were up all night gettin' loud an' playin' cards?"

Nash kept staring at Grizz since he was having a hard time getting anything past the lump in his throat. When he opened his mouth to push out a "yeah," nothing but a rush of air came out.

Grizz nodded, not waiting for an answer. "Did that plenty of times in my younger days. Up all night partyin' an' havin' a good time. Raisin' hell with my brothers an' buddies. Now, sit the fuck down an' Momma will get you ice for that eye an' bring you some breakfast."

"Grizz."

Grizz lifted a hand and shook his grayed head. "Don't gotta explain nothin' to nobody, boy. Nothin'. Not to me. Not to anyone. Got me?"

"Grizz."

"Got our colors on your fuckin' back, don't you?"

"Yeah."

"That's all that matters. Remember that. We're family no matter fuckin' what."

Then Momma Bear came charging out of the kitchen with a bag of ice in one hand and a plate of food that looked and fucking smelled delicious enough it made Nash's stomach growl.

He began to fork the food into his gullet while Grizz went back to nursing his beer.

A couple of minutes later the old man got off his stool, went over to the unconscious former prospect and pissed on him.

Chapter Thirteen

CROSS LIFTED his hand to knock on the motel room door, but as he did so, it swung open. A man stepped out, wearing a baseball cap low, his head down and his hands shoved deep into his pockets as he elbowed past Cross.

Cross had to take a step back so he wouldn't be bowled over. As he watched the man jog down the stairs at the end of the second-floor landing, he heard, "What're you doin' here?"

His gaze swung back to the open doorway where Nash had his hand planted high on the corner edge of the door and was leaning into the door jamb, his shoulder pressed to the molding.

Nash wore no shirt, even though it was November. Without his belt, his jeans rode low on his narrow hips. His feet were bare, and his messy hair hung loose.

Cross turned again and watched the man who had rushed out of Nash's room get into what he would consider a road hazard on four wheels and drive away.

"You shouldn't be here," came the low rumble.

Apparently.

"You don't fuckin' give up."

Cross wished he could. Some days he'd wished he never saw Nash across the bar at The Cockpit. He'd never been like this with anyone before.

He needed his fucking head examined. No doubt about it.

"Why?"

Cross met Nash's hazel eyes and told the truth. "I wish I knew, then I'd be able to give you an answer." He jerked his head toward the now-empty parking spot Nash's "friend" had vacated. "You fuck him?"

Nash ignored the question, turned on his heels and went deeper into the motel room but left the door open. Cross took that as an invitation.

After stepping inside, he closed and locked the door. He watched Nash's lean muscles ripple as he tugged an Ocean City Bike Week hoodie over his head and slide his bare feet into a pair of old sneakers, not bothering to lace them up.

He grabbed something off the small desk and kept walking to a sliding glass door on the other side of the room. Then he disappeared outside.

It took a few seconds for Cross to unstick his feet. When he did, he stepped out onto the small balcony where the air felt a little warmer than normal for fall since that side of the motel room was engulfed in the afternoon sun. That motel room was also located in Virginia where it was a little warmer than back home in Pennsylvania.

Nash probably thought Cross was desperate since he tracked him down two states away.

But it hadn't been hard to find him. All Cross had to do was look online for Dirty Deeds' tour dates. It also wasn't hard to locate the motel once he contacted the band's manager and asked where Nash was staying, saying he needed the info for a police matter.

Once again, the man who now was settled into a lounge chair made him lie.

It turned out the item Nash had nabbed from the desk was a tin, and in that tin was a small bag of weed and a few rolled joints. Along with what looked like a marble bowl and a pack of wrapping papers.

Cross closed his eyes and took a deep inhale. When he opened his eyes, Nash already had a joint tucked between his lips.

"Seriously, you're just going to fire one up in front of a cop?"

"One, don't think this is your jurisdiction." Nash flicked his lighter, lit the end of it, took a couple of puffs, holding the smoke deep, then let it roll out of his open mouth. "Two, it's legal now."

"Due to my profession, I know whether it's legal or not. In PA it's not, unless you have a valid medical reason and carry a card."

Nash tucked the joint between his lips, squinted to keep the smoke out of his eyes as he dug out his wallet. He pulled out a card and flipped it at Cross.

Cross caught it—barely—and read it. "This is a Get Out of Jail Free card from Monopoly."

"Yep."

"That's not—" Cross dropped his head and shook it. "Never fucking mind."

"We're not in PA," Nash reminded him.

"No, we're not." It wasn't legal in Virginia, either. But that was also a reminder Cross didn't need, that he'd followed the man to a different state.

"Which makes me wonder what you're doin' here." Nash pulled the joint from his lips, tipped his head up, blew the smoke toward the ceiling of the balcony and then offered it to Cross. "Puff, puff, pass, baby."

Nash might as well have been holding a python the way Cross looked at it. "Uh. Do not pass go, go directly to jail, *baby*."

"You're not arrestin' me."

"Like you said, I'm out of my jurisdiction. And, honestly, I think the feds should legalize it. However, I can't be smoking it, I'll lose my damn job."

"Pity. Some of you pigs need to mellow out a bit. Unjam those sticks from your asses. This shit ain't hurtin' anyone."

"Won't smoking fuck up your voice?"

Nash lifted one shoulder lazily. "It's rock. Nothin' wrong with a little rough in my voice."

No, there wasn't. Cross liked the rough in Nash's voice, especially when they were having sex.

Cross dragged a second lounge chair closer and settled into it. "That guy—"

"This an official Porky Pig investigation?"

Cross pressed his lips together.

Nash shook his head, jammed the joint back between his lips and grabbed his guitar, which was leaning against the balcony railing. "I didn't fuck him." Nash settled the guitar in his lap and picked at a few of the strings. "Sold me some weed."

Great. While he was relieved Nash hadn't fucked the man... "It's illegal here, too, you know."

"Only if you snitch." After a few more long drags, Nash crushed the lit end of the joint into an ashtray on a small round table next to him, putting it out and leaving it there, picking up a notebook and pen instead.

Then he shifted forward in the lounge chair and sat straight up, tucking the notebook between his spread thighs and reading what was handwritten on the open page.

"Those lyrics?"

Nash's eyes slid from his notebook, to Cross, and back to his notebook. "Yeah."

"You always write your own stuff?"

"In the past we've mostly done covers. But since we got a manager and went on tour, we're scramblin' for more original stuff. Tryin' to get Jazz to help pen some songs for us. Maybe even join the tour as a special guest. She's got a fuckin' voice like an angel. Sultry, though."

"Jazz?"

"One of the ol' ladies in the club."

"And will she?"

"No. No way her ol' man's gonna let her hit the road with us. He keeps an eagle eye on her. Also, she's knocked up. She's got talent. Afraid it's gonna go to waste."

Cross studied the man as he played his guitar and hummed along, a few words escaping here and there.

A thin line of smoke still rose from the joint in the ashtray, catching Cross's eye. Then he noticed something else. Something that must have fallen out from between the pages when Nash had moved his notebook, and it landed under the table.

He couldn't read it from where he sat, but Cross recognized it. It was the business card he'd given Nash the night they first kissed in the parking lot of The Cockpit.

It was dirty, wrinkled, the corners bent. But it was there.

Right there.

In this motel room, in Virginia, with Nash.

Nash must keep it in his notebook of lyrics, something he probably took everywhere with him, in case creativity hit him.

Cross leaned back in the chair, a smile curling his lips. He closed his eyes, feeling the warmth of the sun on his face, and was content to sit quietly and listen to Nash strum his guitar and create magic.

But that voice... That smoky voice swirled around him until it permeated every cell of Cross's body. Until it flowed through his veins and he inhaled it into his lungs.

That voice became a part of him.

I need to break free
Shed these heavy chains
Let the world see me
Take away this pain

NASH SCRIBBLED two more lines down onto the page, then lifted his head, letting himself finally look at Cross.

The man had to be asleep in the lounge chair by now. His face was relaxed, but his lips were curved up.

Like he knew a secret.

Like he was content.

Why the man had shown up today, Nash didn't know.

How Cross found him deep in Virginia, Nash didn't care.

Even so, he'd be having a conversation with his manager about giving out his motel information. He wondered what bullshit Cross told Darren to get that info.

Did it really matter?

It should.

Nash studied the dark chunk of hair that fell over Cross's forehead, the short, dark wiry hair that ran along his jawline and around his mouth.

That mouth. Nash had imagined that mouth on him many a night.

He could see the steady rise and fall of his chest through the open black leather jacket. His gaze slid over his crotch and down his denim-covered legs to a newer pair of black leather biker boots.

Wannabe.

Nash grinned.

Yeah, he was a wannabe. All the Blue Avengers were. They wanted to be bikers on one hand but hated real bikers on the other.

Cross showing up here today proved he didn't hate one particular biker.

Cross showing up here today proved Nash didn't hate one particular pig.

Just like Nash hadn't expected Cross to show up in his room at church that night, he certainly didn't expect him to show up at his motel room in Virginia.

But it made sense in a way. They weren't close to home. The only risk of anyone seeing them together here was his band manager and bandmates.

It had been six weeks since Nash told Cross to get gone. Six. It hadn't been easy. There had been plenty of times Nash had pulled out Cross's card and had been tempted to call or text him.

He'd resisted.

But at the back of his mind that whole six weeks, he'd hoped Cross, being a stubborn and bossy fuck, would show up somewhere where Nash was, like he had today.

Nash just didn't realize how much he'd wanted that. Until now.

To see him standing outside his motel door...

Fuck. It had taken everything he had not to pull the man into his room and throw him on the bed.

In one way they hardly knew each other, in another they knew each other too well.

They were opposites who fit together. However, the imperfect "whole" they made didn't fit in their reality. Which was their everyday lives.

Cross didn't fit into Nash's.

Nash didn't fit into Cross's.

He had no idea what to do about that. And he was pretty fucking sure Cross didn't know, either.

While the man laid there on a lounge chair just a couple feet away, Nash had finished up a song, putting music to the lyrics, while tweaking some of the lines he'd written.

He put his guitar to the side, closed his notebook, and noticed Cross's card had fallen under the table. He picked it up and tucked it in between two blank pages, before pushing to his feet and stepping over to the other chair. He squatted next to it and whispered, "Hey."

Cross shifted but his eyes remained closed. He was out. Dark half-moons colored the skin under his eyes where his long, black lashes laid.

Nash reached out and lightly touched Cross's lips. His warm breath puffed over his fingers, and Nash curled them into his palms before pulling his hand away.

He stared at what he wanted but couldn't have.

What he needed but had to live without.

Everything between them was just fucking wrong.

Cross knew it, too, but kept ignoring it.

But Nash couldn't.

They both had too much to lose.

Even so, he let his fingers travel down Cross's chest and under his leather jacket, where he felt very warm to Nash's cold fingers. Nash brushed the tips over Cross's nipples and down his stomach.

Until a hand stopped him. Cross squeezed his fingers and pressed Nash's hand flat against his belly.

Nash lifted his gaze from their hands to Cross's face. "You fell asleep. Hope it wasn't my singin'."

Cross's voice sounded rusty when he said, "Did a double, then drove straight here when I was done at zero-fuck-oh-clock this morning. Hadn't slept in a couple days."

Nash nodded, then stood, breaking their connection. "Bed's more comfortable than the lounge chair."

Cross hesitated, searching Nash's face. He made sure to keep it neutral and not give anything away.

"You got a gig tonight, right?"

Nash nodded again. "Yeah. Then we're gettin' a break for a few days. My voice could use it. Supposed to check outta here tomorrow mornin'. But thinkin' I won't."

"You're going to stay here?"

"We're gonna stay here," Nash corrected him. Fuck him, it was wrong, but he didn't give a fuck.

Nash didn't miss the flare behind Cross's light blue eyes. "For how long?"

"When do you gotta go back to the pigpen?"

"It's my long weekend. Not until Monday first shift."

Nash fought his smile. "Need to be back for our club run on Sunday. Not sure if it'll be the last one before blue balls weather hits, so don't wanna miss it."

"Plus, they'll want you to play afterward."

"That, too."

Cross tilted his head and studied Nash, his expression becoming cautious. "You wanted me to lose your number."

"Didn't work. Didn't need my number to show up at my door."

"You also didn't slam that door in my face."

"You just woulda kept knockin' like the bossy, stubborn fuck you are. Can't help I'm irresistible."

Cross's lips twitched. "Do you have groupies?"

"Just you."

Cross turned his head away, but Nash saw the tell-tale shake of his shoulders. He snorted softly, grabbed Cross's hand and pulled him from the chair. "It's fuckin' gettin' cold out here. Gotta grab somethin' to eat before we play tonight. You take a nap, I'll grab grub and bring it back."

Cross planted a hand on Nash's chest and leaned in. Nash met him halfway, their lips brushing, their beards tangling, then their tongues doing the same. Once again, he was tempted to throw the man on his bed and fuck him. Fuck food, fuck tonight's gig, fuck everyone.

But that wasn't going to work. He pulled back. "Sleep. Eat. Fuck. Sing. Fuck some more. Then fuck for the next few days 'til we can't fuck anymore."

"Sounds like a country song."

"Bite your fuckin' tongue," Nash growled in jest.

"How about I bite yours?"

"Need it tonight. Then it's yours 'til Sunday mornin'."

That flare turned into a flickering blue flame. "You mind if I come to your gig tonight?"

"If I say fuck no?"

Cross grinned. "I'd still show up."

Nash shook his head, pretending to be annoyed. "Bossy motherfucker."

"If I was bossy, I'd have you on your knees right now sucking my cock."

"Don't gotta be bossy for that." Nash made a point of glancing around the balcony. "Right here? Out on the balcony?"

Cross reached for the glass slider and opened the door, pushing Nash inside. "The carpet will be easier on your knees. Then I'll take a nap while you pick up some *grub*."

———

THEY HAD DRIVEN SEPARATELY to a popular local brewery where Dirty Deeds was playing. Cross arrived a half hour after Nash since he had taken his time in the shower after they got each other off only using their mouths before Nash had to leave.

They didn't fuck because they didn't have enough time. Or they did, but not the kind of time both of them wanted to take with each other.

So, it was tough to be patient while watching Nash up on stage when Cross knew what was coming after they went back to his motel room.

It was also tough to watch the women in the audience trying to get Nash's attention. Smiles. Winks. Tits spilling over tight, low-necked tops. Short skirts. Anything they could do to get his and his fellow bandmates' attention.

Nash wasn't wearing his colors tonight, Cross assumed it

was because it wasn't a biker bar. Instead he wore shredded, worn jeans, the black belt with the big-assed DAMC buckle, boots and an open, unbuttoned black shirt so it showed off a good portion of his lean torso. His sleeves were rolled up past his elbows with one corner of the shirt haphazardly tucked in at his waist.

He was fucking hot. And Cross could see why the women would throw themselves at him.

Every inch of exposed skin was slick with sweat because when he was on stage, he worked it. He not only felt that music, he *lived* it.

It flowed from the very center of his soul.

And because it did, everyone in that brewery could feel that power and charisma.

Cross was impressed. Also, hard as a fucking rock.

He sat far from the stage, simply taking it all in. His eyes only leaving Nash when a waitress would bring him another drink. The man knew how to play to a crowd, especially those women.

Cross wondered if he wasn't there tonight, whether Nash would be hooking up with any of them.

His best guess... probably.

But the fact was, Cross *was* there, and Nash extended his stay at the motel because he was. He could easily have gone back to Shadow Valley and told Cross to fuck off.

While he was excited about the fact they'd be spending time together, dread also played with his mind. Spending a few days with Nash could make this whole thing for him much, much worse.

Three or four days of "all Nash, all the time" could take Cross down a path he was reluctant to go.

Sex? Yes. Something more? It scared the shit out of him.

He had a feeling that spending all that time with Nash would make it impossible to go back to their real lives and keep things the way they needed to be kept...

Neat.

Nash on his side of the line, Cross on his.

That line being the one outside forces were making it difficult—if not impossible—to cross.

Cross would love to settle down with someone, possibly even raise a family. He'd never have that with Nash, even if Nash wanted the same things.

Though, Cross doubted he did.

Nash had it free and easy right now. Nothing tied him down, nothing kept him from doing what he loved to do, which was play his music, when and wherever he wanted.

Why would a man like that want to tie himself down to one place, one man—or woman—and give up his freedom?

Between sets, Nash hopped off the low stage and made his way through the few women who thought it was acceptable to touch him as he passed. Nash kept his eyes on Cross as he worked his way around people and occupied tables, though a couple women continued to trail him.

Nash stepped up to the high table where Cross sat alone and nabbed his ale, downing half of it before putting it back down.

"Want me to get you one?"

Nash shook his head. "Yours is fine." Beads of sweat rolled down the sides of his face, his shirt clung to him in spots.

Out of the corner of his eye, Cross saw the waitress heading their way. He pointed to the beer and lifted two fingers. The waitress stopped short, nodded and headed the other direction.

Nash gathered his damp hair and held a handful to the top of his head. And out of the blue, a woman was there blowing on the back of his neck.

What the fuck?

"This normal?" Cross asked, not sure whether to be appalled or amused.

Nash dropped his hair and twisted away from the woman. "Not always."

"You look really hot up there, honey. Wanna go outside and get some air?"

Cross pinned his lips together as the woman leaned into Nash's chest and the fabric straining over her tits became stained with his sweat. She laughed and then brushed at her nipples like the dampness would simply brush right off.

Cross cocked a brow. "Are you going to answer her?"

"By not answerin', I'm answerin'."

Cross nodded and picked up his beer, taking a sip to hide his grin.

"Lemme see that necklace," the woman said, her words slurring a bit.

As she reached for Nash's copper guitar pick pendant, he snagged her wrist in a tight grip and stopped her. "Get lost."

She snapped her spine straight and planted her hands on her hips, looking indignant. "I juss wanna see it."

"Can see it from where you're standin'."

"You're an asshole."

Nash shrugged and smiled. "Yeah."

The woman frowned, stomped her foot and almost fell over when she spun on her three-inch heels. The waitress, in passing, caught her elbow so the woman wouldn't topple over, and then gave her a little encouraging shove back toward her waiting friends. Then the server dropped off the two beers and a cold bottle of water for Nash. Cross threw a ten on her serving tray.

Nash stared at the water and beer, then at Cross for a long moment before picking up the beer and taking a long pull on it. When he put it back down, wiped his hand over his mouth and said, "Afraid I was gonna get spit in yours?"

"Plan on swapping spit with you later. I just wanted to get you a cold one."

"Thanks," Nash said quietly. He stared at Cross for a few more beats then reached for the leather cord around his neck. After pulling the necklace over his head, he then slipped it over Cross's.

Cross's heart skipped and then began to thump. "Nash, that's yours."

"Now it's yours.'

"But it means something to you."

"Yeah."

After settling the necklace around Cross's neck, Nash flipped the pendant over, so the words faced outward. But he left his hand there.

Cross placed his hand over Nash's. After a few seconds, Nash pulled his away and stepped back, shaking his head. "Wrong place."

Cross nodded, though wishing it wasn't true. "Agreed."

"Gotta go back on stage."

"Take your beer."

"Yes, Daddy," Nash teased, making his voice low and extra deep.

"Don't give me ideas."

Nash stared at his lips. "Fuckin' wanna kiss you right now."

Cross inhaled to try to slow his racing heart. "I want to do a lot more than kiss."

The tips of Nash's lips curled up, he snagged his beer and the bottle of water and went back up on stage.

His band members straggled onto the stage one by one, returning to their instruments. After playing another hour straight, Nash thanked the audience for coming out to see them but stated they had one more song.

Before they could start playing it, Nash raised his hand, called the other guys together in a circle and spoke to them. A couple of them shrugged and when they parted ways,

Nash headed toward the microphone stand at the front of the stage.

He leaned into the mic, announcing, "Gonna play a song next that isn't an original. Hope you all be okay with it but fuck it if you ain't." A loud roar filled the brewery and the crowd teemed at the front edge of the stage. "In case you don't know this song, it's *Secret* by Heart."

Nash stepped back, jerked his chin up toward Cross before dropping it to his neck to begin playing his guitar. Then he moved to the mic again and began to sing.

Cross had heard the song before, but never paid attention to the lyrics.

Until now.

Until they flowed over Nash's lips as he stared over the crowd, across the room at him and spoke to him through the music.

Cross was floored by how fucking perfect those lyrics were for their situation. He sang about how they lived two different lives and a line was drawn between those lives that was never crossed. How it was dangerous to be together, but they risked it anyway. How hard it was to hide what they want and to keep it a secret. That they knew from the beginning they'd have these problems.

The whole song was fitting, but it killed him to hear it. And from where Cross sat, he could tell it killed Nash, too.

The last line he sung about being doomed to stay apart made his voice crack and then he stepped away from the mic as the band played the last few notes.

Then the spotlights aimed at the stage went dark and Cross could only see shadows moving off to the side.

Cross waited there for another half hour, but Nash never came back to his table. Finally, he figured he'd gone out the back of the brewery.

Cross's phone lit up and vibrated on the high-top table with an incoming text. *W8n on U. Doors open.*

Cross dropped his head, smothered his smile, and tapped his phone against his thigh.

They had until Sunday morning.

He didn't know if he was going to be grateful for that time or regret it.

The only way he would find out was to open that door.

Chapter Fourteen

CROSS OPENED the motel door to find the room empty. At first, he figured Nash was out on the balcony smoking pot, since he hadn't seen the man actually smoke a legal cigarette yet. Which was a good thing.

Smoking turned Cross off. Even worse than someone smoking a joint.

Weird, but true.

He dropped his backpack on the floor by the door and put the bag of items he purchased at the twenty-four-hour drugstore on the small desk.

There was no doubt that the night cashier knew what Cross's plans were for the weekend. The couple bottles of Powerade and water, a few protein bars, plus the large box of condoms and two tubes of Astroglide were probably a dead giveaway.

The twenty-something cashier had given him the eye and a smirk. Cross returned it with a chin lift and a smile. While the young guy probably thought he knew who Cross would be using those items on, he'd be wrong.

Now, he stood in the motel room, his cock flexing in his pants with anticipation, but no Nash.

Then he realized the bathroom door was shut and he heard the shower start.

So, the man hadn't changed his mind and run far away from Cross.

The door was flung open and a naked Nash leaned through the doorway. "Fuckin' comin'?"

Cross shot him a grin. "Isn't that the plan?"

Nash snorted, returned the grin, and said, "Get the fuck in here. Need you to wash my back."

His back. *Riiiiight.*

Cross started removing his boots, hanging onto the desk for balance so he wouldn't fall on his ass. "That it?"

"Nope."

Cross tossed his leather jacket on the bed, ripped his shirt over his head, and quickly dropped his jeans and boxers to the floor, all while Nash's eyes were glued to him. And that alone made his cock stand at attention. "What else?"

"Stop jawin' and get in here to find out." He disappeared.

Cross's grin widened into a smile and he *jogged* into the bathroom to find out.

CROSS KNEW what he was doing. He *definitely* knew what the fuck he was doing.

Never, ever had Nash wanted to be a bottom. He still didn't. But, for fuck's sake, if he had to, it was worth it with Cross.

Nash was on his knees, facing the wall while gripping the headboard. Cross was behind him on his knees as well, his hips a powerhouse as he drove up and into Nash. One of his hands was wrapped around Nash's cock and he was stroking it with a lubed, tight fist. The other was wrapped snugly around the front of his throat, his fingers digging into Nash's flesh to keep his head back and pinned to Cross's shoulder.

And the man was moving in a way that hit all the right spots. Well, the one spot he liked in particular.

Cross had ordered Nash not to move once he had a hold of the headboard and, fuck him, he hadn't. He obeyed that order. Which was so fucking unlike him.

He didn't get it. He couldn't wrap his mind around the power Cross held over him. He'd always been the one wanting the control during sex. But slowly... *Fuck*... Slowly he was handing that control over to Cross.

Maybe it was temporary insanity. Awesome fucking sex could drive a man mad sometimes.

A hell of a lot of foreplay occurred in the shower earlier, but they'd kept it at that since both wanted to keep their erections so they could fuck each other. However, Cross insisted on taking the lead first. And now Nash was so close to blowing his load in the man's fist.

He didn't even give a fuck if he did.

Did he want to fuck the man's tight ass? Hell, yes.

But he was in no rush. They had the next three days to take their time and take their turn.

Give and take.

Cross had whispered that into his ear while they explored each other in the shower.

Give and take.

Right now, Cross was giving it to him good. So fucking good.

His own cock twitched with every stroke of Cross's dick in his ass, with every stroke of Cross's tight fist up and down his length.

He ached. He throbbed. The pressure becoming even more intense with every stroke over his prostate, every swirl of Cross's thumb over his swollen, leaking head.

They were back to chest, skin to skin. Their sweat

mingling, their heat merging, their groans and grunts filling the air around them.

He opened his eyes and turned his head until his mouth pressed against Cross's ear. "You tryin' to make me lose it?"

His voice didn't sound like his own. It was raw, husky. And it wasn't from singing for hours. It was from what Cross was doing to him.

It took a few seconds for Cross to answer since his breath was coming as hard as his thrusts. When he did, it was only a hissed, "Yes."

Before Nash could say anything else, Cross twisted his head and the angle made their kiss awkward, though their tongues could still touch and taste.

Their position didn't allow them to kiss like that for long. Plus, Cross had slowed down and that was not what Nash wanted. "Fuck me," Nash moaned in encouragement.

Cross gradually picked up his pace again, eventually slamming his hips up and against Nash's ass, sliding his hand from Nash's throat down to his nipples where he snagged one, twisting it so hard, Nash jerked from the sharp pleasure radiating through him and pulling his balls tight.

Fuck, he was ready to blow. "Again," he forced out.

Cross captured his other nipple, rolling it roughly between his fingers before tweaking it hard.

Heat and shock waves swept through Nash, from his very center to the outer edges of his body.

And he was *done*.

Done.

So. Fucking. Done.

Cross's grip tightened even more on his cock to the point it became almost uncomfortable. It rode that thin line. His voice was rough, and his words hitched when he said, "I feel you. Don't you fucking come yet. I'll tell you when."

Nash thought he was mad, but maybe it was Cross. He

was to the point of no return; he wouldn't be able to control anything. Not if Cross kept doing what he was doing.

"A few more..." Cross's hips tilted and drove upward. "Just wait..."

Fuck. He was crazy. Telling him to wait?

Cross pressed a damp cheek against his and groaned, "Now, baby. Fucking come now."

Jesus.
Fuckin'.
Christ.

Nash cried out as Cross surged up one last time, taking Nash with him, almost shoving him right into the headboard. He swore he blacked out for an instant as he came, hot cum shooting straight up in long streams and landing on him and the sheets. He exploded like an out of control fountain as Cross came, too. But Cross didn't stop, he kept riding him, drawing the head of his cock over Nash's prostate again and again, milking him dry until nothing was left.

The head of his dick was too sensitive to touch now, making Nash relieved when Cross finally released it, but remained deep inside him, their bodies pinned together while they both struggled to stay on their knees.

Nash wanted to collapse to the bed, to enjoy the satisfaction that permeated deep within his bones. Within his soul.

He wanted to curl up with the man who just made him come like a geyser and fall asleep within his arms.

They had the next few days to forget who they were. He wanted to take advantage of every minute of it. Even if it was simply sleeping together in the same bed. Something he'd never done with anyone before.

He'd had sex in back alleys, in cars, in motels, in many various locations. But not once had he stayed afterward and woke up with someone the next morning. Not once.

He couldn't wait to do it with Cross.

"Are you mad—"

"No," Nash cut him off. He was mad but not the angry type of mad.

"You didn't get to—"

"Later."

Cross hesitated. "You sure?"

"Said later."

"You sound mad."

"I'm not fuckin' mad, Cross." *I'm so fuckin' goddamn scared, that's what the fuck I am. There's nowhere good for this to go. We were doomed from the fuckin' beginnin', just like the song said. We knew. We're lettin' it happen, anyway.*

What doesn't kill you makes you stronger, right?

Fuckin'-A-right.

"I'm going to pull out," Cross said softly, giving Nash's waist a squeeze. "Ready?"

No, I'm not. Don't fuckin' go. "Yeah."

Cross slipped from him, and the mattress shifted as he got off the bed and headed toward the bathroom.

Nash continued to stare at the wall, his hands gripping the headboard so hard, his fingers had seized. He pressed his forehead to the edge of the cool wood and blew out a breath.

This weekend was such a bad fucking idea. It would only make things worse. It was like offering a line of cocaine to a druggie and before the addict could snort it, you took a mighty breath and blew the powder away.

After freaking out, what would that addict do? Lick every fucking surface to capture every grain of coke he could find. Because even those few scattered particles might dull that sharp edge.

This weekend would be just like that. Licking the mirror of any residue just to capture whatever high they could find. In the end, it wouldn't satisfy them, it would only leave them wanting more. It would just be a tease.

In the end, they'd both be hungrier for more.

When Nash heard the water shut off in the bathroom, he straightened and moved. He needed to clean up.

And then feed his fucking addiction.

———

NASH STARED at the wallet sitting on the nightstand next to a partially empty box of condoms and tube of lube Cross had picked up on his way back to the motel last night.

It wasn't Nash's wallet.

It was Cross's.

And he knew what was inside.

He rolled closer and snagged it, then rolled back.

Flipping it open, he slid the piece of fabric away from the badge, then ran his finger over the embossed metal that even shined in the limited light.

The fucking sex with Cross was amazing. Even though in the past he'd hated being a bottom, it was worth it just for the opportunity to top Cross.

But it wasn't just sex. Or at least, it wasn't anymore. It had started out like that, but now...

Fuck. Things were getting more complicated.

Nash snorted softly. Not that they weren't complicated from the start. They fucking certainly were.

He knew it was a bad idea to invite Cross to stay holed up with him in this motel for the weekend. And after he did it, he tried to talk himself out of it. But he couldn't.

He couldn't because he wanted to spend more time with the man.

This had never happened to him before. With anyone.

No one had ever piqued his interest enough in the past where he wanted to spend any other time with them than the time it took to fuck.

He had no idea what it was about this cop. Especially since he was a bossy motherfucker, too.

Maybe that was it. The cop was a challenge. One he had sort of won.

Sort of.

Because Cross won, too. But like that addiction Nash thought about earlier, Cross wanted more.

"I don't want to stop seeing you, Nash."

He didn't want to stop seeing him, either.

"We'll just be careful. We'll find a place to meet. Away from your club, away from my townhouse. Somewhere neutral. I'll also meet you on the road when I can. When I have a stretch of days off."

That was the conversation they had last night before Cross fell into deep sleep, probably exhausted from a lack of it.

Nash had noticed the faint dark circles under the man's eyes when he'd first arrived at the motel yesterday, but when he'd walked into the room after the brewery last night, they were darker, deeper.

And for some reason that pulled at Nash.

Was he actually worried for the cop?

Yeah, unfortunately, he was.

Fuck him. His whole life was majorly fucked right now.

Everything had been running smoothly. He had a path he was following.

Until Cross.

Now that path was full of bumps and pitfalls.

It was a dangerous road to travel. But neither of them wanted to take a different route. Neither of them.

Nash had remained quiet while Cross had talked about continuing to see each other.

He felt that strong urge to lick the mirror, just like Cross did.

Nash closed the wallet and quietly set it back on the nightstand before rolling to his side to study Cross as he slept.

It was almost noon, though it was difficult to tell since the curtains were drawn, blocking out most of the early November sunlight.

He hadn't had a chance to fuck Cross yet, but that would change soon. He just hated to wake the man up since he'd been so exhausted.

Even so, Nash needed food soon. But he needed Cross first.

The wrinkled top sheet was only pulled up to Cross's hips. Nash hooked a finger at the top edge and slid it farther down. The cop's dick was soft, nestled in trimmed dark, wiry hair. While he manscaped, he didn't shave himself bare. Nash liked that. He hated totally bare balls or shaved-bare pussies.

He leaned over Cross, who was sprawled on his back, but didn't touch him with anything but his tongue. He licked a path from the man's center downward, circled his navel, before following the narrow trail of hair even lower. Until he nuzzled his nose into that lower dark patch of hair.

Fuck, that slightly musky, masculine scent filling his nostrils made his dick harden within seconds. He couldn't resist taking a warm, soft Cross into his mouth.

Nash knew the second Cross woke up. His cock grew as Nash worked it with his mouth and tongue. Fingers curled into Nash's messy, snarled hair, not discouraging or encouraging, but simply holding on.

Cross's breath hitched and quickened. A low groan was pulled from him as Nash palmed the delicate, silky skin of the man's sac. When he squeezed gently, Cross's hips surged upward, driving his cock deeper into Nash's mouth.

Nash went with him, sucking more intently and increasing his pace.

"Jesus, baby," Cross moaned.

The "baby" thing was new. Since last night, in fact. It kept catching Nash off guard since no man had ever called him "baby" before. He'd never used it himself on a man, either. He wasn't sure how to react to it, or whether to ignore it.

For now, he'd ignore it and continue doing what he was doing. He was so fucking hard just from Cross's reactions and sounds he made from getting head.

The fingers in his hair tightened and Cross tried to take control, driving upward, trying to fuck Nash's mouth. Nash wrapped a couple of fingers around the root to keep from choking but allowed Cross to set the pace, which was getting quicker by the second.

The salty tang of precum coated Nash's tongue. His own dick was leaking all over the sheets, too. In fact, every thrust of Cross's hips upward resulted in Nash thrusting against the bed.

He needed to fuck Cross and needed to fuck him now. So when Cross warned, "I'm going to come," Nash's silent response was, "Thank fuck!"

Cross drove his hips up one more time, pulling Nash's head down as he did so, hot cum shooting down the back of Nash's throat with each pulse of Cross's dick.

When Cross's hips finally fell back to the mattress, Nash licked his dick clean before sitting up and reaching for the lube and wraps on the nightstand.

"On your fuckin' stomach," Nash ordered, his voice as strained as every other part of his body. "Makin' that ass mine."

Without a hesitation, Cross rolled over, burrowing his head in his arms, his back still rising and falling rapidly since he hadn't caught his breath yet.

Nash suited up, slathered lube over his dick, then squeezed a generous amount onto the end of two fingers. He climbed in between Cross's muscular thighs and, without warning, slid those fingers inside.

Cross tightened around them as Nash worked the lube

deep, not quite being gentle but being thorough. Then he curled his fingers and found Cross's prostate, massaging it until he writhed against the mattress.

"Fuck," Cross groaned into the bedding.

"Yeah, that's what you're gonna get. Fucked."

Cross turned his head until their eyes met.

"Got a problem with that?" Nash asked, his fingers still stroking that walnut-sized spot.

Cross's eyelids got heavy and he answered with a thick, "No."

"Right answer." Nash's heart was thundering in his chest, his cock was throbbing in the wrap. He was dying to be inside Cross, but he was forcing himself to wait.

Just a little longer.

The anticipation was sweet but agonizing. However, it would make that first thrust inside even better.

He slipped his fingers from Cross. Using his knees, he shoved Cross's right leg higher up the bed, then the left leg, until he was in a frog-like position, low to the bed, legs bent, but ass slightly raised.

With one hand on his cock, Nash lined himself up, then used his other hand to push Cross's head deeper into the bed, holding him there. Showing him who was in control at that very moment.

It wasn't Cross.

Nash teased him by pressing the head of his cock against his puckered hole but going no further.

It was killing Nash and he could tell it was killing Cross, too. The cop wanted it as badly as Nash did.

"Stay in that position unless I tell you otherwise, got me?"

"Yes," came muffled from the bed.

Every line and curve of the man waiting to take Nash's cock made him lose his breath. Cross reminded Nash of a song. His breathing a melody, his movement full of fluid energy, every inch of him rich with meaning.

This man was fucking with his head. There was an ache deep inside Nash which was spreading from his center and overtaking him.

When he played his music, when he sang, it flowed through him, through his veins, his heart, his mind. And Cross was suddenly like that music. Swallowing him whole. Becoming a part of his being, a part of his soul.

Nash's heart was beating so hard in his chest, he worried he was either having a heart attack or a bout of anxiety.

He was still on the precipice of taking Cross, pressed against him, but hadn't gone any further.

He could end this here. He could stop this now.

He could save himself.

But could he really?

Could he save himself? Or was it too late?

Chapter Fifteen

CROSS HAD no idea what was going through Nash's head. But the man had been frozen in place, the tip of his cock still pressed against Cross. Not moving forward, not retreating.

He wasn't teasing Cross, this was something else.

Cross kept quiet and still, letting Nash work through whatever he needed to.

Nash hadn't said much when Cross mentioned last night how he wanted them to keep seeing each other.

He knew it would be difficult. And he'd actually expected Nash to shut that idea down right away.

He hadn't.

But he also hadn't agreed, either.

Cross had hoped by the end of the weekend he would. Hoped Nash would see the connection they had, even though they were such polar opposites and living in their own worlds.

But they did have something in common. Cross was used to hiding who he was, so was Nash. So, they'd just continue to do what they've been doing their whole lives.

Hide.

Keep secrets.

Pretend they were someone else.

Play the game their environment and their life choices made them play.

They could do this. They were used to it. It wouldn't be anything new to either one of them.

But they could do it together, in a round-about way.

They could have each other without anyone else knowing. It wouldn't be easy but it would be something. And something was better than nothing.

Yes, *something* was better than fucking *nothing*.

He had nothing and he wanted that something with Nash.

But Nash needed to want it with Cross. Cross hoped to fuck that he would.

Then Nash's cock was gone, and he was covering Cross's body with his. He growled, "You fuckin' tempt me. You make me..."

He didn't finish that sentence and Cross needed him to finish it.

Cross made him what?

What was Nash feeling? What was he fighting?

Nash worked his way back down, his tongue sliding along the back of Cross's neck, the top of his spine, following that path back down, only ending at the top edge of his crease. Then his cock was there again, nudging, pressing.

"Make you what?"

After a long hesitation, Nash said, "Make me wanna fuck you."

No, that wasn't it. That wasn't what it was. It was something else he didn't want to admit.

But Cross had patience. He could wait. Nash would figure it out.

They both would.

They had time. Hell, they had until Sunday for certain.

Then they could go from there.

But now... Right now, Nash was pushing forward, filling him, making Cross his. Just like Cross had made Nash his last night.

Lines were blurring.

Neither was a top; neither was a bottom.

They were just...

The two of them.

Together.

Connected.

He suddenly wanted to know everything about Nash.

His real name.

His past.

His future.

Why he was who he was.

But not right now.

Not right then.

Right now, right then, Nash was fucking him slowly, completely. Taking his time, taking careful strokes. Making it good, making it great. His hand released Cross's head, he no longer held him down.

Whatever Nash had planned, it had changed.

Each push suddenly had meaning; each pull had purpose.

Every forward movement and every retreat had significance and consequence.

Like his music.

Like the lyrics he sung last night.

Then he was gone. He pulled out. And Cross felt that loss.

Before he could ask, Nash said, "On your back."

With a hand to Cross's hip, Nash helped roll him over. He stared down at Cross for the longest moment, his hazel eyes dark, possibly even troubled.

When Cross opened his mouth, Nash just shook his head. So, Cross said nothing and waited.

Nash spread Cross's knees, then ran his hands from his ankles, up his calves, along his inner thighs, causing a shiver to rip through Cross.

Here was a dominant man, a biker, a rocker, tattooed and hard-edged, being uncharacteristically tender.

Once again, Cross didn't know what was going through Nash's head. Even if he asked, he was sure Nash wouldn't answer.

So, once again, he waited.

But Nash revealed nothing, instead just lined himself up and pushed inside Cross once more.

Cross accepted him. Welcomed him. Reached up, hooked a hand behind Nash's head and pulled him down, taking his weight, taking his mouth, taking all of him.

Nash continued to fuck him lazily as they kissed, their tongues and lips fused together. Once more creating a connection between the two.

Then it got to be too much. Too heavy. And their kiss broke. Nash pressed his forehead to his and they simply breathed.

Cross closed his eyes to savor that connection as Nash continued to move, his pace slow, deliberate.

Almost... *painful*.

It hurt. Because he wanted this so badly. He wanted it to be...

Them.

The two of them.

More than simply sex.

So much more.

Something was building, growing.

They could fight it but it would be a losing battle, a war neither would win.

They just needed to accept what was happening and deal with it. Deal with the fallout. Or learn to hide it well.

Either way, it would be difficult.

But Cross was willing. However, Nash needed to be willing, too.

He slid his hands down Nash's back, over the large tattoo that defined his life. Which told the world who he was. Where he belonged.

But he also belonged here. With Cross.

Inside him. A part of him.

It was overwhelming, this deep ache. This intense need.

It was raw. Tangible.

Nash's rhythm continued to be excruciatingly slow. Too cautious. Now, too deliberate.

Cross wasn't breakable. He could take whatever Nash could give him. But right now, Nash wasn't giving him anything but heartache.

He dug his fingers into Nash's ass and demanded, "Fuck me."

"I am."

"No, you're not. You're giving me a taste of something you might not be willing to give in the future. You're showing me how it could be and not what it is."

"You're seein' things."

"I'm seeing how things could be, if you'd let it. How it could be between us, if we wanted it."

"What do you want from me?"

"What you're giving me at this very moment. And I don't mean the sex. The rest of it. You're giving me you."

"It's wrong."

"To others, maybe. To us, no, it's not. It's right. What we are defies everything we know and what's expected of us. But I feel what we have. I know you do, too."

Instead of answering, Nash pushed up on his hands and locked his eyes with Cross as he began to thrust more earnestly. Harder, faster. Pounding deep. Cross saw Nash's nostrils flare, his jaw tighten.

He was fighting back his emotions. He was attempting to smother them.

But he lost the fight.

Cross watched Nash's stony expression change into shock and defeat. Reaching up, Cross brushed his fingers over the jaw that turned slack, over the lips that parted, over the throat that worked.

Cross could only imagine the words Nash wanted to say were stuck due to a lump in his throat, because Cross had one, too.

Curling his fingers around the back of Nash's neck, Cross pulled him back down, tucking Nash's face against his neck. Holding him close as the man continued to move, to give Cross what he wanted.

Which was him in all ways.

Would life be difficult? Fuck yes.

Would it be worth it? Hopefully, yes.

A few minutes later, a low grunt was smothered against Cross's skin as Nash arched his body one more time, driving deep and staying there.

Cross buried his fingers into Nash's long hair, pulling his head up until they were face to face. Then they kissed. Long, deep, thoroughly. Until they both needed to gasp for breath.

After their breathing evened out and their heartbeats settled a bit, Cross asked softly, "Do you feel it?" And this time, Cross got his answer.

"Yeah."

Cross wrapped his arms around Nash, holding him tightly for a few moments, until Nash had no choice but to slip from him and go clean up.

But as he watched Nash cross the room, the large Dirty Angels tattoo which covered the man's back reminded him once again how difficult this would be.

They sat outside on the balcony watching the sun set, bottles of beer in their hands, disposable plates of Chinese food perched on their laps. A half-smoked joint in the nearby make-shift ashtray.

Nash's long hair was up in a man-bun. Cross wasn't sure what to think of it when Nash put it up like that. He understood it kept the hair out of Nash's food and face, which the man said could get annoying.

Cross never had long hair, never would. But it fit Nash to a T.

Nash's feet were propped on the balcony's top railing, his legs encased in worn, soft denim. He wore a navy long-sleeved thermal which had seen better days. Cross also wore jeans, and a Southern Allegheny Regional PD sweatshirt. Nash had made a face when Cross put it on before leaving to get take-out.

But in response, Cross had given him a smirk and the finger before walking out of the room. He might have heard a laugh as he closed the door behind him.

When he'd returned with the food and the beer, he found Nash barefoot and smoking outside.

How the man could tolerate being barefoot with the chill in the air, Cross didn't know. But he couldn't stop sneaking peeks at Nash's long toes and beautifully shaped feet. He didn't know if he'd ever seen such sexy ones. And he was in no way a foot man.

No, he was an ass man. And Nash definitely had that going for him, too. That ass in Levi's looked like art. Those dimples above that ass made it fine art.

Cross dropped his head and grinned at his own boot covered feet. He shoveled another forkful of chicken *mei fun* into his mouth to hide that grin.

"Hopefully, you're not one of those who likes to suck

toes," came the rumble next to him.

Fuck, he was busted. "No, but if I was, you'd have the perfect toes for it."

"I'm not stoned enough for you to do that."

"Neither am I."

Nash burst out laughing, catching his plate before it tumbled to the floor. Cross smiled at the rich, genuine sound coming deep from the other man's chest.

After taking a long pull of his beer while still chuckling, Nash set it down to concentrate on his General Tso's chicken. But after a moment, he snuck a peek at Cross, who caught it.

"Didn't think cops could have beards."

Cross ran a hand over the whiskers on his face. "Why? You don't like it?"

"Didn't fuckin' say that."

"My department allows it as long as we keep after it. Not all departments do. So, you like it." He hid his grin with another forkful of food.

"Yeah."

Cross couldn't fight the grin anymore, so he pointed it at his plate, saying, "I've been told I've got a baby-face, the beard makes me look more badass."

Nash snorted. "Right."

"Unlike your scrub."

"Don't like it?"

"Like it against my balls when you suck my cock."

"Same here. With that shit around your mouth, when you're suckin' me, it reminds me of a hot, wet pussy."

Cross choked, then laughed. "You keep giving me reasons to try pussy."

"Take it from me, pussy's a hassle."

"Men are easier?"

Nash lost his grin and took a long guzzle of beer.

They sat there quietly for a few minutes, filling their

bellies with good Asian food and domestic beer. While he enjoyed the companionable silence just sitting next to the man, Cross wanted more. So, he swallowed another mouthful of rice noodles and asked, "Where do you go next?"

Nash wiped his mouth with the back of his hand even though he had a napkin sitting on his thigh. "Back to Shadow Valley."

"I meant on tour."

"You should know since you musta stalked our website."

"I only looked to see where you were playing last night. I didn't take the time to plan my stalker route."

Nash's expression became dead serious. "Just a warnin', got a homo hater in my band. So, if he catches wind I'm bi, it could be an issue. Can't afford to lose him right now while we're gettin' our new guitarist up to speed. That'll screw us up one side and down the other. Not a good idea to be followin' me to gigs. Need the band to be solid to see if we can catch a label's attention."

That was a whole lot of words for Nash. Singing was one thing, talking another. "That what you want?"

Nash lifted a shoulder and put his now empty plate on the floor. "Dunno. Depends on the deal."

"It would be a lot of pressure," Cross murmured.

Nash turned his hazel eyes to him. "Yeah."

"People would be watching you closer than ever."

Nash's lips flattened out. "Yeah."

"You might eventually be outed."

Nash closed his eyes and his jaw worked. He turned his head away before he opened them again, staring through the aluminum railing into the line of trees behind the motel.

"Would it be worth it?" Cross asked cautiously.

"To get signed?" Nash huffed out a breath. "Dunno. Maybe. Easy to replace a drummer, I guess. Not so easy to replace my club and family."

"Think the club would have a problem with it?"

"Don't wanna find out. They're my family. Even if some wouldn't care, some might. Shit could get sticky. Don't need that hassle."

"I get it, believe me. I know a couple guys who were out, or who've come out, in other PD's and they've taken a beating. Not physically, but the underlying harassment's there. Other officers are fake as shit to their face but rip them a new one behind their backs. I worry about them if they would ever need backup. This day and age, you'd think things would be different. In truth, things haven't changed, intolerance is only kept hidden more. Like your brothers, some of mine wouldn't give a shit, but some might. And the few who would could cause trouble. I want this promotion. I've worked hard for it. It's a nice bump in salary and responsibility. I shouldn't be passed over because of who I choose to spend my time with outside of work."

"You say choose, but it's not a fuckin' choice. At least for you. I could choose to stick with women. There have been times I've done that to keep under the radar." His jaw flexed. "Truth is, after a while, a restlessness starts deep down inside me, and I need to find someone to settle it."

"Then it's not a choice for you."

Nash dropped his feet to the floor and straightened in his chair. "No, guess not."

"Were you feeling that restlessness when you went to The Cockpit?"

"Was there to check out the lead guitarist. Wasn't lyin' about that."

"Were you feeling that restlessness when you showed up at my townhouse?"

Nash didn't answer. Instead, he grabbed the joint from the ashtray and kicked his feet back up on the railing before lighting it, taking a deep inhale, holding it, and finally blowing it out on a long breath.

Cross watched the smoke dissipate into the cool evening air. He lifted his beer to his lips and waited. He was learning if he waited Nash out, he might get an answer to his question. Not always, but sometimes.

This was one of those times.

After a couple more tokes on the joint, Nash said, "Was feelin' somethin', not sure if it was restlessness."

Cross decided not to push that topic any further, even though he wanted to explore it deeper. He didn't want to shut Nash down by asking about his feelings, which was not a normal guy thing, especially when you were a cop or a biker. Instead he asked, "Your parents know?"

Nash's head twisted toward him. "Know what?"

"You're bi."

His expression turned to concrete, and he turned back to face the railing. "No."

"Are you afraid to tell them?"

Nash's hesitation was too long for Cross's liking, which made his gut churn.

Nash's words sounded as stiff as he looked. "No. They're dead."

Damn. To lose both his parents had to be tragic. "Sorry."

"Nothin' to be sorry about."

He waited for Nash to shut down this line of conversation, but he didn't, so Cross asked, "You miss them?"

"No."

Interesting.

After Cross's mother died of pancreatic cancer when he was twelve, he missed her terribly. He still missed her. "I miss mine. My father's alive but wants nothing to do with me. He couldn't accept me as I am, so..."

"You told him?"

"Not so much told him but made a major mistake by bringing home a guy during my Christmas break from the police academy."

"How'd he know the guy wasn't just a friend?"

He'd grown up thinking his father was a fair and tolerant man. He learned the hard way he'd been mistaken. *Live and learn.* "Because I didn't introduce him as a friend. I had no reason to believe my father wouldn't be accepting since I never heard him say one bad thing about the LGBTQ community. Not one word. He either hid it well or he was accepting of it as long as his son wasn't a part of it. Especially a son who was following in his footsteps. I was making him proud by attending the academy and becoming a police officer. But after that Christmas I was nothing but an embarrassment and a disgrace to his name. My... *friend* and I left not even a half hour after we'd arrived there. I haven't seen or talked to my father since. I've tried, but he's shut me out completely."

"He's a fuckin' asshole," Nash growled.

Maybe. But that didn't make the loss of his father any easier. The man he looked up to his whole life and who he wanted to emulate turned out to be a major disappointment. He was devastated to find out the truth of how his father felt about his son not being straight.

He'd said some nasty things Cross had tried to erase from his memories. But he couldn't, they were seared there forever.

After reaching out a few times and getting nothing back, he'd given up. He had no siblings, his mother's family lived in California, so he hardly knew them, and his father's brother and sister had become distant after that Christmas, too.

That meant he had no one.

Nobody but his law enforcement and Blue Avengers MC brotherhoods. Because of that, he understood how Nash's MC had become his "family." He also didn't blame the man for not wanting to alienate them.

Live and learn.

Brotherhood.

The DAMC colors permanently inked onto Nash's back. All those tattoos made sense. As well as the music themed half-sleeve. What Cross hadn't figured out yet was the reason for the "never quit" tattoo. Did he get it for some particular reason?

"Never quit," he murmured.

"What?"

Cross shook his head. "We shouldn't have to hide."

Nash stared at him for a few seconds. "We don't. I'm a biker. A musician. You're a cop and a wannabe. Ain't hidin' any of that."

"You know what I mean."

"Take out the obvious fact we're both men... Say you were a woman, think this would be any easier? You're a fuckin' pig. I'm," Nash shook his head, "me. Remember how the fuck I was treated by your so-called brothers? Think they woulda treated me with respect if you were a bitch instead and a 'dirty' biker was fuckin' you?"

Nash was right. More than one reason existed which could create issues if they were discovered. There were multiple.

Cross reminded him, "And your brothers would want to kick my fucking ass, too." Especially The Incredible Bulk.

"Yeah."

Yeah. He didn't even bother to deny it because Nash knew it was true.

"We got the weekend," Nash reminded him.

Right, they had the weekend. "And then what?"

"Then we head home and get back to our real lives."

"Think about what I suggested."

Nash cocked a brow at him. "About seein' each other on the sly?" He shook his head. "Fuckin' stupid, Cross. Deep down you know it."

"We could get a place to meet."

Nash dropped his feet from the railing and twisted in his chair. "Soundin' like a desperate motherfucker right now, *baby*. Expectin' miracles that ain't gonna happen." He grabbed his beer bottle and jumped to his feet.

Before he could open the glass slider, Cross was out of his own chair and blocking the door with his arm across it. Nash came to an abrupt stop and lifted his narrowed eyes to his.

"Take what you can get, Cross, and be happy with it."

"It's not enough."

"Tough shit."

"You're scared."

"Damn right I am."

"Not just about getting caught and being outed."

Nash set his jaw and his eyes slid to where Cross's hand was planted on the door frame.

"Tell me something..." Cross started.

Nash's hazel eyes hit his again. Yes, fear that this could become bigger than either of them could control filled his eyes.

"What's your real name?"

"Didn't look when I got arrested?"

"No. Didn't have the chance. Everyone was calling you Nash, so I just figured they were using your last name."

"They were."

"What's your first name?"

"Does it fuckin' matter?"

Did it? Fuck yes, it did. It was a piece of Nash Cross wanted for his very own. "It does to me."

"Why?"

If he told Nash the truth, he'd spook him, so he didn't. Cross jerked his shoulder up. "You know my first name." That was a lame excuse but the only one he could come up with on the fly.

"Aiden."

Fuck. That was the first time Nash used his name. Nobody used it anymore. Cops typically called each other by their last names. "Yes."

"That doesn't change shit."

"You're right. It doesn't. But I'm asking. Will you give me that?"

"No."

"Why?"

"Because if I give you that, it makes this shit all too real."

And there was the truth, the fear. "And that's a bad thing."

"Yeah, *Aiden*, it's a motherfuckin' bad thing."

"But it *is* real, Nash. You want to ignore it, but it's real. It's hitting you like a fucking two-by-four just like it hit me."

"You're trying to make this to be somethin' it's not."

"Is it not?"

"Fuck you."

"Same to you, baby."

"Don't call me that," Nash growled, leaning closer until his face was just inches from Cross's.

"Then give me your name," Cross whispered.

"I give you that, doesn't mean you can use it."

They were at a stand-off. Cross kept blocking the door with his arm and Nash refused to give in.

Again, Cross waited him out.

"Bossy motherfucker," Nash finally muttered under his breath, straightening up but not moving away.

That pulled a smile from Cross and he shrugged. "Feet cold?"

Nash blinked at the sudden change of topic. "Nope."

"Sure you don't want to go inside?"

"You don't let me inside, I'm gonna force my way in and takin' you with. Then I'm gonna bend you over that desk in there and fuck you raw."

Cross's smile dropped. "Raw, as in no condom?"

"Yep."

"That's not going to happen."

"Try me."

The thought of Nash taking him bareback sent both a prickle down his spine and heat swirling through him.

He never fucked without a condom. Ever.

Both parties involved would have to test clean before Cross would ever consider it. He'd also have to trust his partner completely.

Nash and he were nowhere near that point yet. And might never be.

So, for Nash to threaten that...

But that's what it had to be, simply an empty threat. Nothing more. Something to shock Cross into moving away from the door.

He dropped his hand and unblocked Nash's path. And, like he was getting used to doing, he waited.

Nash didn't disappoint. He wrapped his fingers around the back of Cross's neck and leaned in again, this time Nash's lips just a fraction away from his. "Graham."

Cross had taken a sharp breath at the shock of Nash's cold fingers touching his skin. And when Nash said his name, Cross inhaled it.

His heart skipped a beat. What Nash gave him was small, simple, but also huge at the same time.

Graham.

Graham Nash.

Wait. He'd made a joke about that when they first met. Now he understood Nash's reaction at the time. "Your parents named you Graham?"

"They were assholes."

Cross's lips twitched. "It's a great name for a musician."

Nash rolled his eyes. "Now you're bein' the asshole."

He pressed his lips together, trying not to laugh. "I take it you don't like it."

"Haven't used it in twenty years."

"Bet you won't be able to use it if you get signed to a label."

"Probably not. But not gonna cry about it."

"You could be like Prince and just use one name."

"Or you could just shut the fuck up and kiss me."

"Or I could just shut the fuck up and kiss you." His smile was smothered when Nash crushed his lips to his, pushing him against the glass door and sliding a knee between Cross's thighs.

It wasn't long before they were both sporting erections and out of breath.

They didn't break the kiss as Nash reached behind Cross, slid the door open and shuffled him backward until they were inside. He had one hand still wrapped around Cross's neck as he maneuvered the slider closed, cutting off the cold air.

Cross twisted his head to end the kiss as Nash continued to back him up until his legs hit the mattress. After he fell backward onto the bed, Cross rose to his elbows and said, "Thought you wanted me over the desk."

Nash stood between Cross's parted knees, undoing his belt, his eyes dark, locked with his. The sound of the bulky belt buckle clanking, the soft growl of the zipper being lowered, the whisper of Nash's jeans being shoved down his legs, all of it made Cross's blood rush, not only to his ears, but to his cock, making it flex in his jeans.

Which meant he was still dressed when he shouldn't be.

As he reached for the button on his jeans, Nash stopped him. "I'm gonna do it."

Cross lifted his hands up in surrender and leaned back onto his elbows to watch Nash finish getting undressed.

Never quit.

He needed to know what that tattoo meant. He was afraid if he asked, he'd get some bullshit story. He'd find out eventually if he had patience and waited.

"Boots off."

Cross's attention snapped back to Nash, who was stroking his hard-on.

"Wasn't a suggestion, *Aiden*."

Cross pushed to a seat and leaned over to untie his boots. He yanked them and his socks off, tossing them out of the way.

"Stand up."

Cross's cock was dripping precum in his boxer briefs. But he kept his mouth shut and listened.

"Take that motherfuckin' sweatshirt off and hand it to me."

Was he going to destroy it?

Cross pulled the sweatshirt over his head and held it out. Nash snagged it from him and, after stroking his cock a couple more times, wiped his own precum off on the lettering that said Police Department.

"Jesus," Cross whispered.

"What?"

He shook his head.

"Didn't think you said anythin'. Turn around."

Cross's breathing was coming a little faster now. His cock was pressed painfully against his zipper.

"Turn around."

With a slight nod, he did what was demanded of him.

"Hands behind your back."

Cross opened his mouth to question what the hell Nash was planning, but he snapped it shut when Nash repeated more firmly, "Hands behind your back."

Okay, what the fuck?

"Don't like commands barked out at you like you're a

criminal? Sucks, doesn't it? You won't be treated like I was, though. Keep your wrists like that."

A prickle of worry slid through Cross as Nash used the sweatshirt to bind his arms. It wasn't like cuffs, so it wasn't tight even after Nash knotted the fabric, and Cross knew he could easily break out of it or even slip his hands from the tied cotton. But it wasn't the fact Nash was trying to keep him from escaping, he expected Cross to *want* to remain bound.

He dug into Cross's back pocket, pulling out his wallet that held his badge, and threw it on the bed. Then Nash reached around him to unbutton and unzip his jeans. Nash shoved them to Cross's knees.

Fuck, he was being hobbled by his jeans, too.

Again, if Cross really wanted to, he could escape. Unlike when Nash was handcuffed and thrown into the back of one of the department's cruisers that day. But Cross didn't want to escape. He wanted to see where this went even though he didn't like giving up control like this. But then, neither did Nash.

Give and take.

Nash kicked Cross's feet as wide as they could go even with being bound by his jeans, which were now gathered at his ankles.

Then he lost his breath as Nash planted a hand at the top of Cross's back and shoved him forward.

"Should take you over the desk."

Before Cross could respond, Nash yanked Cross back up with a hand to his shoulder and spun him around, shuffling Cross forward until he was standing in front of the desk, which had a large mirror above it.

Before his face was shoved down, Cross caught the reflection of the two of them. Nash naked, his face unreadable, standing behind him. A flush on his own face. Then he saw nothing as Nash shoved him down until Cross's right cheek was pressed against the cool surface.

"Hold your ass open for me."

Cross stretched his fingers, finding he could just reach his ass cheeks. He grabbed his own flesh and did as he was told, exposing himself.

He waited for Nash to move away. To grab a condom and the lube. But he didn't.

"Nash..." He tried to rise, but Nash shoved him back down.

"Keep holding yourself open. Wanna see what you're offerin' me."

"Not going to be offering you shit if you don't grab a condom."

Nash ignored Cross's demand. Instead, he spat on Cross's hole, then into his palm.

Cross's heart began to thump so hard, it pounded in his ears. "Not just spit." *Please, for fuck's sake.*

Nash's palm at his center back kept him pinned to the desk. "Thought you liked it rough."

Cross could break free if he needed to, but if he did, it might cause a fight he didn't want to start. Why was Nash doing this? "Not just spit, Nash. *For fuck's sake.*"

Spit could be used in a pinch, but they had plenty of lube and Cross had never been taken with just saliva before.

"Don't move," Nash growled, releasing him.

If Cross wasn't already lying over the desk, he would've collapsed when his knees buckled in relief. He locked them again when he heard Nash return.

Then he heard the tear of the wrapper and the cap of the lube.

Thank fuck.

He was still holding himself open when the cool lube dribbled down his crease. Nash threw the tube of lube on the desk right next to Cross's face. Then he heard the man's voice in his ear. "Would you have stopped me?"

Was this a fucking test?

But, fuck him, in truth, he didn't know that answer. He didn't know if push came to shove, whether Cross would have stopped Nash, not only from fucking him bareback but without lube.

Did he want Nash that badly?

Had he become fucking stupid over the man?

Had he lost all sense of reason?

No.

No, he was a fucking cop and he needed to keep his sense of reason in all things.

Even Nash.

No matter how much he wanted the man, no matter how much he wanted this to continue after Sunday when they walked out of this room and headed back home, he needed to keep his head on straight.

So, he answered Nash truthfully. "Yes, I would've stopped you."

"Wanna fuck you without a wrap."

"You know what that would take. We could plan that in the future..." Cross let that trail off and waited.

Finally, Nash straightened up and Cross felt the pressure of his cock at his now lubed entrance.

"Yeah... We'll see," Nash grumbled, before taking Cross.

Was Nash actually considering it?

Cross sure as fuck hoped so.

Chapter Sixteen

NASH TURNED his head on the pillow and glanced at the time. It was way earlier than he normally woke up and even Cross was still asleep. But he needed to get back. The club had a run today and then a pig roast afterward. He was expected to show up for both.

Not that he minded. Spending four hours in formation with his brothers riding through the countryside was a great bonding experience. And it made him feel like he belonged

And he did. To something great.

He also didn't want to fuck that up.

The man lying next to him could fuck that up.

He didn't know why he pushed Cross last night by taking him over the desk and pretending he was going to fuck him raw and unwrapped. In the end, he wouldn't have. But he felt a strange need to see how much Cross wanted him.

How much Cross would give him before he said no.

It had been stupid, and he regretted it but Cross let the whole thing drop.

Cross had mentioned doing it in the future.

The future.

Why was the man so determined for this to continue?

It was reckless.

Nash rubbed a hand over his eyes. He knew why Cross kept pushing.

Nash was feeling the same way. He was just doing his best to ignore it.

It was hard to do so when he watched himself in the mirror while fucking Cross over the desk. Even though the cop could easily escape, he remained bound only because Nash wanted him to.

He did it for Nash.

Watching them fuck in the mirror had been difficult in more ways than one.

While he had no doubt he was bisexual and liked to fuck men, he'd never watched himself actually doing it. Like in that mirror.

That moment hit him hard. Watching made it real.

Everything had become way too real.

And it wasn't just because he was fucking a man. It was because he was fucking Cross.

And it wasn't because Cross was a cop. It was because they had some crazy fucking connection Nash couldn't figure out. He couldn't wrap his head around it.

After he had come, he stared at himself in that mirror a long time with Cross still bent over the desk.

He didn't hide his expression because Cross wasn't looking. But Nash saw it.

Fear. His eyes, his face held fear. He was scared.

So fucking scared.

Nash had untied the sweatshirt from around Cross's hands and helped him rise while they were still connected. Not only intimately, but skin to skin.

But he saw it then. That fear engulfed both of them.

Nash's came from Cross wanting it to continue between them.

Cross's came from Nash wanting it to end.

But, fuck him, he didn't want it to end.

At the beginning, he thought he could fuck Cross and walk away like he'd done so many times before in his life.

But this one, the one in bed with him, was making it difficult for him to leave Cross in the dust.

For them to go their separate ways.

To never see each other again.

Nash rubbed his hand over his chest at the swelling ache.

He twisted his head to look at Cross who was sleeping on his back, one bent arm thrown over his head, the sheets barely covering him.

He noticed two important things. Two things that clashed. The Blue Avengers' colors tattooed on Cross's arm. And the necklace Nash had given him. The only time the man had taken it off since Nash gave it to him the other night was when he was in the shower.

Even now, Cross had the pendant within his curled fingers. He touched it a lot. He'd brush his fingers over it or hold it in his hand, but he'd stop as soon as Nash noticed.

Cross wanted too much from him.

He wanted everything. But they couldn't give each other everything.

It was impossible.

This room held a fantasy, not a reality.

They were headed back to reality soon.

Nash rolled into Cross, brushed his lips over his mouth and whispered, "Hey."

Blue eyes blinked open. "Hey."

"We gotta go soon. Or I do. You can stay. Room's covered 'til eleven."

Cross yawned and stretched both arms over his head, his back arching away from the mattress. "But I got this." He grabbed his morning wood over the tented sheet.

He wasn't the only one sporting a hard-on. "Yeah. Me,

too. But I gotta hit the road soon. It's a long ride north and gotta be at church in time."

"Sounds like a wedding," Cross teased.

"Thank fuck it's not. Been too many weddings in our club the last few years. Everyone's been gettin' tied down and knocked up."

"Except you."

Except him. "Me and some other hold-outs."

"The club's in your blood."

"Yeah."

"You'd never give it up."

"Fuck no."

Nash stared down at him. What was he getting at?

"Even if your music career took off."

"No."

"Not if you met the right person."

"Not even then." Nash looked him right in the eyes and asked, "Would you give your career up for the right person?"

"No."

Nash nodded and rolled onto his back. It was Cross's turn to roll into him, his face blocking Nash's view of the ceiling.

"I'd never ask you to give up your music career or your brotherhood, Nash. Just like I wouldn't expect someone to ask me to give up who I am, which is a cop. Whether you like it or not, that's who I am."

"Whether you fuckin' like it or not, being DAMC is who I am."

"I respect that."

"Do you?"

"Yes. But I'm sure I respect that more than you respect me being a cop."

"You wanted somethin', you went after it, you achieved it. Gotta respect that."

"Just not what that something is."
"You blame me?"
"No. We're not all bad."
"You're not all good," Nash reminded him.
In turn, Cross reminded him, "Neither are MC's."
"Yeah."
"Axel Jamison has ties to your club. His wife. His family. How do they treat him?"
"Depends who it is. But that's not our only problem, Cross, you fuckin' know it. And, I explained this shit before, Axel's granddaddy was one of the DAMC's founders. His wife is DAMC born and bred. His brother is prez. That holds a lot of fuckin' weight."
"He gets a pass for that."
"A reluctant one, but yeah, he does. I got no blood ties to the club and neither do you. You're also fuckin' gay. A gay cop. Couldn't pick a worse choice if I tried."
"When I first saw you at The Cockpit, I thought you were a free spirit. That you lived your life the way you wanted to, didn't give a fuck about anything. I was envious but now I know I was wrong. My instincts were totally off. You're not free. You are chained like the rest of us."
You are chained like the rest of us.
That was too fucking true. His freedom only went so far then that chain jerked him back.
That was because, blood or not, born into it or not, that fucking club was everything to him. When he had nothing, they took him in and gave him anything he needed.
But that *anything* also had limitations. And he was staring right up into the blue eyes of a big one.
"If we head out now, do we have time to stop somewhere for breakfast?"
Cross was good at that, changing subjects. Keeping Nash on his toes. Dropping conversations when they became too heavy.

Like now.

But he also had a way of circling back around and getting the answers he wanted if he waited long enough.

"Yeah, we roll soon, we can stop."

Cross smiled, dropped a quick kiss on Nash's lips, rolled away and out of bed.

Though, watching the man's bare ass as he bent over to pick up his clothes made Nash want to drag him back into bed and say fuck it to breakfast.

He reached down and gently squeezed his aching balls before reluctantly getting out of bed.

"We hit Shadow Valley's town limits, we gotta go our separate ways. Got me?"

Without pausing as he pulled on his clothes, Cross said, "I hear you. It's a good idea."

Yeah, it was a good idea.

But it still sucked.

———

THEY ALMOST MADE IT.

They were at the intersection where Nash planned on taking a left when Cross made a right.

At the stop sign, Nash cursed as he planted his boots onto the pavement and Cross rolled his sled up next to him.

Cross lifted his visor. "Okay, I'm going to—"

Cross stopped talking when he noticed what Nash was staring at. Not what, who. Nash was sure he had a pained expression on his face, which he quickly wiped away as the two bikes approached from the right.

"You lose your fuckin' cut?" Dawg yelled at him over the loud exhaust coming from the straight pipes as he came to a stop.

Nash jerked up his chin at him, then at Crow. "In my bag."

"Why the fuck ain't you wearin' it?" Dawg asked with a growl.

"Wasn't tryin' to catch the pigs' attention or the Deadly Demons. Had to roll through their territory."

"Ain't in their territory now," Crow mentioned the obvious, his face neutral but his almost black eyes observant.

No, they fucking weren't.

"Pull into that lot and put it on," Dawg ordered. "Fuckin' any of the executive committee sees you, you're gonna have some explainin' to do."

Fuck.

Crow and Dawg rode into the lot. Nash watched them go, then his gaze slid to Cross.

"We busted?"

Nash shook his head. "I'll make some shit up. Just get the fuck outta here."

"I'll call you."

Nash didn't answer but watched Cross slap his face shield back down and take off, going in the direction Dawg and Crow came from.

He put his sled in gear and rolled into the lot, kicked the stand down, and shut off his bike.

Crow and Dawg were both sitting on their now quiet sleds. Just staring at him.

Did they fucking know? Was it obvious he'd had sex with Cross all weekend?

Was it tattooed onto his forehead?

Nash yanked his goggles off his face and hung them on the handlebar before moving to his saddlebag.

"Who was that?" Dawg asked.

"Buddy I met at a gig."

"He's got a badass sled. He wanna prospect?" Crow asked.

Nash pressed his lips together as he dug into his side bag and pulled out his cut. He shrugged it over his two layers of thermals, then finally turned to face them. "Doubt it."

"Local?"

"Not sure. Didn't ask him where he lived. We weren't goin' on a date or nothin'."

Dawg barked out a laugh and hit his Harley's ignition button, letting it roar to life. "Sure 'bout that? Thought you, Crash an' Rig did circle jerks on the regular. C'mon, we gotta get to church."

Dawg took off and Nash mounted his sled, waiting for Crow to take off, too. He didn't.

He just sat there, so Nash, wanting to break the uncomfortable silence, asked, "Where's Jazz?"

"Meetin' us there. She might stay at church an' watch the kids so some of the ol' ladies can go on the run." He still sat there, staring. The longer he did, the more it made the hair on the back of Nash's neck stand up. "Guy looked familiar."

Nash's heart began to race.

"Even wearing a brain bucket, wasn't hard to remember him. Wanna know why?"

"You saw him talkin' to Axel at the last pig roast?"

Crow's eyebrows rose in surprise. "No."

Fuck.

Crow planted his hands on his thighs and gave Nash a hard look. "'Cause a lot of people show up at my shop. They want the best ink slinger in the area."

Which was Crow hands down.

"Don't matter to me what or who they are. It's scratch in my pocket an' also the club's. 'Cause of that, I rarely turn away work. But there's a breed of customers who come through my door I don't forget. Especially when they get certain ink. So, when a cop walks in an' wants a biker to give 'im a tattoo, I take notice," Crow tapped his temple, "an' I don't fuckin' forget."

Now, not only was Nash's heart thumping, he had a lump restricting his throat. "You think he's a cop?"

Crow's dark eyes narrowed on him. "Think I'm fuckin' stupid?"

"No."

"Weren't wearin' your colors, not because you were afraid of catchin' any pigs' attention but because you were with one. That right?"

"I met him at the gig."

"Your gig was a coupla nights ago. Jazz says—"

"Fuck," Nash groaned, grinding the bandana he had wrapped around his head into his forehead. "Fuck."

Crow ignored his outburst and continued, "Jazz says there's somethin' restless 'bout you. She sees it. Now I'm seein' it. You wanna give up your colors? That why you're hidin' your cut an' hangin' out with a pig?"

"No. Fuck no. Ain't givin' up anything, Crow. You've got this all fuckin' wrong."

"Make me get it right."

Nash glanced over his shoulder in the direction Dawg went, which was toward church. "We gotta go."

"Ain't goin' nowhere 'til you tell me what the fuck's goin' on."

He turned to look at Crow, whose dark eyes were intently focused on him.

"Why the fuck are you hangin' out with 5-0? Do I need to give Z a head's up?"

"No. It's nothin'. Met him and we hit it off, that's all."

Crow tilted his head, his long black braid falling to the side. The man's hair was almost to his waist. "Thinkin' it's more than that."

"What are you fuckin' sayin'?"

"Just what I said. Hawk told us what that former piece of shit prospect spouted. Had to give us a reason why the fucker got his colors yanked. Was it true? Did you have a pig upstairs at church?"

Crow didn't ask if he had a "man" upstairs, but a "pig."

"You're more worried about me havin' a cop in my room than a man?"

"More worried about havin' a fox in the hen house. Don't give a shit who you're fuckin' as long as he ain't a cop."

"And if he is?"

"Know he is. Just told you I put that tattoo on his right arm. Think I don't know what that MC stands for? Think I don't know Axel an' Mitch wear the same colors?" Crow shook his head. "Jesus fuck, Nash. That's some sticky fuckin' shit."

"It's nothin'."

"Not sure who you're lyin' to. Me or yourself."

In truth? Both.

"Brother, don't care if you like bonin' men. If that's your thing, it's your fuckin' thing. You've been part of this club for a long fuckin' time. Almost as long as me. You're family. Ain't throwin' out family because he likes," Crow shook his head, "what he likes. Don't get it, but it's not for me to get. But that's the least of your problems when it comes to bonin' that one." He jerked his thumb in the direction Cross went. "Bet there ain't a day where D doesn't think about curlin' his fingers around Axel's throat an' snuffin' out his life. He's forced to tolerate him an' that chaps his fuckin' ass. He won't be forced to tolerate some outsider. Not for you. Not for anyone. You got me?"

"Yeah."

"Best this truly be nothin' like you said."

Nash nodded, his gut churning. "It's nothin'. A mistake that won't happen again."

Crow gave him a nod. "We gotta go." He kicked his sled

to life, then asked, "Is Dawg right? You do circle jerks with Crash an' Rig?"

Nash shook his head, grinning. "No. They'd get a fuckin' complex if they compared their dicks to mine."

Crow burst out laughing and hit his throttle, pulling out of the lot.

Shortly after, Nash did the same. Only he wasn't laughing.

Chapter Seventeen

THEY SAT around the long table, the one with their insignia carved into the center. The symbol that represented them all.

As president, Zak sat at the head, Hawk, the VP, to his right, Diesel, as Sergeant at Arms, to his left. Then Ace, Dex and Jag filled the rest of the seats. Nash stood at the other end of the table nearest the door, facing the executive committee.

Nash's eyes locked with Dex, trying to get a read on him. Turned out the brother was a kinky fucker who liked his woman to dominate him during sex. He might be his only ally in the room. However, Dex's face gave him nothing.

He wasn't told why he'd been called into the executive meeting. But he had a good idea why. Like Crow, the rest of his brothers weren't stupid.

Nash's skin prickled as he imagined having a knife filet the colors off his back.

"Need you to move outta church," Z started.

Fuck. Were they turning their backs on him? Not only removing him from church but from the club?

"Got a perfectly good fuckin' house sittin' in the

compound empty." Zak rapped his knuckles on the table. "Got new prospects bein' patched in, movin' upstairs. Need the space."

Bullshit.

Most of the patched members kept a room upstairs only for a place to crash, but for the most part, they all went home after runs, parties or whatever. Nash was the only one who had a house in the compound and never went there. Home to him was still upstairs.

Nash studied his prez's face. "There are plenty of empty rooms up there. None of you use your rooms anymore. I use mine."

"You arguin' with your prez?" Diesel barked, planting his knuckles on the table and leaning forward.

"No."

"Sure as fuck sounded like it."

Nash ignored Diesel, even though he was difficult to ignore. He kept his gaze locked with Z's. "What's this really about?"

If it was what he thought it was, he might need to get it out in the open and get it over with.

"Time for you to move outta church," Hawk repeated. "That issue we had with the prospect is tellin' us you need more privacy than you're gettin' here."

Nash shook his head. "This all's comin' from that prospect's bullshit?"

"Was it bullshit?" Zak asked with a cocked eyebrow. "You sayin' he lied?"

He wasn't sure how he could face these men, these bikers, his brothers, and tell them the prospect didn't lie, but what was between Cross and him was only sex. Would that confession—hell, that true lie—make them consider him less than a man?

To confess he was bi... Would they look at him differently? Treat him differently? Or worse, strip him of his colors?

He could say the prospect lied since the asshole was long gone, if he wasn't the only one who "knew." Axel saw Cross at church that night and even talked to him. Nash figured Hawk had a suspicion. He wasn't sure what Linc thought. Then there were Grizz's unexpected words of wisdom.

Not only that, Crow knew something was up. Dawg might have guessed, too.

This was all because Nash met a fucking cop in a gay bar outside of Pittsburgh. All because he couldn't resist that fucking cop.

What he worked hard to keep buried from his brothers was rising to the surface.

But he could trust everyone in that room, couldn't he? And even the rest of his brothers who weren't there?

Revealing the truth still scared the fuck out of him.

Around the table, all eyes were on him, waiting. A technique Cross had used on him too many times.

"He wasn't lyin'."

Nash didn't miss when Jag and Dex exchange looks and so did their VP and president.

He also didn't miss Ace staring across the table at his son, Diesel, with concern. That was because Diesel's thick fingers had clenched into fists on the table top and his face became...

Scary as fuck.

"Was it that fuckin' pig I caught talkin' to Axel?"

Nash opened his mouth, but nothing but air escaped.

"You bring that fuckin' pig inside our church an' upstairs?"

He didn't, no. Cross had snuck up there all on his fucking own. But he wasn't going to split hairs on that with the big man. Nash also didn't kick him the fuck out. In the end, it was Nash's responsibility to do that.

"Swore I saw you gettin' head from Mini that night," Jag said softly, staring at the carved insignia at the center of the table.

"Yeah," was all Nash would say to that.

"Are you guys just buddies or somethin'?" Jag lifted his gaze to Nash's.

Out of all of them, even Diesel, Jag might be the hardest to confess to. Jag might think back to when he first brought Nash to Shadow Valley and remember how Nash was with him.

Completely, totally fucking infatuated.

Wishing Jag swung both ways, too. He didn't and once Nash recognized that fact, he let it go. But it took a while.

However, he never told Jag. And Jag never guessed.

Now he might.

Even so, he told Jag the truth. If anyone deserved it, it was the man who helped him find a home and family. "No."

A look of surprise crossed Jag's face before he could hide it.

Nash let his gaze slide around the table, to judge their reactions.

"A switch-hitter, huh, son?" Ace asked, scratching his bearded chin. "This somethin' new?"

Yeah, because he got fucking bored one day with pussy and decided to try dick instead.

But he couldn't say that, and Ace also didn't deserve that kind of attitude. They were just trying to get to the bottom of what the hell was going on. He didn't blame them. If he'd been sitting around that table, he'd want to know the same thing.

"Not new. Always been like that."

"Always?" Jag asked.

Nash met his eyes and nodded. "Always."

Jag ran a hand over his hair. "Huh."

He needed to get all of this the fuck over with. He felt

like a death-row inmate walking to the electric chair. He turned his attention back to Zak. "So? Now what? You wanted me to move outta church an' into my house. But now you know that..." He hesitated, then finished with, "That. You gonna strip my colors?"

"We figured that part out when the problem with the prospect came about," Zak told him. "Don't got a problem with you takin' dick. Got a problem with you takin' dick attached to a badge."

Maybe Zak didn't have a problem with him being bi, but he wondered about the rest of them. Not that he was going to ask. No fucking way. He didn't want to extend this conversation in any way, shape or fucking form.

"This is why you need to move outta church, Nash. Think it's best, this way you'll have more privacy to do... whatever with whoever. But—"

Diesel leaned forward, interrupting Z. "No pig's gonna be sneakin' into the compound for dick. No pig's gonna be livin' in the compound 'cause he likes *your* fuckin' dick. Long as he's a badge-wearin' pig, he ain't fuckin' welcome. You need dick, find it elsewhere."

The king had spoken. All hail the fucking king.

"Can't be sleepin' with the enemy, Nash," Ace said, backing Diesel up.

"Can't be fuckin' a pig with either a dick or a pussy an' be loyal to the rest of us. Can't be loyal to the colors on your back or any of your brothers," Diesel added with a shake of his head. "Must be outta your fuckin' mind."

Z steepled his fingers in front of his face and stared at the table. Then he rapped his knuckles again on the surface. "Not likin' any of this. Not likin' the choice you've made. Not likin' the choices you're gonna hafta make. Not likin' any of this shit." His eyes circled the table. "Don't like forcin' his hand but also don't like 'im forcin' ours," he said to the members at the table, then sat back in his chair and addressed Nash. "Spent ten fuckin' years in the joint. Ain't ever gonna do that again. Tryin' to keep the club right-side up. No guarantee it won't tip, some days more than others. Don't need 5-0 breathin' down our fuckin' necks. Got a good hold on Axel now. For fuck's sake, even Mitch has been bitin' his tongue an' wearin' blinders. But this guy's a wild card." Zak lifted his gaze and hit Nash's. "You might like takin' dick up the ass, but I don't. Got kids to protect. We all do. Not one of us sittin' at this table wants to be taken from our ol' ladies, our kids, our future. An' it's up to us, sittin' at this table to protect that."

"So, what I'm hearin' pretty fuckin' clearly is, you don't mind I swing both ways. You only mind who it's with."

"Thought that was made pretty fuckin' clear," Z murmured, his brows raised.

"Axel—"

"Is a fuckin' cross we gotta bear. Axel's at the point now where he's got a good life, good wife, an' Z's woman steppin' up to bear his an' Bella's children." Hawk looked at Zak. "So, he's willin' to keep his fuckin' mouth shut to keep all that."

Diesel butted in again. "Your boy's got no ties to this club, got no DAMC blood runnin' through 'im. The only thing DAMC in 'im is your fuckin' dick. Got me?"

Jag said next, "Got a good life, Nash. Got it easy. A life of playin' music an' no other responsibilities. Where else you gonna get that shit? Where else you gonna get the freedom to do the things you love without worryin' 'bout scratch?"

Nowhere. He got to live the life he wanted to live. For the most part.

"Need to choose a path, brother," Dex spoke up. "You like what you fuckin' like an' we don't plan on stoppin' that, but gotta—"

"Find another dick to ride," Diesel finished for Dex. He pointed a finger at Nash. "But tellin' you now, when you do, he ain't gonna be on the back of your sled durin' rides. He ain't gonna be hangin' out here at church. You move out, move into the compound. We won't care who comes an' goes. Here, yes. There, no. Just long as that dick ain't a pig."

"Don't care what the fuck you do behind closed doors, Nash. Dex's proof of that with his nip rings an' his whip-wieldin' woman." Hawk snorted and Dex sighed loudly. "But out in the open, yeah, we care. Gotta rep to maintain. We might not see you fuckin' another guy as a weakness, but other clubs might. Don't need to open us up for any territory challenges. Got too many ol' ladies an' kids to protect now to get into another fuckin' war."

That's the last thing Nash wanted, to be the cause of a war between the DAMC and another club. After decades, the one between them and the Shadow Warriors was finally over. Not that anyone had let their guard down. Especially Diesel, since he was the Sergeant at Arms and the club's enforcer.

Nash didn't need to be the reason to call attention to their club. Too many people would be at risk.

They were saying if he moved out of church, they were fine with anyone he brought home, as long as it wasn't Cross.

Or maybe he could remain above church if he didn't bring men into his room at all. Which he never had before, anyway.

"If only females are in my room, I can stay here?"

He didn't think anyone expected that request. In fact, it took a bit for anyone to respond.

"Got a fuckin' great house in the compound," Z reminded him.

"It's too much for one person."

"You're gonna give up dick just to remain in that dump upstairs?" Z asked, not hiding his surprise.

He didn't say that. He just wouldn't bring men "home."

He'd continue with how it had always been. If he got that itch, he'd go scratch it elsewhere.

"I get to stay upstairs, you won't ever see me again with another man."

He would have to stick with random fucks. Not men who would track him down where he lived.

No names exchanged. No phone numbers. Nothing.

Totally fucking anonymous.

"Let us discuss it, have a vote. We'll let you know," Zak finally said with a frown.

Nash continued to stand there until Diesel slammed his fist on the table and barked, "Get gone."

He got gone.

———

Nash sat on the edge of his bed at church. Even though he was fucking exhausted from the local gig he had earlier tonight, he couldn't sleep. He scrolled through the phone log on his cell and began to count.

Twelve.

Twelve missed calls. Twelve voicemails.

An average of two a day for the past week. That didn't include the texts.

With a sigh, he deleted his voicemails without listening to them, then the call log before going to his text app and counting again.

Twenty-six.

Twenty-six fucking texts.

Before he could think about it too hard, he deleted those, too, without reading them.

However, what he did notice was the calls, the texts, they all stopped two days ago. Just stopped.

Nash didn't think Cross would give up. But maybe he finally did.

Maybe the cop finally got a fucking clue.

Nash went to his photo gallery on his phone next. He pulled up the only photo he took that weekend. One Cross didn't know he had taken. One of the cop sleeping, sprawled out on his stomach on the bed in the motel in Virginia.

The top sheet had fallen to the floor and Cross was totally naked. Nash zoomed in on the picture and stared at the man's perfect ass, his thighs, his back.

The tattoo on his arm caught his attention.

Fuck.

Fuck.

Fuck.

He closed his eyes and remembered the exact moment he took that photo. It had been Saturday night between rounds of sex.

Cross's words whispered through his head. *Give and take.*

They had given. They had taken. Now nothing was left to give.

His finger hovered over the little trash can icon in the top corner of the photo. He set his jaw and hit it. And before he could think twice, he went to his contacts list, scrolled down to the C's, found Cross's name and deleted that, too.

A sharp pain not only shot through his chest but his temples.

Nash thought about the phone call he'd made to Cross two weeks ago, the day the committee voted on whether Nash could remain in his room at church.

Jag had come to him afterward and said they had reluctantly voted he could. So here he was, sitting on his bed, thinking about that painful conversation with Cross.

"We had a good weekend. That's all it was."

"You're fucking fooling yourself, Nash."

"No, Cross, you are. You're foolin' yourself if you ever

believed this would work. It won't. Sex was one thing, the rest…"

"I can get sex anywhere. I want the rest."

Nash had blown out a breath, buckled down and said, "Can't give it to you. Been clear about it from the beginnin'. Not sure why your head's so fucked you think we can make this work. We can't."

Before Cross could say anymore, Nash had hung up. He turned off his phone, then crawled back into bed and slept for over twelve hours, hoping when he woke up the ache would be gone.

It wasn't.

Over two weeks later, it still wasn't. So, he needed to purge Cross from his life and forget him, forget everything that happened. He needed to concentrate on his music, his band and their tour, his club and family.

That was enough.

He didn't need anything more than that.

He could live without having a steady man in his life. Plenty of pussy was always available and he could occasionally continue with his random hookups with men. Just on the DL.

That was fine.

It had worked in the past. It would work in the future.

That was enough.

He didn't need anything more than that.

Maybe he should call the band's manager and schedule a tour on the west coast. Hit Los Angeles, maybe San Diego.

Yeah, that's what he would do. Get far away. This way he wouldn't be tempted to show up at Cross's door late at night after a gig. Like he had been tonight. When the urge was the strongest. Not for sex. Fuck no.

But to be around Cross. To talk to him, to touch him. To inhale his now familiar scent.

To see his pendant hanging around the man's neck. Like he'd been claimed.

Because, fuck him, Nash didn't realize when he did it, but that night at the brewery, when he put his necklace over Cross's head, that was what he'd been doing.

Claiming Cross.

Now he had to let him go.

Nash belonged to the Dirty Angels MC, he belonged to Dirty Deeds. He did not belong to Aiden Cross, officer with the Southern Allegheny Regional Police Department.

No, he fucking didn't.

They spent some time together, got it out of their systems.

So, now they were done.

For fuck's sake...

If only that was true.

Chapter Eighteen

CROSS GRABBED his helmet out of the closet. Being late March, he was ready to hit the road with the only girl in his life, hear the purr of her exhaust pipes, feel her power between his legs.

He was already wearing his Blue Avengers cut over a thick SARPD sweatshirt with a long-sleeved tee underneath. A T-shirt he'd bought online on the Dirty Deeds' website.

Sometimes he wore it, along with Nash's pendant, when he wanted to feel closer to the man who walked out of his life and never looked back.

Even four months after the last time they talked on the phone, Cross still couldn't let go.

He was a fucking fool.

He knew it. And being a fool, he also accepted it.

He had hit The Cockpit several times during those months, as well as a few other gay bars, but he'd walked back out each and every one of them alone.

And when he was feeling really foolish, he'd try calling Nash again.

The man never answered.

He'd followed the band's path online for a few weeks.

But once he saw they'd gone out to the west coast for a couple of months, he stopped.

There was no need to keep torturing himself any worse than he already was.

For example, by wearing that fucking pendant. And that damn T-shirt.

And staring at the photos on his phone he took of Nash when the man wasn't looking, during the gig at the brewery and also during those days at the motel.

He kept hoping one day he'd just wake up and be over Nash.

It wasn't this morning. And it probably wouldn't be tomorrow morning, either.

But he kept hoping it would be soon.

Please, let it be fucking soon.

After locking up, he jogged down the interior steps and into his two-car garage, which made up the lower level of his townhouse.

His girl was waiting for him there. Tuned up, prepped and freshly washed. Cross was itching to feel the wind against them as they traveled the roads north of Pittsburgh with his brothers.

At least, he had them.

Not that any of them warmed his fucking bed at night.

About an hour later, he rolled into the parking lot of the restaurant and parked behind it in the long line of bikes. Every month they hit up a different one for their monthly "chapel" meeting. Their law enforcement MC was huge, and their regional chapter covered everything in Pennsylvania west of the Susquehanna River. So, they moved the meetings around that side of the state to make it fair for everyone.

This time chapel was north of Pittsburgh in New Castle. He couldn't wait to get a few cups of coffee in him, not only because he needed the caffeine but to warm up his blue balls and frozen fingers.

Fuck, he should've worn a third layer of clothes.

Even so, he was ready to hit the road for the Blue Avenger's first monthly run of the year. Or he would be once everyone was done stuffing their face and socializing for a bit. Today Cross wasn't sure how much patience he'd have to wait around.

It had been an endless, lonely fucking winter. A long, chilly ride should clear his head.

Two hours later, Cross was gritting his teeth because they were still there. BAMC president and Shadow Valley PD sergeant, Mitch Jamison, stood at the front of the banquet room conducting club business along with the rest of the club officers. One being Corporal Axel Jamison, the club's vice president.

Cross had a few words with Axel prior to the start of the official meeting. But the man didn't mention Nash at all.

No surprise. But even so, Cross had hoped he would.

Finally, after they adjourned, everyone pushed to their feet, the large room rang with raised voices, chairs squealing and good-natured ribbing as they funneled out toward the front of the family restaurant.

Mitch and Axel were walking shoulder to shoulder ahead of Cross and he noticed their body language change as they passed a booth along the front windows of the restaurant. Mitch's pace quickened while Axel's slowed down, then he glanced over his shoulder back at Cross.

Cross frowned as Axel raised his eyebrows at him, then turned and continued toward the exit.

As Cross filed with the rest of his brothers through the narrow aisle between tables and booths, he spotted what Mitch had ignored, and now understood Axel's silent warning.

It wasn't a "what," but a "who."

And that "who" had his back to the exit and faced in Cross's direction.

Even with his back to the booth's padded seat, his cut was clearly recognizable. As was his hair, face and everything else about him.

Cross's chest compressed, and he abruptly stopped two booths away, causing one of his brothers to slam into the back of him.

"Hey!"

Cross could barely squeeze out a "sorry."

With a coffee mug paused halfway to his lips, Nash spotted Cross.

Their eyes met. Held.

And, at first, neither of them noticed when one of the older BAMC members, a retired sheriff's deputy, stopped right at Nash's table.

Nash's gaze broke from Cross and slowly lifted and as it did, the sheriff spit a hocker right into Nash's raised mug, muttering the words "biker trash." The two other guys at the table, sitting opposite of Nash—who Cross recognized as two Dirty Deeds band members—jumped to their feet, yelling at the man.

Nash only set his coffee mug down and stared at Cross, ignoring the ruckus when two other Blue Avengers grabbed the retired deputy and pushed him away from the table, while two more instructed Nash's bandmates to "sit the fuck down and shut the fuck up."

While the rest of his brothers pushed past him, knocking into him as they did so, Cross remained frozen in place.

They both ignored the waitress rushing over to Nash with a fresh mug of coffee and taking the other one away, while apologizing.

She had no reason to apologize, it wasn't her being a dick.

No, once again this was one of his brothers in blue

treating Nash like trash when he'd done nothing to warrant it.

Cross could see the other two guys at his table talking animatedly, but Nash sat there quietly, just looking at Cross.

"You coming?" another BAMC member asked as he stepped around Cross.

"Yeah," he answered, then shook himself mentally and moved forward. His feet felt like they were encased in concrete and he forced himself to move past the table without stopping. Nash's eyes followed him until Cross could no longer see him.

He stopped at the front door to the restaurant, his hand on the push bar, but he was having difficulty engaging it. His mind was screaming at him to go back, to talk to Nash. Something he'd wanted to do for the last four months.

But his common sense was telling him to walk out the door, not only for self-preservation, but to avoid creating any more problems for Nash.

If he went back to talk to Nash, questions would be raised.

Now was not the time.

He pushed outside and the late morning sun hit his face. He took a long breath, sucking in the still crisp air, filling his lungs, trying to clear his head.

But then he saw it.

Nash's Harley.

Parked next to a full-sized cargo van with the band name painted on the side. And that bike was on its side on the macadam.

Some asshole had tipped it over. Whether the mirrors snapped off when it fell or someone kicked them off, they were broken. And he was sure there were scratches and dents in the custom gas tank and chrome exhaust.

He glanced around the lot and noticed none of his brothers were around. They'd all headed around to the rear of the restaurant where their line of bikes waited. And instead of following, he walked over to the downed bike, picked it up, set the kickstand and placed the broken mirrors carefully on the seat.

It wasn't much, but it was something.

Four months of silence.

Today was a good reminder of why.

Cross closed his eyes and ground his teeth.

Reality and fantasy were two different things.

The fantasy being he and Nash could be together. That they could make it work.

The reality being their situation was hopeless. That it would never work.

Cross would never give up being a cop.

Nash would never give up being a biker.

He opened his eyes and with a last look at Nash's damaged bike, turned on his heels and went to get his own and get in formation with the rest of his MC.

NASH WAITED.

It was getting dark. He was half-frozen from the late March night air.

Not to mention, pissed.

For several reasons...

One, Cross not standing up for him. He knew it was unreasonable to be pissed about that, since it would be stupid for Cross to defend him in front of other law enforcement, but still...

Two, his sled was fucked up. It didn't fall over on its own. Someone kicked it over and broke off the mirrors on purpose. Now, he'd be without a sled while Jag or Crash fixed it.

And three, Cross was the last person he expected to run

into on his way back from a gig in Cleveland. It had shocked the shit out of him. He had no idea why they kept crossing paths, but it was like fate kept fucking with them.

He'd been waiting there for an hour, his ass numb from sitting on the concrete steps to Cross's townhouse. The cold had settled into his bones and chilled his blood.

For fuck's sake, he needed to leave.

But he couldn't.

Seeing Cross earlier had just about killed him.

When he had, he'd lost all sense of what had been happening around him. Dangerously so. All because he was focused on the man who stood frozen in shock at seeing him.

Nash had been just as surprised.

He didn't realize how fucking much he missed Cross, how fucking empty his life was without him, until the very second their eyes met and locked.

He fought the urge to leap out of his seat and go talk to him. Hell, touch him. But he was glad he didn't. Something worse than his coffee being spat into, or his sled being kicked over and the mirrors being broken off, might have happened.

Cross's "brothers" might have taken Nash approaching the man as a "threat."

But really, Cross was the threat.

To Nash's whole motherfucking psyche.

He thought he was good. That he'd moved on. That heading out to California had purged his need to be with Cross.

That the nameless, faceless female groupies who sucked and fucked him after gigs had pushed Cross mostly from his mind. And what remained afterward, he did his best to fog out with pot.

But no. None of that shit had apparently worked.

Which was why he was now sitting there with his balls pulled up into his body retreating from the cold.

However, he had no idea where Cross was, what time he'd be back or even if he would return. Nash could be sitting there like a motherfucking fool for nothing.

He needed to go before Cross *did* come back and find him there like the stupid fuck he was.

Getting his fix of Cross wouldn't help anything. It would just make it all worse.

Stir up the shit he'd been fighting for months.

The regret.

The constant wishing things could be different.

They couldn't.

Not without one of them making a major life change.

Neither had been willing to do that. And neither should. What either of them would have to walk away from was more than anyone should ask for.

Career. Family. Brotherhoods.

Loyalty.

Nash couldn't give up many for one.

Cross had a path he was traveling. A good one. Nash wasn't worth causing him to step off that path. Especially now the man had been promoted to corporal like Cross hoped.

Nash had seen it on the "department news" tab of the Southern Allegheny Regional PD's website. Cross's picture was up there, in a uniform with a new stripe on his arm, shaking hands with his chief.

He had a smile on his face. But it looked hollow. Empty.

Which it shouldn't be. Cross got what he wanted, what he worked for. He was climbing his way up the ladder.

He was a good man. A good cop. Nash would never ask him to give that up.

He might as well ask the man to give up his right nut instead.

Cross's asshole father was a pig near Harrisburg and

Nash hoped the man choked on his own spit when he heard the news about his son.

The son he was proud of until he found out Cross was gay.

Being gay didn't make Cross any less of a person, any less of a man.

Any less of a cop.

Just like being bi didn't make Nash any less worthy, either.

Whether in his father's eyes or his club's.

Jazz's words came back to him. *"I found my happy, Nash... You need to find yours, too."*

He stiffly rose to his feet as he heard the low rumble of Cross's Sport Glide and the beam of the headlight swept over him.

The garage door rattled as it rose, and Cross pulled his sled inside. Then it went quiet.

Nash didn't move from the steps next to the garage. He remained there. And he waited.

Cross was good at waiting.

Nash was getting just as good.

He learned if you waited long enough, you might get what you wanted.

Might.

But not always.

Sometimes you had to grab life by the balls and just take what you wanted.

Today was that day.

Or so he hoped.

Finally, he moved slowly down the steps and around the corner into the garage, where Cross was waiting for him.

He looked good. The man had stolen Nash's breath when he saw him at the restaurant earlier and he managed to do it again. The leather cut he wore emphasized his broad shoulders, his Levi's his narrow hips. And Nash already knew how they fit on that ass of his.

Pure fucking perfection.

"I'd ask what you're doing here, but that would be stupid." Cross's voice was hoarse, holding a whole bunch of hurt.

He wasn't the only one fucking hurting.

Nash was tired of that feeling, but he just had no clue how to make it stop.

Being with Cross could cause a whole lot of fucking pain.

Being without him already did, too.

Hopeless.

It was all motherfucking hopeless and he wished like fuck, he'd never walked into The Cockpit that night. It would have made life so much easier.

But he did.

And now they were here.

Connected but disconnected.

Drawn to each other, but separate.

Two halves that might never be a whole because the pieces didn't fit perfectly. They were jagged and rough when they needed to be smooth.

"You just going to stand there?" Cross asked softly.

"Not sure why I'm here."

"That's a lie."

And that was fucking too true. "It would be best if I just fuckin' go."

"That's another lie."

"Actually, that one's more true than we wanna fuckin' admit."

Cross sighed, dropped his head and raked a hand down his beard. "Sorry about today."

A muscle in Nash's jaw popped. "'Sorry about today. Sorry about that time you were tased and tied to a bench like a mongrel.' Didn't see you steppin' in and doin' anything about it either time."

"I'm a total fucking asshole," Cross said, lifting his head. "I have no fucking excuse."

Nash hated to be that harsh on him, but anger helped drown some of the pain. He sighed, disappointed in himself, with his words, with the whole situation. "Yeah, you do. You got a life you're livin' I don't fit into."

"You've got a life you're living I don't fit into," Cross echoed.

"What're we gonna do about it?"

Cross blew out a breath. "I wish I fucking knew." He took a step closer to Nash and grabbed his wrist, pulling him closer. "One thing I do know is these past four months sucked. I feel like I'm living my life with a big chunk of it missing. I don't even care if that makes me sound like a pussy."

"Yeah," Nash whispered. It was the same for him. Easy women, pot, even his music hadn't filled that void. Only one person could. "Missed you, motherfucker." It hurt to admit that, but it needed to be said.

A grinning Cross yanked on his wrist and pulled him until they were toe to toe, eye to eye. "Missed you, too, motherfucker."

Nash beat back his grin. "Probably not smart to be standin' here with the garage door open, me wearin' my colors, you wearin' yours."

"Right now, I don't give a shit."

Nash didn't, either. "Later you might."

"How about a pact? When we're together, neither of us wear them."

If only it was that easy to hide who they were. "Still got a badge in your back pocket."

"And you still have your colors inked into your skin." He tilted his head and met Nash's eyes. "Again, I might sound like a pussy, but I don't give a shit... I think we're worth fighting for."

Fuck him, Nash did, too. "Not gonna be easy."

"We just have to be careful," Cross said.

"Meanin' we need to hide."

"Might be the only way."

Unfortunately, it *was* the only way, but... "You wanna hide from your people, your brothers, I don't give a shit. Not gonna ride on the back of your sled durin' one of those pig runs, anyway. Not gonna go to some pigs' fuckin' Christmas party. You're on your fuckin' own for that shit. But I want you in my bed. I wanna be in your bed. I want you waitin' for me when I come home from a tour. I wanna be there when you come home from a midnight shift. Problem is, don't wanna go behind my brothers' backs. That could cause a major fuckin' issue."

"So, you'll tell them?"

"No choice. It'll be worse if I don't and they find out. It could get ugly."

"We could get a place of our own."

"Yeah, we could get a place for when I'm in town. Neither of us wear our colors in or out of that place. Give up my room at church. Give up my house in the compound."

"House in the compound?"

It was something Nash never talked about with Cross, since it was just an empty house and not a home. "Yeah, got a house sittin' empty. A big one. In our club compound. Never felt as if it was home. It isn't. Now I know why."

Cross's eyebrows shot up. "You stayed in that fucked up room when you had a nice house?"

Nash's lips twitched. "Yeah. Just said it didn't feel like home, Cross. Need your ears cleaned the fuck out?"

Cross's lips twitched, too. "No, heard you loud and

clear." He jerked his head toward the door in the garage. "You coming up?"

"Yeah. We got a lot to figure out."

"Not sure we'll get it all figured out tonight."

"No, but that's not the only reason I'm here."

Cross grinned. "I didn't think so."

"Best we get inside, before I bend you over that wannabe's bike and scar your fuckin' neighbors for life."

"I'm not thinking you're getting the first shot."

"We'll see."

"Yes, we will." Cross got serious. "We have a lot to talk about."

Yeah, they did. Most of it wasn't going to be easy, either.

Cross continued, "I'm not talking about what went on in our lives for the last four months, either. I don't want to know since I can guess. I'm talking about our future."

Nash nodded. "Gotta know, no matter what happens with my club, I'll never give up my music. Also gotta know, I'll be gone for long periods of time. If you got a problem with that tell me now and I won't go up those steps with you."

"And you have to know I never plan on giving up my badge willingly. So, if you have a problem with that, I won't be inviting you up those steps."

"Also gotta be clear, club business is club business. You don't ask, I don't tell. You wanna talk about my band, my tour, I'm good with that. Anything DAMC, I'm not. You wanna talk about your day bashing heads and arrestin' people, I may listen, may not. Don't get bent if I don't."

Cross shook his head, the lines at the corners of his eyes crinkling. "I won't get bent if you don't want to listen about my day of community policing and writing jaywalking citations."

Nash huffed out a breath. "Then we're good."

"I sure as fuck hope so."

"Now... We got a lot of time to make up for. Not sure why we're still standin' here in your garage jawin'."

Cross walked over the interior door that led up into his townhouse and hit the automatic garage door opener. "You have me thinking about you taking me over my *wannabe's bike*."

"Could do that. Got a wrap?"

Cross nodded. "You?"

Nash nodded.

"What about lube?"

Nash raised his eyebrows, held his hand out and spat into his own palm.

"Oh fuck no," Cross said on a groan.

"Need a sense of adventure."

"I think our life from here on out will be one, but I'm putting my foot down on that, unless..."

Nash cocked a brow. "Unless?"

"Unless, you let me fuck you with a little bit of spit first."

"I can take it like a man."

Cross barked out a laugh. "Right. You don't even like when you're the bottom."

"I like it."

Cross's eyes widened. "Since when?"

"Since you."

"So from here on out, you always want to be the bottom?"

"Fuck no. Give and take, remember?"

Cross gave him a single nod. The hollow look in his eyes Nash had seen in that promotion picture was nowhere to be found. "Give and take," he whispered. "Never quit."

"What?"

"Never quit. Your tattoo. I never quit hoping," Cross admitted softly.

"Never quit what you love. Never give up on your

dreams. Get knocked down and pull yourself back up and try again."

"With your music?"

"With everything."

Cross released the tight grip on Nash's wrist and grabbed his face, pulling him into a kiss.

Nash parted his lips to let him inside. Let their tastes mingle. Let their breaths merge. Reconnect.

Fuck, it was like coming home.

That house in the compound would never be home. Not without Cross in it.

Cross was now home to him.

Even though it might not be right to the people that surrounded them, it was right for the two of them.

The hard truth was, they needed more than that. They couldn't hole up and just be with each other. That wasn't living life. That was completely hiding.

His brothers needed to accept Nash as he was. Accept, like them, that he found his partner.

Even if they disagreed with his choice.

But they needed to be solid first.

Right now, they weren't. They'd been apart for four long fucking months.

But that was ending there tonight. They'd start working on solid.

When Nash approached his brothers, he wanted no doubt at the back of his mind. He wanted to know there was no one but Cross for him.

When Cross released his face, they kept kissing, and Nash hooked an arm around his waist, pulling him even closer. Their cuts were crushed together, and he was surprised they didn't self-combust, or lightning didn't strike them.

Things couldn't be more wrong between them, but they also couldn't be more right.

No, he was wrong, they could be a lot more fucking right just by getting naked.

He loosened his arm around Cross and tipped his head back enough to break their kiss.

Cross's blue eyes were darker than normal, his eyes hooded, his breath rapid. His erection unmistakable.

Nash was sure he had a similar expression on his face. And he certainly had just as much of a raging hard-on.

They needed to get upstairs before he really did bend Cross over his sled and just use some spit.

"Think we need to go upstairs," Cross said.

"Would be better for you if we did," Nash answered, then pressed his lips together to keep from grinning.

Wearing his own grin, Cross pulled away from Nash and headed toward the interior door. "You coming?"

"Damn right I am."

Chapter Nineteen

CROSS FELT the bed move and the warm body he'd been curled around disappear. "What's going on?"

"Gotta go."

Cross's heart skipped a beat. "What? Where?"

In the six months they'd been together, not once had Nash crawled out of bed at an early hour.

In fact, Cross's daylight shift was usually half over before Nash woke up and sent him his first text of the day. Sometimes it was just a dick pic, showing off his mid-morning wood.

Sometimes it was a video clip of Nash doing something with that wood.

And all those *sometimes* made Cross want to rush home to help ease the man's "suffering."

"Church."

"Like church with a crucifix? Or one with sleds parked outside?"

"The second one. Never stepped foot in the first kind."

Amazing. Even after six months, they were still discovering a lot about each other. Which was one reason Nash hadn't addressed his club yet about the two of them.

They were still sneaking around, doing their best not to get caught from either side.

Though, Cross was going to tell his sergeant soon. Not that he was with a biker, but that he was gay. It was the first step.

"Coming out might affect your future promotions," Nash had warned him, even though Nash had joked in the past that if Cross got fired, he could become Nash's personal bodyguard when he became famous.

"I made corporal, they can't take that from me. I'm not going to throw it in their faces. And I'm certainly not going to tell them you're DAMC. But I don't want rumors starting in case someone sees us together or us coming and going from our house."

Our house.

Cross was determined for that to be soon, too. They were still using his townhouse. A good chunk of the past few months Nash had been on the road, touring with Dirty Deeds and they were finally starting to make some good money. Between that and Cross's corporal pay, they should be able to get a decent home. Maybe not like the house in the DAMC compound Nash had showed him a picture of. But they didn't need all that.

He dragged his thoughts back to the current conversation. "Never been in a real church? Not even for a wedding or a funeral?"

"That's not how we do it."

That's not how we do it.

Interesting. Cross was resigned to the fact he'd never be invited to any of the DAMC's events to see for himself how they did it. How the club functioned as an organization, a brotherhood and a family.

He stretched and yawned. "What time is it?"

"Eleven."

"Fuck," Cross groaned rubbing a hand over his eyes.

He'd worked a middie and only crawled into their bed around seven-thirty that morning.

Their bed.

Not really, but it felt like it since Nash was crashing at his townhouse more and more during their "trial" period.

"I need more sleep. Got two more nights of this shit... Why do you need to be at church?"

"For a meetin'."

"About?" He asked anyway even though he had been told club business wasn't his business.

"About nothin'. Gonna make it about somethin'."

Cross jackknifed up in bed, his heart beginning to thunder. "What's the something?"

"Us."

"Fuck," Cross groaned again, dragging his hands down his face.

"It's time."

"Are you sure?"

"Yeah. Said I'd wait. I waited. Spendin' more time here than in my room at church. If they haven't guessed why by now, they're gonna soon."

"You could tell them you found a girlfriend."

Nash turned around at the dresser, where he was sliding his bulky rings back onto his fingers, to frown at Cross. "Don't wanna lie."

"Nash..."

"Cross."

"I know we said we'd wait, make sure things were solid with us first..."

"Are they?"

He fought to keep his voice from rising an octave. "Aren't they?"

"Fuck yeah."

Cross breathed easier at that answer.

"Cross," Nash slipped the last ring on, grabbed his

Sturgis T-shirt and pulled it over his head. When his head popped through, his hair was practically standing on end. "Ain't lookin' forward to it. But it's time."

Cross didn't feel good about it. This could change everything for Nash, and he didn't want to be the cause of Nash losing a brotherhood he'd been a part of for almost twenty years. His only family. But if he thought it was time...

They knew it was heading in that direction. Cross didn't think Nash would do it only six months after the day they crossed paths in New Castle. Six months seemed like only a blip in time. "Are you going to be okay?"

Nash grabbed his jeans from the floor and tugged them up over his long legs, the heavy DAMC belt buckle clanking as he did so.

"Do you want me to go with you?"

Nash didn't finish fastening his jeans, instead he put his hands on his hips and his eyebrows knitted together. "You there's gonna make it a million times worse."

Cross's lips flattened out. "Thanks."

"You know why?"

"I'm sure I can guess."

Nash snorted, shook his head, and fastened his jeans.

"They won't hurt you, right?"

Nash finished buckling his belt and tipped his head up. "No."

"You're not lying about that, right?"

"Cross..."

Cross jumped out of bed and stepped up to him. "I'm worried."

"Know you are, baby," Nash murmured.

Every time. Every single time Nash called him that, he lost his breath. It wasn't often. But when he did, it really hit home.

It reminded him how much he loved the man who couldn't be more opposite of him.

"You are, too."

"Yeah," Nash admitted softly.

"I need you to call me as soon as it's over."

Nash hesitated. "I'll come straight back here."

Cross grabbed his chin and forced Nash's hazel eyes to meet his. "No, you will call me as soon as it's over."

"Fuckin' bossy motherfucker," Nash muttered.

"I need to get more sleep, but it'll be impossible now knowing what you'll be doing. So, phone call first, then get back here. In that order, Nash."

"Right. Call. Get back here. You gonna be waitin' on your knees at the top of the steps?"

"Guess you'll find out when you walk up those steps."

Nash leaned in, his lips close to Cross's. "Better be on your knees waitin'."

A shiver slid down Cross's spine and his cock stirred in his boxer briefs. "I'll be waiting."

Nash pressed a quick kiss to his lips then moved away to hunt down his boots. "Now I'm gonna have a hard time concentrating durin' that meetin'. Wanna give me a little taste before I go?"

"No, because waiting will encourage you to get back here ASAP."

"That it will," Nash muttered under his breath as he pulled his cut out of Cross's closet and shrugged it on.

"You know the rule," Cross reminded him.

"Gonna put it in my saddlebag before I open the garage door."

Cross nodded. They'd been careful. Nash always tucked his cut away in one of his saddlebags before entering the townhouse complex. And he never wore it out.

So far, it's worked. And when one of the neighbors inquired about who he was while giving Cross the side-eye, he just explained Nash was an undercover vice detective. And when the nosy neighbor wanted to know why Nash was living there, Cross told him Nash was recently separated and just needed a place to stay until he could get his life in order.

This was going to be their life. Being prepared to lie. Telling stories.

The last six months hadn't been easy. The rest of their lives wouldn't be, either. They had no illusions it would ever be different.

"Hey," Cross called out as Nash headed toward the bedroom door.

Nash paused and glanced over his shoulder at him.

"Never quit," Cross whispered.

"What?"

Cross cleared the rough from his throat. "Never quit on us."

"Don't plan on it," Nash said, then disappeared.

IT HAD BEEN six months and things between him and Cross were solid, for the most part. Cross wasn't going anywhere. Nash wasn't going anywhere.

That meant it was time. He was tired of lying, he needed to tell them the truth.

Nash knew it would be rough. He wasn't wrong.

"Got two choices. He gets rid of the badge or you get shot of 'im. Got me?"

The king had spoken.

"You talkin' for Z now? Since when d'you become president of this fuckin' club?"

Diesel's head jerked back, and his broad shoulders tensed.

"Anybody on this board can have their fuckin' say," Z reminded Nash quickly but quietly.

"But you make the ultimate decision."

Z shook his head. "No, we vote. You fuckin' know that."

"Do I have to claim Cross at this table? Because I will."

"Don't mean we'll pass that vote, son," Ace murmured, sitting back in his chair and brushing a hand down his beard. "He can't become an ol' lady. He could prospect an'—"

Diesel's chair shot back and crashed into the wall behind him as he surged to his feet. "The fuck if some pig's ever gonna prospect for this club!" he roared.

"Sit the fuck down, D," Diesel's father said firmly. Ace stared down his son. "Sit. The. Fuck. Down."

Ace waited until D settled back in his seat to continue. "Not sayin' he should prospect. Sayin' that would be one way for us to accept 'im, *if* he wasn't 5-0. But he is. So that's out." Ace tilted his head to look at Nash. "Unless he's willin' to give up his badge for one of our cuts?"

Diesel dropped his head and shook it. Both his hands curled into fists on the table.

"He's not gonna give up his career just to be with me, just so you all accept him. You need to fuckin' accept him as he is or don't. He loves his fuckin' job."

Ace continued to stare at him. "You love this club, brother?"

Nash's gaze circled the table starting with Ace. Then it slid over Zak, Hawk, Diesel, Dex, finishing up with Jag.

"Gave me everythin' when I had nothin'," he said to all of them, but did it meeting Jag's eyes.

Jag gave him the slightest chin lift but said nothing.

For the past couple of weeks, he'd thought long and hard about what he'd have to do if they didn't accept Nash's relationship with Cross. "I can give up my colors."

D slammed back in his seat, making it creak dangerously. But before he could begin bellowing, Diesel's father, Ace, spoke up. "You've been DAMC a long time, son. You're gonna give up your family just for some dick? Plenty of other dicks out there without badges hangin' off 'em."

Ace dropped his head and shook it, muttering, "Never thought I'd be saying dick instead of fuckin' pussy. Fuckin' times have changed."

"It's not my fuckin' choice. Was plannin' on movin' outta church, givin' up the house in the compound. Don't need it anyway. Gettin' a place outside of town. Somewhere with some privacy. On the road a lot now, anyway. Was gonna do my best to be home for the runs, play the roasts. Was plannin' on keepin' him out, keepin' him separate." He let his gaze land on Diesel. "Seein' that's not gonna work."

"He mean that much to you?" Zak asked.

"Fuck yeah."

Nash's eyes circled the table once more.

He set his jaw and shrugged out of his cut. He stared at it in his hands for a long moment. The room in dead silence.

No one spoke. No one moved.

If they did, Nash couldn't hear it over the breaking of his heart.

He placed it on the long table, staring at it because he couldn't look at any of them.

Then he lifted his head and forced his gaze around the table once more, pausing on each one of them for a moment.

"You all claimed your ol' ladies at this very fuckin' table. Every fuckin' one of you. You all found the one who made you a better man. You all found the one who made you a father. You all found your fuckin' heart and soul. I found that, too. Never expected to. Never thought I'd give up my colors for anyone. This club became my family when my own didn't want me. I'm forever grateful. It made me who I am today. Gave me my music. But I need more.

"Every one of you loves your ol' lady. Know every one of you would fuckin' die to protect her, break your fuckin' back to take care of her. I'll never have an ol' lady. Never find that woman who's the other half of my soul because she doesn't exist. My other half isn't a woman, it's a man. And, unfortunately, he's a cop.

"I get that one or both of these things might be unacceptable to you, but I had to accept it and I have. Love this fuckin' club. Love this brotherhood. Love this family. But I also want Cross to be a part of my life. Will pay my buy-out, whatever you think I owe. I'll get my colors covered." With a sting in his eyes, he drew a shaky breath, trying not to break down in front of everyone. "Done talkin' now."

Jag shifted in his seat. "Brother, didn't bring you in an' set you up for you to turn your back on us over someone you're fuckin'."

When nobody said anything for a few uncomfortable moments, Dex said, "It's not just fuckin'. It's more than that."

Nash met Dex's eyes. "Yeah, it's more than that."

"Leave your cut there an' step out. Gotta talk 'bout this, maybe take a vote," Zak said.

Nash nodded, gave them all one last look and stepped out, closing the door behind him.

NASH RODE up to Cross's townhouse. The man was going to be pissed. Nash hadn't called first.

He couldn't talk right afterward, anyway. The lump in his throat had made it impossible.

As the garage door lifted, Cross was standing there next to his own sled, arms crossed over his chest.

"Fucking told you to call me," Cross shouted, a catch in his voice.

Nash ignored him and pulled his sled next to Cross's. Nash kicked the stand down and before he was even done dismounting, Cross had his hands fisted in Nash's shirt and was pulling him off his bike and into his arms. "I was fucking worried, goddamn it."

Nash closed his eyes and wrapped his arms around Cross's waist. "Needed to take a ride, clear my head."

"I called you like fifty fucking times," Cross said into Nash's neck, squeezing him even tighter.

"Was ridin'. Couldn't check my phone."

Nash waited for Cross to give him more shit. But he didn't, instead he asked, "Where's your cut?"

"In my saddlebag."

Nash not only heard but felt Cross's breath hitch. "They let you keep it?"

"Yeah," he whispered. "They let me keep it."

Cross pushed him away, holding him out with straight arms to search Nash's face. "As a memento? Or as a member?"

"Knew you'd rather me not be a part of the MC—"

"They're your family, no matter what they think of me."

"Yeah."

"I'd never want you to give up family."

"Good."

Cross's blue eyes hit Nash's. "Good?"

"Yeah. 'Cause my family is a pain in the fuckin' ass."

Cross dropped his hands from Nash's shoulder and bent over at the waist, an arm covering his gut. "Fuck, I've been wanting to puke for the past few hours."

"Me, too," Nash admitted.

"I was worried they'd kill you and bury you somewhere no one could find the body."

"They set some rules. We follow them, they'll let me continue to breathe," Nash teased.

"That's not even fucking funny." Cross tilted his head and planted his hands on his hips. "What rules?"

"Ones I expected. Givin' up my room at church, givin' up the house. Not talkin' DAMC shit with you. Not bringin' you around." He gave Cross a serious look. "You need to stay off DAMC property. All of 'em. They made that crystal fuckin' clear. Not The Iron Horse, not church, not even Sophie's bakery in town. You won't fuckin' exist to them 'til you retire. Once you do, they'll reconsider. But not before then."

"They have a lot to protect."

"We have a lot to protect," Nash corrected. "Family, businesses, future generations."

"I get it. I kind of admire how fiercely loyal and protective you all are."

"Unlike real blood."

"We both know that too well."

Cross knew the truth about Nash's father now. Nash hadn't told him every detail of that last day in his childhood home, but he'd told him most of it. Enough in case Nash had nightmares.

The rest just needed to be forgotten.

They had the rest of their lives to make up for family who rejected them. They had the rest of their lives to make better memories.

Life wasn't going to be perfect, but it was going to be damn good.

Epilogue

THEY BOUGHT a small house on the edge of Shadow Valley on a private, wooded lot. It actually backed up to the hundred acres of woods the DAMC owned behind the compound. While they lived close enough to the DAMC, it wasn't enough for their living arrangement to "touch" the club.

Where they were, they didn't have a lot of neighbors but that didn't mean the ones they had wouldn't be nosy. They'd still need to be careful. Now not so much for Nash, but more for Cross and his career.

Cross's sergeant had taken the news he was gay as well as expected. Said he'd keep it to himself but couldn't guarantee no one else would find out. Right. Which Nash pretty much figured the man would run his fucking mouth. That worried him. He worried none of the other pigs would come help Cross out of a jam. Like the day Cross fought for his life on the side of the road what seemed like so fucking long ago.

Cross had gone to the closing that morning on the house while Nash had woken up three states away after playing two weeks straight of gigs in Georgia and the Carolinas.

He fucking missed him.

And he couldn't wait to get home to open the door to their future. Even if it was a fucked-up future, it still belonged to them.

Whatever shit would be chucked their way, they'd handle it together.

For the most part, no one treated him differently in the DAMC, but they also didn't ask about Cross. Not one thing. They knew but they didn't want to *know*.

Cross knew and accepted that he wasn't welcomed there, not because he was gay, but because of his shiny silver badge.

Until he retired in fifteen years, it would remain that way. With him unwelcome and on the outside.

But the day he turned in his badge and became a civilian, Nash had no doubt he'd be welcomed as part of the family. D might hold some grudges, but he wouldn't want to kill him. He'd save that urge for Axel.

Nash smirked.

His phone beeped. Nash recognized the tone he used for Cross.

Snagging his cell from the nightstand in the motel room, he shoved one hand under the sheets and scratched his balls before running his fingers up and down his still-resting dick a couple times.

He might have time to pull one off before hitting the road.

He hit the power button to read the text. *What time R U getn home?*

Nash sighed as he reluctantly released his dick so he could respond. *Whenever I get there.*

He knew that response would drive Cross batshit crazy. He'd learned quickly Cross was a detail type of guy, especially being a cop, so he liked real answers. Not vague ones.

Try again came the next response.

Nash snorted, glanced at the clock, then tried to figure out how long of a ride it would be back to Shadow Valley.

In VA. Same motel. Ready 2 jackoff in the same bed we fucked.

U shittn me? came back immediately. *Didn't know U were nostalgic.*

"I'm not," Nash whispered to the empty room. "But I'm missin' you."

Nash threw the sheet off his now mostly hard dick and snapped a picture of it with the motel's desk and mirror in the background. He hit Send.

It was a long minute, maybe even two, before he got a response. *Meet me @ The Cockpit @ 8. Gives U time 2 do that & get there w/o speedn.*

Why there? Nash texted back. While it was one of the safe places for them to hang out as a couple, they hadn't been there in a while.

A picture popped up in a text. It was of a set of keys hanging from Cross's very familiar, very recognizable finger captioned with *celebratory drinks.*

Would rather get celebratory head, Nash answered, now stroking himself with one hand, awkwardly texting with the other.

Same here. We'll negoti8 over drinks.

Nash liked the sound of that. Though their form of negotiating was usually done while they were naked, which would not be happening at The Cockpit.

While Cross was a bossy motherfucker, Nash could be, too.

Give and take whispered through his mind.

Another text popped up. *Love U.*

Nash closed his eyes as warmth filled his gut, filled his chest and a weird sense of peace filled his mind. It always did when Cross told him that.

Yeah, he texted back. "Love you, too," he whispered to the ceiling.

Still w8n.

Nash rolled his eyes and texted back, *Luv U 2, U bossy motherfucker.*

CROSS SAT in the back corner of The Cockpit, waiting.

He was always waiting on Nash, but the man was worth the wait.

Except for when it took Nash forever to admit he loved Cross.

On that, Cross had been impatient, but he still waited it out. Until he couldn't wait anymore, so he nudged Nash a few times about it.

While he knew Nash loved him, Cross needed to hear it.

Especially since he was the only person in Cross's life that did.

Nash was never going to be a man who brought home flowers or chocolate, or even declared his love openly. In fact, if Nash started throwing the L word around too often, Cross would probably get suspicious, even though he had no reason to be.

He trusted Nash. Even being on the road weeks at a time, he didn't worry about the temptations that were thrown at him at the Dirty Deeds gigs.

And it wasn't because Nash occasionally mentioned that he loved Cross.

No. It was because Cross felt it. Deeply and with all certainty.

And no relationship would exist between them if there wasn't trust.

He never questioned Nash while he was on tour. Cross just believed he was Nash's one and only.

Because Nash was *his* one and only.

They bought a house, they were living a life together.

Nash had come clean to his club. Cross had come clean about his sexuality at work. The only thing Cross hid was who he was in a relationship with. And, of course, Cross stayed clear of Nash's club.

It all worked for now and he hoped it would continue.

Cross kept his eyes peeled to the entrance of The Cockpit and he knew the second Nash stepped inside.

Nash's gaze slid right through him like Cross wasn't there and he worked his way through groups of men having a good time to head toward the bar.

Cross watched as curious and interested eyes followed him. Even without wearing his cut, Nash looked like the ultimate bad boy rocker.

One that was his and no one else's.

Cross tipped his head down and smirked at the table when Nash climbed onto the same bar stool Cross had first seen him at about a year ago. Then Nash turned his back to the rest of the bar, including Cross, as the burly bear bartender approached to get his order.

Cross waited.

Once Nash had his drink, Cross rose from the table and made his way over.

He waited for Nash to lift his glass and then knocked into his elbow, the whiskey splashing slightly over the rim.

"Fuckin' watch it," Nash muttered, turning on his stool with his eyebrows pulled low.

Cross fought his grin. "Problem?"

Nash set his glass down slowly on the bar and grumbled, "Yeah."

Cross leaned in to ask, "What?"

Nash gave him the side-eye. "You."

Cross raised his palms up in surrender. "Didn't mean to bump into you, man. Got shoved from behind."

Nash glanced behind Cross and grumbled, "Whatever."

"Is broody asshole still a thing?"

Nash knocked back half of his whiskey before slamming the glass back onto the bar and raising a brow at Cross. "Don't know, is it?"

"Haven't been out looking, so I'm not sure what's hot right now."

"Wouldn't know, either."

Cross liked the sound of that. He leaned closer to Nash again to make sure he was heard over the loud voices and the DJ's music. "Name's Aiden. Got a name?"

"Everybody's got a fuckin' name," Nash answered.

"Then I'd like to hear it," Cross prodded.

"Graham." Nash couldn't hide the slight wince when he said it.

Cross smiled since he hadn't been expecting that answer. "Great name."

"So's yours."

"Want to get out of here?"

"Thought you'd never fuckin' ask," Nash said, downing the rest of his whiskey.

Cross fought the upward curve of his lips.

Nash pushed to his feet. "Got somewhere we can go?"

"Yes." Cross dug into the front pocket of his jeans, pulled out a single key on a Harley keychain, then tucked it into Nash's front pocket. "A place called home."

"Sounds fuckin' perfect."

Cross couldn't agree more.

Turn the page to read chapter one of Rip Cord: The Complete Trilogy

Read a sample of Rip Cord: The Complete Trilogy

If you love m/m, turn the page to read a sample of my novel: *Rip Cord: The Complete Trilogy* Available now in ebook, paperback and audiobook!

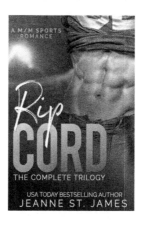

About the Rip Cord Trilogy

The Reunion:

Gil Davis hated high school. Ever the geek, he has no intentions of attending his tenth year class reunion. The last thing he wants is to relive the taunting and teasing he received during his teenage years. However, there is one thing he misses from high school: the star Varsity football player. The one he had a crush on from the first day he laid eyes on him. But the last thing he expects is the now-pro football player to come back to their home town to attend a lame high school reunion. Known as the Bad Boy of the NFL, Ripley "Rip" Cord not only shows up, but shows up without a date...*and* an eye for Gil.

The Weekend:

Geek extraordinaire Gil Davis hooked up with his long-time crush Rip Cord, the Bad Boy of the NFL, during their tenth year class reunion. It was a dream come true for Gil, so when Rip surprises Gil with a trip to the pro football player's cabin on the lake two weeks later, Gil looks forward to their weekend alone. Since Rip is still deep in the closet due to his career, Gil will take any stolen moments they have. Little does Gil know, those moments will be filled with a blindfold and ropes, as well as a bad tumble down the mountain. A few bumps and bruises won't stop Gil from spending precious time with Rip and his toys. But when the weekend ends, will Rip disappear again? Or will Rip want to take their relationship to the next level?

The Ever After:

Rip Cord, the infamous Bad Boy of the NFL, ends up on Gil Davis's front porch drunk as a skunk. Not only has he been fired by his franchise, but also his sports agent. His last brawl on the football field during a prime-time game was the final straw.

Accounting geek Gil Davis hasn't seen his on-again, off-again lover since the summer when the professional football player whisked him away for a kinky, sex-filled getaway weekend. But immediately after, Rip returned to the NFL and was on the road leaving no time for Gil.

Now Rip wants to come back into Gil's life one more time, this time to not only make a future with him, but to finally admit who he really is deep down inside. After hiding his sexual preference since he was a teen, Rip realizes he's made too many bad choices along the way. It's time to make the right choice with Gil.

But is Gil ready to forgive Rip for keeping him at a distance? And more importantly, after two false starts, can they finally live happily ever after?

Rip Cord: The Reunion - Chapter One

Gil Davis couldn't believe it had been ten years since he'd last walked through these doors. Where had the time gone?

When the invitation to his class reunion had come, he'd almost tossed it out, just as he had with the notice of his five-year reunion.

He was not into reliving his high school years.

No way, no how.

But something on the invitation had caught his eye. This time they were holding it at the school. So instead of immediately pitching it, he had thrown the invitation on his kitchen table. Unfortunately Katie, his best friend and roommate, found it and hounded him relentlessly until he agreed to RSVP.

And, of course, Katie insisted on being his date.

Which thrilled him to no end...*not*.

Now he wasn't so sure if he wanted to go in.

He wasn't sure he was ready for a night of teasing from his former schoolmates.

Yet, here he stood, just inside the double doors of his old

high school, staring at the registration table by the gymnasium doors.

Someone grabbed his elbow. Firmly.

"You're not chickening out, are you?"

Gil shook his head and swallowed hard. "Did you find the restroom all right?"

"Fine," Katie said in her little no-nonsense tone. "Let's go."

The harder she tugged on his arm, the more he dug in his heels. He didn't want to leave his little corner of safety yet. "Hold on."

"No, Gil. It's not going to get any easier. You look fine. We've—okay, *I've* worked really hard to get you to this point." She smoothed the hair back from his eyes. Gil was surprised she hadn't spit on her fingers first like a hovering mother hen.

The problem was, he was still a nerd at heart.

"Now, get your shit together and *let's go!*" She gave his arm one last hard yank and dragged him over to the table.

Sucking in a breath, he steeled himself for what was to come.

The two women sitting at the table wore big predatory smiles.

"Gilbert? Gilbert Davis, is that you?" the toothy piranha on the right asked. "I swear I didn't recognize you without your bottle-bottom glasses and pocket protector."

Those glasses were long gone, thanks to Katie forcing him to the optometrist for contacts years ago.

Gil leaned forward to read her name tag. *Bonnie (Trusk) Smith.*

Bonnie Trusk. He remembered her. She had been part of the homecoming court their senior year.

And had *accidentally* run over his foot one day in the parking lot with her Eddie Bauer Explorer. Why? Her excuse had been she hadn't seen him. Yeah, he had been the invisible man, "invisible" to all the popular kids.

"Just Gil," he corrected her.

She laughed and waved a hand toward him, clearly dismissing him.

The other woman, Patti Petroski-Harrison, shoved a *Hello! My name is…Gilbert Davis* sticker at him. "And your hair! It looks…" Gil expected the next word out of her mouth to be *normal*. Her face showed her internal struggle. "Nice."

He was a geek. He knew it. He had been one ever since he could remember. And his classmates had always teased him about it.

She sized up Katie. "Are you his wife?"

Katie laughed and patted Gil's arm. "Oh no."

Gil shot her a quick warning look.

Katie gave him a sugary smile and a noisy kiss on the cheek.

"Well then," Patti said. "When you go through the doors, Gilbert, there will be a table with place settings. Find your name, and that will tell you where you're seated."

"Just Gil," he corrected again, but by then both women were flashing their beaming smiles at another couple who had come up behind them.

Katie tugged him to the side to avoid being crushed by the new arrivals' hugging and squealing. Gil didn't recognize the newcomers. But then they had probably been a part of the "in" group.

Gil had been a full-fledged member of the "out" group, but not the "out of the closet" group.

A woman's shrill scream shot a bolt of pain through his head.

"Did you hear Rip Cord is going to be here? Can you believe it?" Patti asked, her question ending in a squeal. She looked as if she would bust a vein.

Gil stumbled back a step from the table, barely avoiding Katie's toes.

Holy hell, he never should have agreed to come to this thing. Especially if he'd known Rip would be here.

Gil had a crush on Rip since high school. Unfortunately Rip was definitely of the heterosexual persuasion. Being captain of the football team, he'd had every girl in school chasing after him, one way or another.

So Gil had admired the well-built, handsome jock from afar. Very afar.

Hearing Rip's name brought all those old feelings back to the surface.

All the insecurities.

Gil certainly had never expected his secret crush to come back to town for a ten-year class reunion. Rip had become way too famous for that.

Gil grabbed Katie's arm and, with her squeaky protest, dragged her through the double doors into the gym.

"Jesus, Gil. What's going on?" she asked as he pushed her against the wall just inside the doors.

"Did you hear that?" He struggled not to hyperventilate.

"What?" Katie peeled the backing off Gil's name tag and slapped it onto his chest. Not so gently either.

"Rip is going to be here."

"Rip?" She wrinkled her nose. "What the hell is rip?"

"Not what. Who!" Gil swallowed hard and blew out a long breath. He realized then he was squeezing her upper arms. Way too hard. He relaxed his fingers.

"Okay, okay. Calm down. And let up a little more please."

He released her and wiped his sweaty palms along his slacks. He never should have worn slacks. Slacks were nerd wear.

Why didn't Katie talk him out of wearing them? He should have worn torn jeans or leather pants or—

"So is Rip a band? I would've thought they just would've hired a DJ. It's cheaper."

"Wait. What?" Gil shook his head. "First of all, why would they need music?"

Katie pointed a finger upward. "Hear that, nerd-o? Music. You know, it creates atmosphere and gives you something to dance to."

"Dance?" Gil swallowed hard. He cocked his head. He did hear music. He hadn't noticed it because he'd been too panicked about Rip being there. "Okay, just don't ask me to dance."

"No can do, Gilly. We will be dancing. I didn't come along to be a wallflower."

"Katie, you know I can't dance," he hissed, inches from her face.

She had the nerve to laugh. As if his lack of rhythm was something to laugh about. His coordination left something to be desired. Gil considered it a handicap—maybe not one recognized by the government. But no one should make fun of the handicapped!

Gil frowned. "I didn't see anything on the invitation about dancing."

Katie sighed. "Gilly, don't worry, we'll fake it."

"Don't call me Gilly here. It's bad enough people will be calling me Gilbert."

"Okay, *Gil*. So if Rip isn't a band, then who or what is it?"

A low murmur throughout the room behind him caused Gil to look up. Coming through the doors…

Gil pressed a hand to the wall to steady himself. His legs had suddenly lost all strength.

Coming through the doors was…

"Him," was all Gil could get past the lump in his throat.

"Him?" Katie turned the direction Gil was staring, and her mouth made a little O.

Gil had expected Rip to walk in with a tall, leggy blonde on his arm—one who was enhanced in various places. He hadn't expected Rip to come…alone.

Ripley "Rip" Cord was just as tall as Gil remembered. Around five inches taller than him, not that Gil was a squirt. The football player was at least six foot two.

And every inch of him was muscle. Not lean muscle, but heavy muscle. Heavy, rounded, lickable muscle.

Gil glanced at Katie. "You're drooling."

Katie wiped her mouth with the back of her hand. "As if you aren't."

Gil snagged her wrist and backpedaled until he rammed into something hard. It was the table with the place settings.

Gil peered over Katie's shoulder to see if his klutziness had caught Rip's attention.

Luckily it hadn't. The man was completely surrounded by their old classmates clamoring for his attention.

Throughout the years, he'd followed Rip's career in the newspapers, on the evening news, on ESPN.

And in the tabloids.

Rip was well-known. Unfortunately it was as the "bad boy" of the National Football League. He started out with a great career in the NFL, drafted straight out of college. He was one of the best wide receivers in the league, but it was all his rumored problems that kept him in the spotlight, not his stats.

And that famous wide receiver was here. Now.

"C'mon, Katie! Don't stare."

"Why?"

"Because—"

"Jesus, Gilly, because you have a crush on him!"

Heat crawled up Gil's neck. He was glad the lights were turned down in the gymnasium. He didn't want anyone seeing him blush.

Hell, he was twenty-eight years old. He shouldn't be blushing. He felt seventeen all over again.

He pulled away from Katie to study the name cards remaining on the table. Of course, he read the same card over and over before Katie squealed.

"*Oh. My. God.* Here he comes!"

Gil nervously tugged Katie next to his side and threw an arm haphazardly around her shoulders.

"Ouch," she yelped as her curly red hair got caught on the button of his cuff.

"Sorry," he whispered and straightened up just as Rip arrived at the table.

Gil swore he saw spots. He was not going to faint. He was not going to faint.

His knees buckled, and he grabbed for the nearest solid thing: Rip.

Rip grasped his forearm and held Gil steady. "You all right, buddy?"

Gil looked up—and up—into deep blue eyes. Eyes he had never forgotten. To this day they haunted his dreams.

Dreams he usually woke up from with a raging hard-on.

Gil opened his mouth to answer, but nothing came out. Rip smacked him hard on the back.

"Are you sure you're okay?"

Gil nodded.

"Did you find your name card yet?" Rip asked, flashing him a bright, white smile.

Gil shook his head.

Rip moved closer, almost hip to hip with Gil, to study the table of white folded cardstock. Gil fought the urge to lean in and nuzzle the larger man's neck, inhaling his manly scent. Roll around in it like a dog.

Hell, he'd probably end up sporting a black eye if he tried.

Even so, Rip's large hands, his long fingers, fascinated Gil as he reached out to snag a card off the table.

"Here you are." He lifted Gil's hand, cupping it from the bottom.

Gil could feel the rough, calloused palm against his knuckles. A thrill ran down his spine as Rip tucked the tented name card into his curled fingers.

Rip remembered his name? He must have if he had picked Gil's name out from the place settings.

Gil quickly glanced down at his own chest. Crap. He'd probably read his *Hello. My name is…* sticker.

Rip's deep voice broke into his thoughts. "I've dreamed of you, Gilbert."

Gil looked up at him in shock. "What?"

"I said, I remember you, Gilbert. Don't look so surprised."

"G-Gil."

Rip lifted one brow. "Again?"

"He goes by Gil now," Katie butted in. "I'm Katie." She held out her hand.

Instead of shaking it, Rip lifted it and brushed his lips over her knuckles.

"Oh, a gentleman, huh? Hard to find these days."

"Hardly." Rip laughed, then pinned Gil with a stare. "Is she your girl?"

Gil's gaze flicked to Katie, who stood entranced, staring at Rip. He knew the feeling.

Rip had a strong square jaw, currently covered in a super-short beard since it wasn't game season. He sported shoulder-length dirty-blond hair with sun-kissed highlights due to the time he spent outdoors.

His long legs were encased in black jeans, which sinfully hugged the muscles they covered. He had on a tight black T-shirt under an equally black but very worn leather jacket. A biker jacket, not a designer jacket. Heavy leather with rivets, sporting buckles and zippers.

He looked bad. So bad, he looked good.

Even so, Gil couldn't help thinking it was way too warm out for a leather jacket.

"Where are *you* sitting?" Katie piped in, tearing Rip's attention away from Gil and onto her.

Damn. Rip had always liked the ladies, and it seemed to be no different now.

Gil quickly scanned the table and found Rip's name card. Table 15. He looked at his own. Table 13.

Hell. Unlucky thirteen. He couldn't be lucky enough to be sitting with the NFL star. He was sure whoever organized the reunion had Rip sitting with the popular crowd—or at least the former jocks from high school.

"With you guys." Rip plucked his place card off the table. "Have a pen?"

What the hell? Was Rip going to be hitting on Katie all night? Gil didn't know if he could sit there and watch that.

"Don't you wear a pocket protector anymore?" Rip asked him, running a finger over his shirt pocket. Gil's nipples hardened instantly, and he bit back a gasp.

"N-no," Gil stuttered. Katie had forbidden them. Even at work.

"Here. I have one." Katie handed Rip a pen she extracted from her purse.

Rip gave her a smile in thanks and used the pen to scribble out the 13 on Gil's name card. He replaced it with the number 15.

He handed the pen back to Katie and the name card back to Gil, the pads of his fingers lingering on Gil's palm.

Gil fisted his hand, still feeling the tingling sensation left behind.

He had to get a grip.

Rip was a football player. A man's man.
Too bad he wasn't Gil's man.

TO READ MORE, FOLLOW THIS LINK:
The Rip Cord Trilogy

If You Enjoyed This Book

Thank you for reading Crossing the Line. If you enjoyed Nash and Cross's story, please consider leaving a review at your favorite retailer and/or Goodreads to let other readers know. Reviews are always appreciated and just a few words can help an independent author like me tremendously!

Want to read a sample of my work? Download a sampler book here: BookHip.com/MTQQKK

Also by Jeanne St. James

* Available in Audiobook

Made Maleen: A Modern Twist on a Fairy Tale *

Damaged *

Rip Cord: The Complete Trilogy *

Brothers in Blue Series:

(Can be read as standalones)

Brothers in Blue: Max *

Brothers in Blue: Marc *

Brothers in Blue: Matt *

Teddy: A Brothers in Blue Novelette *

The Dare Ménage Series:

(Can be read as standalones)

Double Dare *

Daring Proposal *

Dare to Be Three *

A Daring Desire *

Dare to Surrender *

A Daring Journey

The Obsessed Novellas:

(All the novellas in this series are standalones)

Forever Him *

Only Him *

Needing Him *

Loving Her *

Temping Him *

Down & Dirty: Dirty Angels MC Series™:

(Can be read as standalones)

Down & Dirty: Zak *

Down & Dirty: Jag *

Down & Dirty: Hawk *

Down & Dirty: Diesel *

Down & Dirty: Axel *

Down & Dirty: Slade *

Down & Dirty: Dawg *

Down & Dirty: Dex *

Down & Dirty: Linc *

Down & Dirty: Crow *

Crossing the Line (A DAMC/Blue Avengers Crossover)

Guts & Glory Series

(In the Shadows Security)

Guts & Glory: Mercy

Guts & Glory: Ryder

Guts & Glory: Hunter

Guts & Glory: Walker

Guts & Glory: Steel

Guts & Glory: Brick

COMING SOON!

Blood Fury MC™

Blue Avengers MC™

Dark Knights MC: Magnum

Brothers in Blue: A Bryson Family Christmas

About the Author

JEANNE ST. JAMES is a USA Today bestselling romance author who loves an alpha male (or two). She was only thirteen when she started writing and her first paid published piece was an erotic story in Playgirl magazine. Her first erotic romance novel, Banged Up, was published in 2009. She is happily owned by farting French bulldogs. She writes M/F, M/M, and M/M/F ménages.

Want to read a sample of her work? Download a sampler book here: BookHip.com/MTQQKK

To keep up with her busy release schedule check her website at www.jeannestjames.com or sign up for her newsletter: http://www.jeannestjames.com/newslettersignup

www.jeannestjames.com
jeanne@jeannestjames.com

Blog: http://jeannestjames.blogspot.com
Newsletter: http://www.jeannestjames.com/newslettersignup
Jeanne's Down & Dirty Book Crew: https://www.facebook.com/groups/JeannesReviewCrew/

facebook.com/JeanneStJamesAuthor

twitter.com/JeanneStJames

amazon.com/author/jeannestjames

instagram.com/JeanneStJames

bookbub.com/authors/jeanne-st-james

goodreads.com/JeanneStJames

pinterest.com/JeanneStJames

Get a FREE Erotic Romance Sampler Book

This book contains the first chapter of a variety of my books. This will give you a taste of the type of books I write and if you enjoy the first chapter, I hope you'll be interested in reading the rest of the book.

Each book I list in the sampler will include the description of the book, the genre, and the first chapter, along with links to find out more. I hope you find a book you will enjoy curling up with!

Get it here: BookHip.com/MTQQKK

Printed in Great Britain
by Amazon